BRIGHTNESS

REMEMBERED

by

Carol Williams

PICTON PRESS
ROCKPORT, MAINE

Cover illustration by Betsy Thorne

Published under the auspices of the *Swiss American Historical Society*. This
book is *Swiss American Historical Society Special Publication No. 19*.

First Printing July 2001

This book is available from:
Picton Press
PO Box 250
Rockport, ME 04856-0250

Visa/MasterCard orders:
1-207-236-6565
Fax orders: 1-207-236-6713
e-mail: sales@pictonpress.com
Internet secure credit card orders: www.pictonpress.com

Manufactured in the United States of America
Printed on 60# acid-free paper

∞

Dedication

To Joyce Bethea and Patricia Williams

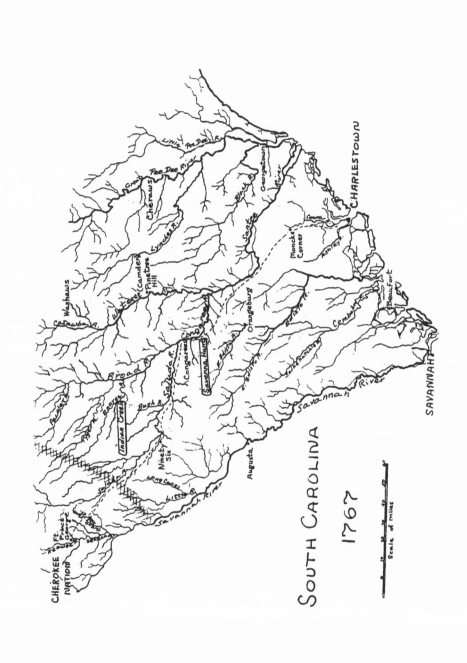

CHEROKEE
NATION
Ft. Prince George
Keowee

Waxhaws
Catawba R.

Cherokee
Broad R.
Pacolet
Tyger R.
Enoree R.
Bush R.
Saluda R.
Congaree River
Savannah Hund.
Indian Creek
Ninety Six
Long Cane
Little R.
Savannah River
Augusta

Green Cr.
Pee Dee River
Little Pee Dee R.
Cherews

Lynches R.
Camden
Wateree
Pinetree Hill

Black River
Georgetown
Santee

Moncks Corner
Orangeburg
Edisto R.
S. Edisto R.
Bridge R.
Salkehatchie R.
Ashley R.
Combahee R.
Beaufort

CHARLESTOWN

Savannah River

SAVANNAH

SOUTH CAROLINA
1767

Scale of miles
0   10   20   30   40   50

Foreword

When I first envisioned a novel about early Swiss immigrants to Saxe-Gotha Township in South Carolina, I thought it would begin in 1756 with the immigration of a young Swiss couple, Johannes and Madle Lienhardt, and would end with Johannes' and his two sons' participation in the American Revolution. But that novel turned into three: *The Switzers* (1981), *Brightness Remembered* (2001) and *By Wonders and By War* (1999). *By Wonders and by War* does end in 1782, but *The Switzers* sees the young couple only through the end of the Cherokee War in 1761. What about the years between? *Brightness Remembered* fills in these middle years.

The genesis of this novel was twofold. First: In my early reading I learned of the Regulator movement, vigilante groups that formed in 1767 to combat the outlaw gangs ravaging much of South Carolina above the Tidewater. 1767-69 was a turbulent period indeed. Second: In talking about patterns of early Swiss and German settlement with historian Horace Harmon, Director of the Lexington County Museum, I learned of the Deadfall Line in upper Lexington County, a generally accepted line of separation between German-speaking and English-speaking settlers. The English-speakers, mostly Scots-Irish, called "Irish," would settle above it; the German-speakers, that is, the "Deutsch" or "Dutch," would settle below it. Mr. Harmon said that trouble had sometimes erupted between the two groups because of Romeo and Juliet situations.

Now, just as there is a strand of Swiss ancestry in my own family, there is also a German strand. In upper Lexington County an eighteenth-century ancestor, Jacob Neese, married Margaret Allen. Evidently this distant grandmother's legacy was a strong one, for the name "Allen" has been repeated down through the generations.

Margaret Allen in *Brightness Remembered* is fictitious, as are the other main characters; yet perhaps she is not wholly unlike her namesake, for both are strong-minded women. I suspect Swiss Rudi Näffels in *Brightness Remembered* is somewhat different from German Jacob Neese, however.

This novel, like the others in the trilogy, is about the blending of cultures and how these Swiss became American. This blending is what happened to all our ancestors–what defines America.

Chapter One

Felled in 1754 and never torched in the Cherokee War, the logs of yellow poplar crackled in the sunshine. Riders churned in the dooryard and yelled to see red tongues flick between the logs. They jerked at their horses and watched cedar shingles catch, flare, and soar into roaring sheets about the chimney. They backed away, moved outside the broken paling, farther into plowed ground and away from the floating ash.

When the roof ridge crashed and the logs showed black ribs, Tyrrel shouted, "Sun's moving, boys! Best make for Bush River and Saludy!"

"Where to, beyond?"

"Back up Cloud's Creek. Old man Howe, his job's yet to do!"

They whooped and kicked up their horses, fifteen of them, and trampled across what was left of green corn and peas, southwest toward the heavy woods.

The band did not hurry because of fear. Few people on Indian Creek, if they saw the smoke, would have courage to chase them.

Robert Allen would not defy them again. Shot in the chest, he had fallen before his barn door five days ago and had not had to watch his cattle slaughtered, his horses driven off, and his young wife dragged screaming, fainting out of the house loft, pretty enough to be taken off, along with the handsome clock brought down the Great Wagon Road from Pennsylvania years ago and with the musket Robert was so luckless as to have left in the house that July afternoon. Perhaps it was as well that a rifle ball had killed Robert. What he'd have had to see done to Janet, it was better he'd been spared. Though after they'd ransacked the house, Tyrrel had knocked down that fool of a Distoe, who'd had no more sense than to shoot Allen before he could be induced to show them the money they thought he had.

Why had they come back to burn the house? Sheer malevolence perhaps, for they had not found money today either. Or maybe the burning was a way of razing the sight of Janet Allen's face as she'd tried to defend herself. She had not taken to camp life as had some of their other young captives.

Now in the afternoon sunlight her hearthstones were warm again. But

1

the great white oak that had shaded her working hours stood trunk-blacked with shriveled leaves, leaves that had dappled her spring comings and goings, leaves that, young, unfurled, had been Robert's planting sign.

Robert's sister, Margaret Allen, stirred in the barn loft and tried to swallow hard pain. The sweat of fear had dried, but her hands still clamped the cudgel with which she'd been going to brain the man who'd find her. God's mercy she'd been in the barn. She'd stopped there to see if a tool or iron piece might have been left, had been standing with curled lip, noting that other scavengers had gotten what the first gang left—roving scum who'd steal anything to sell for a pistreen to buy grog with. But the barn too was stripped clean.

Why hadn't they burned it today? Because it would have taken a little more time or work. And it was the good dwellinghouse that made such a satisfying blaze, the house of a man who'd testified against five of them in Charlestown at the Court of General Sessions in March. What a fine destruction—the firing of hand-hewn planes, of doors, panels, and shelves, product of skilled hands and eyes.

Stiffly Margaret climbed down the ladder on the inside wall beside the doorway. Outside, she gazed at the charred beams smoldering between stone pillars, high now above coals and ashes, foundations laid for a lifetime, for a generation that never would be.

And so it had happened before. She remembered black chimneys in the Valley of Virginia in '55, when she was seven years old. Then it was redskins. And her Granny remembered the desolation of old County Derry in Ireland when the Papists rose in 1689. And years before that, she said, the killing times in the glens of Ayr and all southwest Scotland, when those of the true Kirk had taken to the fields and at last crossed over to Ulster. And, oh, beyond that time, the centuries of raids and wars from Solway Firth to the River Tweed. Not that Margaret knew those names, for if her Granny knew them, she'd never named them.

Margaret went no nearer the embers. She was slightly above a woman's middle height. Her black hair hung rough and loose down her back. Bareheaded, barefooted, she wore a petticoat of dark-dyed homespun over a shift of the same material, undyed. Her blue eyes were light and cold.

So it had ended for her own blood brother. The one she'd half-envied, sometimes resented and quarreled with. Robert as vulnerable as anyone else. Margaret's look was bleak.

Hardworking, ambitious, Robert had brought his bride to this house he'd bought from a woman widowed in the Cherokee War. Now Robert too lay at the edge of his field beside the small graves of his son and daughter. Janet had not borne strong children. Margaret closed her mind to the thought of where or how Janet might lie now.

But no longer could she bear the sight or the smell of such ruin. She turned half-running toward the shadows of the unchanged woods as if green leaves might blot out evil's stench. She set her face toward home and Granny.

Home was a log house two miles up the creek, built by her father and brothers in 1756, eleven years ago, when they'd first come into the country. Then there'd been seven of them. Now there were only two. The others had been carried off by smallpox, apoplexy, marriage, and the lure of land in the west. Now only Margaret and eighty-three-year-old Jane McGrew lived here on Indian Creek. Most of their cleared land was reverting to old field or pasture, and only the garden patches were kept clean and one broad field of corn and peas. Still the two of them managed fairly well with their poultry, cows, and help from Robert.

How would they manage now? She did not know. Or did not want to face it. She knew what she ought to do. It had been expected of her for the last two years. For if at nineteen she wasn't ready, she'd better be getting ready, Robert had told her plainly.

But where was the man she could think of being tied to for life? She shied violently when Bill Lee or Tom Stokes stopped by on various pretexts. The two years in Pennington's Fort during the Indian war had instilled too much repugnance in her for some of the ways of men.

It was not that she disliked all men, she said. It was these hunters, Rangers, these adventurers with their dirt and drunkenness, their careless cruel ways that she could not abide. And she knew what life had been for her mother and her grandmother.

"It's to settle and lead a regular life that he wants to wed you," urged Robert. "He's a good Ulsterman even if he is the bit rough."

"Well, I'll not have a man that can't scratch his name to a bond!" she flared, giving the one reason Robert would respect.

Now she tried to rid her head of thought or remembrance. Her bare feet picked smooth places in the path, avoiding roots and loose rock. It was past midafternoon. Tree frogs shrilled and the songs of wood thrushes silvered the glades. The great chestnuts, oaks, and hickories, the blackgums and tulip poplars cast heavy shade on the forest floor, kept clear of undergrowth by spring burnings and thick now with grass for browsing creatures. But there were still coverts for panthers and wolves along the creek. Margaret carried her hickory cudgel and was not afraid. Yet she hurried, half-wishing she'd ridden the mare.

The thought struck her: What if she *had* ridden? There'd have been no hiding a horse. Her scalp prickled. Normally she'd have ridden Molly. Why hadn't she today? She couldn't remember; she'd just set out walking. ... Granny would say it was Providence. A somber musing hovered over her.

She was still a mile from home, just before where the path rose and wound around the foot of a big hickory. She stopped abruptly. Twenty feet ahead of her, face down, a body sprawled in the path—a man's body in a brown hunting shirt and leather breeches.

Lord God! What in this world! The figure lay as if his legs had buckled under him. How had he got there? She approached slowly.

The black hair, clubbed behind with a leather thong, had a slight curl to it. The skin of his neck was smooth, not pockmarked. Somebody young. Who?

She stooped and gingerly touched a shoulder. *Was* he dead? She knelt and slipped her hand underneath his chest but could feel nothing through his bunched shirt. She braced herself to turn him. As she pulled and lifted, he made a sound between a groan and a sigh.

Margaret drew back. "Who are you?" she asked loudly.

No answer.

She rose. He was sturdily built but was not the great gaunt length of man she was used to seeing. A hunter? a half-breed?

He did not move.

She knelt again and tugged to turn the man's body over. His eyes opened, fever-glazed. A side of his face was bruised black. His bearded lips moved. Then she saw the blood-caked leather, rent at hip and groin, exposing the raw wound.

"Lord ha' mercy!" she breathed. "Oh Lord God!"

What to do? Get Granny.

But who would help them? Their nearest neighbors were three miles off and it would be black dark before she got anybody from there.

That awful place on him. If she left him, vermin would begin to crawl all over him, if they hadn't already, and get in his wound. Could she bind it?

She bent to pull up her petticoat and catch the bottom of her shift. It was strong cloth, but her teeth were strong and she tore a wide strip off the bottom, though not without ruing its mutilation for this vagrant, this—whoever he was. But anybody'd have to do what they could to help him. If he wasn't beyond help.

Oak leaves—or moss to pack the wound? She looked about her. The oak limbs were too high. Then the kind of moss that grew in creek bottoms, that was it. Hurriedly she picked her way down the slope, thrashing with her stick to warn off snakes, and more quickly than she expected she found a boggy patch of light green feathery moss. Quickly pinching off clean tips, she gathered a mass in her skirt.

On the path, he had not moved. She knelt and forced herself to handle the man again, to tear back the leather and look at the great raw gash he'd attempted to bind himself with a piece of his own shirt. The breeches would have to be cut off him. Later.

Well, nothing to do but dress the place the best she could and try to bind it up. She needed a knife. Where was his? She felt about him, found none. Nothing to use but her teeth.

With considerable difficulty, she passed the strips about his body twice and bound a large wad of moss into place. The man moaned a time or two.

"I'm going to get Granny!" she cried close to his head. "We'll be back directly.

She set off running.

She was panting when she saw the chimney and rooftop. She gave a long call.

Granny was in the garden, her little gray-bonneted head barely distinguishable among the bean poles. She listened with still face as Margaret talked breathlessly. "Whe'r he can be saved or not, I can't tell, but I knew you'd think it right we try to get him up from there!"

"Aye, we must get him off the ground."

"Granny, how'll we ever be able to?"

"It'll come to us, child, the way to do when we get there." Granny was already toiling up the high steps. "We'll take the axe. Rope and harness.

And that big old fleece upstairs." She turned and gazed the way Margaret had come, shading her eyes.

"I wouldn't doubt it's more to do wi' the rogues," Margaret said shortly, "one way or another."

"Aye," Granny sighed.

The chestnut mare grazing under the apple trees came eagerly to snuffle at Margaret's hand, at the worn saddle she carried.

"I'd put the plow collar on her too," Granny called, emerging with the fleece and a small leather bag. "I'll get a jug of water. The poor soul's like to be parched wi' thirst."

Margaret rode astride the mare with bunched up skirts, the axe in front of her and Granny behind, holding onto Margaret's waist and the jug.

"It's a good little Molly ye be, to carry us both and all this plunder too," said Granny in the light, loving voice she used for animals and children.

Already sunlight was slanting between the trunks into the shadowed glades.

"Yonder, the other side of that big hickory."

The brown figure seemed already part of the forest floor like the roots and nutshells in the grass, pieces of dead limb, wind-scattered by recent storm.

Margaret slipped off the mare, then helped her grandmother down, feeling the squareness of the small body.

The old woman looked without speaking. She bent stiffly and raised the man's wrist to feel his pulse, ran her hand along the unbruised cheek, drew her fingers across the eyelids. She beckoned for the jug and, lifting his head, put it to his mouth, but the water ran down in his beard.

"He's not already gone, is he?"

"No, he's living, but—" Granny rose. "We'll need some kind of litter to draw him on. It's a rough way, but to lie across Molly's back would be rougher."

"Even if we could get him up there." Granny still had strength of hand and arm but no longer strength in her back. "Cane poles, you think? What kind of poles?" Margaret asked.

"Young gum branches would be easier. Down there a way by that little clearing."

The rays of the sun touched only the treetops as they bound the poles together with deerhide thongs, and the sunlight was gone when they fastened the frame to Molly's harness with long ropes.

Now came the hardest part. "We can't drag him head down," said Margaret.

"No. We'll have to get him turned round. Child, you slip your arm down under his hip bones." They struggled, trying to be gentle. "Oh, if I wasn't such a poor old broke-down creature!" Granny mourned. The man was dead weight and they were hindered by the sunkenness of the path. "Oh, Lord help us. Wait now. Let's rest a bit."

They stood still.

"Granny," began Margaret, "why don't we—"

"Aye. Let's just get him on the litter frame the way he is and let Moll do the turning."

But as Margaret looked at the discolored face, she wondered, Is it any use?

They unharnessed the litter and brought it alongside the man's body. "I'll lift and you slide the fleece under him," said Margaret. "Then between us, maybe we can move him."

Working carefully, shifting him by degrees, they did at last get him onto the litter and bound to it, and as Margaret held up the end his head was on, Granny harnessed it to Molly. "Northward Indians do this way," she said. Margaret was looking at the bruise-shadowed face.

"Now his head's up, if I could just get some of this cordial down him. Hold him up a bit more, Meggie."

As Granny opened the leather bag, Margaret knelt again to cradle the man's head, that was rough with trash from the forest floor. This time it gave Margaret a strange feeling, not that earlier distaste but unexpected compassion. Surely someone sometime had cherished this head, this body once?

He must have been semiconscious, for his throat moved convulsively as the liquid from Granny's vial went down. "Good, sir!" said Granny.

They stood up. They had a mile to go over an up-and-down path in the darkening woods. Making a wide circle, Molly dragged the litter through the rough grass so that at last they were headed toward home. They decided Granny would lead the mare and Margaret would try to ease the burden over rocks and roots. "You be careful, Granny. I wish it was so you could ride."

"Never mind about me, my dear. We must do the best we can. Now come along, Molly!" The old woman spoke with sudden vigor. "Get up, old girl! And young man, ye'll just have to tough it out the best ye can!"

A three-quarter moon was rising when they stopped near the steps of the high porch. Lord, how'll we ever get him up those steps? Margaret had been wondering for the last half-hour.

They did it by lifting the litter from step to step and finally were able to drag it into the big room.

"Now to make up the fire and heat water. We must get something inside him for this fever. And see if there's anything to be done for what's causing it."

The probing and cleansing of the wound caused the man to cry thick words they did not understand. At first it took all Margaret's strength to hold him so her grandmother could cleanse the wound with whiskey and drench it with sugared turpentine, then coat it with a salve of tallow and herbs. But understanding must have come to him, for at last he seemed to try to submit.

"It's a wonder how it missed his bowels."

"Will it heal, you think?"

"As the Lord wills," Granny sighed. The gash was angry with infection. "This moss dressing's as good as any. You can fetch more tomorrow." Margaret saw her grandmother's hands tremble.

They poured hot willowbark tea into him for fever and then camomile tea to make him sleep. "Now mind me, sir, you must drink what I tell ye," Jane McGrew said sternly. "You're in no case to refuse."

They had snuffed the tallow candles, but the firelight was bright. Did the pain-clouded eyes focus? His lips parted. He swallowed.

By the dying fire Margaret told of the other event of the day. "It was that same set. That Jim Tyrrel, John Anderson, Tony Distoe. I knew that Tyrrel's voice. Likely that Govey Black too. It must ha' been at least a dozen."

"Oh my child, you should never ha' set foot there!"

Margaret clamped her jaw. Why must it be so? Why should we have to be afraid on our own land, in our own houses? Why should so many take pleasure in devilry and destruction?

Because some men are of the devil, the minister said. Vessels of and for destruction.

Because there were no courts, no provision for enforcement of laws in these back parts, Robert said. Because the Charlestown gentry would not heed their pleas for courts. And even when the settlers were able to hale known criminals to Charlestown and get them convicted, then ignorant officials as often as not turned them loose. As that new governor had pardoned Distoe and three others last spring.

And because the country was overrun with vagrants, her neighbors said, to aid and abet the gangs, idlers who cared for naught but to hunt and drink and fight.

Like that man on the pallet? The man she and Granny would take turns sitting up by tonight?

Granny was exhausted. Yet she would not hear to Margaret's taking the full brunt of the watching. Not for the first time Margaret pondered: What caused the difference between the Granny kind and the other kind?

She heard the man's regular breathing. He was bathed in sweat and sleeping, no longer in a swoon.

Chapter Two

The hands that held him, that lifted, restrained, that touched his brow, that unclothed and made him clean, they were the hands of someone he had known. Long ago. Light and dark, a light place in a dark room. He groped for the memory. A box. Playing at a box near a glass window. Light. The voice, the knee, the old knotted hands. The grandmother they'd told him of, back in Switzerland—Wildhaus, where they said he came from.

Even his mother he barely remembered. She'd died a year later with the rest of his family who'd survived the voyage to South Carolina. Because what came afterward had almost abraded the memories. Of breast and lap, the big girls' swinging braids; broad shoulders and a deep voice. Yet a gold watch remained an ineradicable brightness. But his later memories had left him in gray and unshaped bereavement. And no woman's hands had touched him since in any personal way. Except his cousin Madle's in her cool, light affection. And Eva's, that lying bitch. But her touch had not been gentle or personal either, he'd come to realize.

He moved and pain knifed his head and flamed in his groin.

The face above him a blur. The young voice distant, severe. "Drink you some more of this tea now."

He was afloat in liquid. He was washed down in sweat.

"Can you raise yourself up?" The hands under his head inexorable. "Granny—" The voice thinned, vanished outside the room.

He turned his head a little toward the source of light. The doorway, a square of green and blue. He watched it a long time.

Irish people. He was still in the Irish settlements above the Deadfall Line. Did they know he was Dutch? They had little use for Switzers and Germans whom they called "Dutch."

He had been making for the road along Broad River that led to the Congarees, hoping his legs would last him to the German settlements on Cannon's Creek. The last he remembered was stumbling along above Indian Creek.

He stilled himself, remembering: the shock, the grappling and throttling, the killing rage. Too many of them. Remembrance gathered in a

10

mass that griped and heaved. He held himself rigid against nausea.

A movement about him as slight as the fall of a leaf. A fragrance of old washworn skirts, an emanation as of camphor and spices. The glass window. The knees. A hand rested on his forehead, light and dry. Bile drained away and the knot dissolved. He breathed a long sigh, tried to see her face.

Very old. Her sunken mouth wide but her chin firm, yet dented with marks like those of a child about to cry. But her faded blue eyes had a light of—merriment?

"Your fever's down. Now you can take you some nourishment."

He nodded slightly.

"A bit of gruel won't harm you. Think you can sit up?"

Again he nodded, braced with his arm, but pain eviscerated him.

"Margaret, you'll have to help me," the old woman called. Two pairs of hands supported him and he found himself resting against the slanting back of a chair turned upside down.

"I'm thinking he must ha' got some blow to his head too."

He closed his eyes as the women moved away.

More than one blow. But his strength of arm had fought off biting and gouging.

The stink of fear assailed him. He clenched his teeth against the everlasting fear of blows, mutilation, and the cursing rage he had known since he was five years old. His only relief was to counter it with his own rage.

...Oh, there'd been a time of respite nine years ago, a place of sanctuary with Johannes Lienhardt and his wife, Madle, who was his only blood kin in this country. The little farm down on Savanna Hunt Creek was a good place. But he did not go there now. Or not often. Not since Eva.

The girl brought a porringer of gruel. His eyes focused better. He saw she was grave-faced and thin almost to sharpness, but if she was Irish, she didn't have their red hair and freckles. As she knelt with the food, English words came to him. "I thank you. For what you done."

Her face softened slightly. "We're glad to ha' found you." She offered him the porringer. "Can you hold it?"

He took it. His hands were steadier now.

He waited for her to ask some question, but she sat back on her heels and watched as he slowly fed himself. It was pewterware they'd given him.

So they were not the poorest class of backwoods Irish. If they'd come by the ware honestly. However, she went barefooted and wore no cap or apron.

For the first time he looked about the room, lighted by the cooking fire, the unshuttered window, and the open door. Cupboards, tables, spinning wheel, the usual household plunder. A shelf of books. A fairly large room with a door to another one. Suddenly he realized that although he lay on a pallet, a sheet was under him. When had he last lain on sheets?

The smell of clean laundry in a dusky room. Johannes' loft-room and Madle's sweet-scented linen.

"I'm Rudi Näffel'." He omitted the *s* on his name.

"Neville?"

He nodded.

"There was Nevilles in Augusty County back in Virginny."

He was silent a moment. "Näffels," he said. "It's Swiss, not English."

Her lips parted. He saw the silent "Oh."

He spooned up all the gruel, though pain stabbed his head every time he swallowed.

"I'll be on my feet to leave soon." The porringer rested in his limp left hand.

She took the dish and rose. "I doubt it's any time soon," she said and was gone.

He closed his eyes. Maybe not. He might be done for this time sure enough. And maybe just as well. Not even his horse left. Loss of horse and rifle of a piece with all else he'd lost in his time. Twenty-seven years old, on his own for the last ten, and what to show for them? Not even a pack of deerskins.

That pack was to have paid the fees for his land warrant and survey. He'd finally decided to renew the land application he'd made five years ago, for the laws were lenient in these matters, and he'd been on his way to Charlestown when the three men with blackened faces sprang at him and left him unconscious. Though not without hurt to themselves.

Now? All he had left was the bare claim to a hundred and fifty acres at the head of Camping Creek on Saluda, where he'd cleared and put up a cabin of sorts after he'd stopped riding with the Rangers. But when Eva left, he'd taken to the woods again. Still wouldn't anybody think that in ten years he could have gained more?

A good strong horse and the best rifle in the country. A friend or two in the Lower Towns of the Nation. ...Increasing skill of hand and eye. More knowledge of beast, rock, and tree. The speed to deliver a blow from which a man might not rise for some time. Long bouts with the jug. Days of oblivion.

But for the last year the thought kept coming to him: A man should have more to show for the time he's served.

Time served. Twelve years stolen from a child-orphan by that conscienceless old man. Twelve years he'd been forced in his ignorance to serve as the old man's bondslave. Twelve years and what to show for it? The scars on his back.

Was that why Eva hadn't loved him? What was wrong with him that a woman couldn't love him? Examining his body, running her fingers over the ridges, the scars of festered sores, she seemed avid for details of how he'd come by them. "And what would you do?"

"What could I do—a shirt-tail boy? Run and dodge? Just made it worse."

"Nobody'd better ever lay a hand on me like that."

Brooding, he thought her words irrelevant. "I told you what I did finally."

"Tell it again."

At seventeen he had gone at Bruger with a piece of firewood, and, past caring whether he'd killed him or not, had taken the old man's musket and left.

"You're strong, aren't you?" whispered Eva. "You're not tall, Rudi, but you're strong." She made him pick her up, wrestled him for the pleasure of being held down.

But it was for a taller man, a great dark hulk of a man that she left him. Luke Altzwinger, whom he pursued but unluckily was not able to come up with and put a rifle ball into. Later it didn't matter. As for Eva, he never laid eyes on her again. Her family sent him word of her death, but he refused all claim in her. Yes, he had married her before God, had taken her down to St. Johns to say his vows before Pastor Theus and the Congaree Swiss and Germans, but he might as well have taken her directly to his cabin for all the difference it made.

Aye-God, what did it matter now? To hold on, to try to hold on to decent ways—for what? As well run with the dogs as be treated like one. And yet— Well.

Never again would he give himself to a woman that way, he'd said. Or be snared by one.

He was slumped against the chairback and needed ease from his position. He tried to lift himself but the effort was too great. Moreover, there were other physical needs. He glanced ruefully at the sheet. A bed of leaves, a shakedown of pine branches was best for him.

He did not want to call the girl. "Margaret," was that her name? Painfully he turned his head. He lay by the wall midway between the chimney and the outer door, not facing the fireplace but in its light.

The old woman, sitting by the hearth, got up.

"Mistress, I need—I need to—" he hesitated, unwilling to use the coarse English word or the German either, "to go out."

She understood. "I'll bring ye something. It's all right. We can take care of that."

Strangely he felt no embarrassment as she helped him, and afterward, out of the agony and the relief a curious peace settled over him. She brought her low chair from the hearth and sat by his pallet, plucking at something in her lap. He couldn't see what she was doing, but her skirt was so near he could hide his hand in its folds if he wanted to.

"Try to get ye some more rest now. The quieter you be, the better you can heal. We won't trouble that place today, but if it goes to paining too much, you tell me now."

Willow bark, she said, Indians used it too. Good for all manner of fever and hurt. As well as camomile. She'd brought camomile from Virginny along with slips of rosemary, mint, and sage. Varmints got into her garden from time to time in spite of the palings they'd put up to keep out fowls as well as the wild things. Her son-in-law used to set traps, but somehow she'd got so she couldn't set a trap for anything, not to break some poor dumb creature's neck or leg. They'd just have to do the best they could and depend on the bounty of the Lord, she told Margaret. The herbs would survive, even flourish, if He willed it. She'd lived in wilderness country over fifty years and she'd come to see a time ago that they lived only by His mercy. She'd learned not to trouble overmuch for mischances....

Her voice moved over, around, and in him, became one with the drowsiness in his head, the dulling of the knife, the immobilizing of the pain in his groin ... the relaxation that crept up his legs, the blessed ease, the quiet that moved under his eyelids. It was the play of sunlight in and out of his fingers. Child fingers moving over wooden toys on a box. Swaddling ease. He slept as she talked and worked with her knotted hands.

Late in the afternoon he grew unbearably warm. They would not allow the fire to go out although it was mid-July. He saw beads of sweat on the girl's upper lip as she gave him more of the everlasting hot tea. He saw darkness under her eyes. Unlike her grandmother she had few words for him.

He wondered about the men of the place. They'd put another shirt on him sometime or other. Was it the young woman's husband's? ...He saw no signs of children either. Strange to be in a house with no men or children. The old woman spoke of a son-in-law but it sounded as if he were gone. Why would a settled man be gone this time of year? Unless.... Men rode in the woods for many reasons nowadays. And such men had houses and women to harbor them too. ... Still, if this were that kind of house, would they have brought him in and tended him? No, no, not the old one. Nor the young one either, he thought. Yet who could understand their impulses?

Stifling hot, he grew more and more restless, tried to move different ways.

"You'd best lie still," said the girl sharply. "You'll just aggravate that wound. You don't want any more commotion than you can help."

"So hot," he muttered, "I die of this heat."

"You're like to die of something else if you take chill," she retorted. "Be glad you're not the way you were yesterday this time."

He was abashed, wondering how they had managed to get him here.

"Granny says you've got to keep that fever sweated down."

Toward evening when she brought him broth and hominy, he asked, "Where's the man here?"

"What?" She seemed startled. Then she said low, "My brother, the only man kin I had here, he was shot down on his own place six days ago." She paused. "And if you have aught to do with such murderers, I'll ask you to keep it to yourself whilst you're under this roof!"

He was unprepared for her cold vehemence. "Why—why—" He did not have the English to express his indignation. "How you think I got—like this?"

"Well, all kinds of things happen to woods-rovers," came her hard voice. "Who's to say how anybody gets hurt in the woods anymore?"

He turned away, the dish resting heavily in his hands.

He heard her clear her throat. Yet she stayed, sitting back on her heels by the pallet. At length she said, "You'd better try to eat that."

Slowly he turned his head to look at her, but as he did so, she rose swiftly.

After a while a wry smile twisted his mouth. Was her suspicion any more unjust than his had been? Admit it: hers could well have had some basis in fact. After all, why was he not now riding with James and Anthony Tyrrel or Govey Black or the Moon brothers? He'd shared fires aplenty with some of their followers. Why hadn't he taken up with them?

He put the bowl aside and fell into a half-drowse, yet all the while his mind moved slowly above his body. Why hadn't he? He did not know. It was something to do maybe with what he had once begun to be—a brightness once in the center of his memory. Or maybe sunlight on willow leaves down on Savanna Hunt Creek when he'd first talked with Johannes Lienhardt. Or maybe—the thought was fresh—the brightness of Dutch guilders before they were changed to Carolina pounds, the guilders his old Swiss grandparents had sent him by Madle. They had given him his new clothes, a bright bay horse, and a new start as he rode to Sabbath worship at St. Johns. He was somebody then those golden autumn days at the Congarees.

Had his life held only loss?

Unaccountably tears welled under his eyelids. Strange because he never cried now.

The empty room was dusky. They were busy with evening tasks, he supposed. If the girl should say anything by way of apology or even if there should be a softening in her manner, he might say something to show he bore no ill will.

But she gave him no occasion.

Chapter Three

Margaret had come to gather muscadines. Since the best ones were clustered high in the trees, she tied up her petticoat about her waist, and hindered only by her short-skirted shift, she caught at a lower limb and pulled herself up into the leaning chestnut oak that grew from the hillside above the creek. She had been climbing this tree for years, not only for fruit for wine and jelly but also because of how the tree grew, its places to sit and stand, where you could look out on the world and just be.

But hardly a morsel of fruit had she picked this summer. The woods offered varied bounty—plums, crabapples, haws, persimmons; all manner of high and low-growing berries; chestnuts, chinquapins, walnuts, and hickory nuts. Their gathering had once been her favorite task. Let the boys shoot game and fowl, let Jean gather eggs and garden truck, but Margaret would harvest the woods. Nowadays, however, there was too much work at the house for time in the woods. But today Granny said, "Seems like I'm in the notion to make muscadine wine if ye can see your way clear to fetch me some fruit, Meggie."

It was good to obey her grandmother, to lose sight of the house, a blessed release to leave cows, poultry, hogs, bean rows, water-pails and woodpile. Here in this spacious shade were only birdcalls, their flights and flutterings, the soft crash of squirrels in the branches, the hover and flit of dragonflies and butterflies. Margaret stood at the joining of limb and trunk, and all sense of obligation fell away.

She climbed higher. She felt the strength of the tree limbs and experienced a surge of strength in her own limbs. She felt she could run, leap, soar, do all she was meant to do. She stood housed by the floatings of green, unencumbered, poised among the light-glazed leaves for perhaps as long as a bird might perch before flitting away.

Then she began reaching among the limbs, pulling at vines, dropping fruit into a pail she drew up and attached to a lower limb. She had only half-filled the pail when the crack of a musket stilled her. She listened. The rustle of a squirrel, the rattle of a woodpecker down the ridge. Then—was it a cry or a halloo from the house? Dread moved up through her legs, unnerved her hands.

She slipped down the limbs and started running as soon as she hit the ground, scuffing her feet on rocks, snagging her petticoat. But when she reached the edge of the woods, she paused. Two horses. No, three. Molly, dear Lord, where was Molly? She began running up the pasture, stopped again. She saw a man in the shadow of the porch, then another. One turned. She exhaled a long breath. Thank God, just Aleck Fraser!

She drew her hand across her forehead and bent to wipe her face on her petticoat, saw the condition of her hiked-up skirts in dismay. A wild heathen she looked! Scratched ankles and tumbled hair, hot and perspiring and ragged as a beggar woman. And oh, my soul, it was Mr. Richardson, the Presbyterian minister from the Waxhaws! And her in such state!

Now whose was the third horse? As she came up the hill, she recognized the blaze on a brown gelding. Dan, one of Robert's horses!

The men saw her. "I made sure you'd hear the musketfire," called the red-haired one with high cheekbones and homely, irregular features. Aleck Fraser, a married man who lived four miles down the creek. He had helped to bury Robert.

"Yes, I came quick as I could, not knowing who it was." She mounted the steps and made a slight, stiff curtsy. "Mr. Richardson, I'm sorry not to ha' been here to give you welcome."

"Miss Margaret, it's well known the straits you're in." The minister's voice was deep and resonant but had a kind of dragging undertone. A tall, pale man in shabby ridingdress, he advanced to take her hand. "We've come to inquire what ways—" he paused, "you and Mistress McGrew can be assisted."

And it's slow anyone's been to come, she thought with a flash of resentment. Robert's house fire two weeks ago, somebody's bound to ha' seen that smoke.

Granny stood in the doorway, neat in her bleached linen apron and her long-eared cap. "My dear, he wishes to speak with us both." Granny's voice trembled.

Margaret stood awkwardly, having no ready word.

Her grandmother said, "It's warm inside the house. We'll bring out chairs. And you'll take a dram of whiskey?"

Margaret went quickly to set out three rush-bottomed chairs and a stool for herself, while her grandmother brought cups.

Margaret waited impatiently as they sipped. What news? She wanted to ask about the horse.

The minister removed his spectacles and polished the scratched lenses. When he looked up, Margaret was astonished, for she had never seen his eyes without spectacles, their melancholy, deepset darkness. Although he had a large congregation of his own, William Richardson spent much of his time traveling about the back parts of the Province, preaching to small leaderless congregations, many without meetinghouses.

"Miss Margaret, I was distressed beyond measure to learn how your brother died." His speech was halting. "I've been meeting with the people on Duncan's Creek." He cleared his throat, glanced at Fraser. "The news we have most particularly to bring you—" He cleared his throat again. "To speak plainly, you must know your brother's wife is dead."

Neither Granny nor Margaret spoke. Margaret looked away in the trees.

"What caused her death, sir?" Granny's voice was frail and high.

"It's said she died the day of her husband's death. By her own hand."

"Oh, God be merciful to her—" The old voice crumbled.

Margaret saw again the rose-fleshed arm of Janet lifted to wave goodbye. "Come again, Meg! Come again soon!"

She rose and turned her back to the men. Her words drove themselves out. "Why is it, tell me, why is it that decent people cannot keep safe in their own houses? Why should my brother be murdered on his own land—and his wife—who harmed ne'er a soul in all her days—why must she come to an end like this?" Her voice was strained thin. "You tell me, sirs, you tell me! Where are the men in this country ... that let such happen?" She turned to face them.

"Never you fear—" began Aleck swiftly.

The minister interrupted, "You know, do you not, these things have happened everywhere, not just here?"

Aleck said, "And I can tell you this: men are gathering!"

The minister continued, "Things worse than this, if you can imagine it. In the Waxhaws, at Pine Tree, in the Welsh settlements on the Pee Dee, and even down in the German settlements beyond the Edisto—"

Aleck cut in again, "And men *are* gathering."

After a small silence Mr. Richardson said, "I must agree with them. Felons must not be let to terrorize the country."

Aleck cried, "Oh, we're going after 'em, never you fear! We're already banded up! We know where they den and who harbors 'em."

"Then I wish you good success." Margaret's voice was lean and dry.

"I thank you, sir," said Granny, "and Aleck too, for coming to acquaint us with these things." She drew a tremulous breath. "I don't wish harm to e'er a creature in the world, but such wickedness—to countenance such wickedness, I cannot believe it right. Not in God's sight."

After a few moments' silence the minister said heavily, "No, the Almighty never meant men to live without law. Though," he added, "there *are* men already appointed to carry out the laws." Aleck made an impatient sound. "But," Mr. Richardson sighed, "in our district they seem helpless."

Aleck snorted, "They've more often hindered than helped. And when we ha' sat back and waited for 'em to act, it's been about the same as giving the villains license. The time for that, sir, is past."

Margaret looked at Aleck. The lines in his bony face were deep-drawn. He had a wife and three little ones, she reflected. Who would care for them if he weren't here?

"Aleck, I'm sorry to ha' spoke so rough while ago," she said low. "It's that I—I had a fondness for Janet Allen—Janet Logan, that was."

"Aye, they were little together," said Granny. "You'll excuse the child's bursting out so."

"It was no discredit to her," said the minister. He cleared his throat again. "Mistress McGrew, with the two of you alone, your neighbors are much concerned for you."

Aleck leaned forward. "Robert gone and all, we know you need help on the place now. Well, my brother, James Fraser, he's more than willing to ride over and give help as needed. He sends this message to you. He's more than willing—if it's agreeable." Aleck looked at Margaret.

Margaret glanced at Granny but Granny said nothing.

Margaret's face grew warm. She looked down to hide her vexation. And why could not Jamie Fraser have come himself? Why would he even *ask* permission when any fool would know their need? But that was like Jamie—ever a kind of stand-offishness in him. He might have more learning than his brothers, but he was downright dull-witted when it came to his own kind.

Aleck said, "We'd thought to send word to David Allen—"

Margaret interrupted, "We sent word. We had good chance to send it and Granny wrote." Bill Lee was good for carrying messages if nothing else. "It's like he's got the letter by now." Yet the coming of her older brother she did not care to think of either.

She shifted. Well, just saying the man could come on the place needn't mean anything else, did it? Though there were worse men, she thought soberly. He was a far cry from Bill Lee. "We'd be obliged for what'er help our neighbors could spare us," she said formally. "Tell James Fraser we'd be glad of his help. Though we'd thought to manage for ourselves." She glanced at her grandmother.

But Granny had a faraway look. "Margaret's a brave girl, Mr. Richardson. But oh," she said softly, "how I wish it was so I could take her elsewhere. I've lived in these back settlements many a year now; yet I ha' known other ways too. Long, long ago afore I came here. I wish we could go back—somewhere eastward or northward. Not for my sake but hers."

Go back. How many times she had thought of it.

Again the minister took off his glasses. He too knew other ways. He had been born in England but educated at the University of Glasgow, had come to Pennsylvania as a young man and studied under the great Dr. Davies.

His deepset eyes gazed beyond the rough-planed boards of the porch, past the rooftop of chestnut, oak, and hickory on the horizon. Endless were the hills, valleys, and streams of this land and countless the souls lost among them. Here, at home, everywhere—more and more he was oppressed by the dreary endlessness of it all. Every journey opening up more savagery than before.

Aleck said vigorously, "But it won't always be this way. Once we rid ourselves of thieves and vermin, it'll be a different country, you'll see."

Granny said, "I pray God I may see it. If He spares me."

They were so taken up with their thoughts that they did not notice the man who came hobbling up until he stood at the foot of the steps. He carried a piece of harness and was looking at the horses tethered at the edge of the yard.

Margaret observed him almost with shock. It was as if some woods animal had followed her home from the ridge. His dark hair had the spring of tendrils on a muscadine vine, his eyes the glint of light in a rock-strewn creek. She drew a long breath like someone stepping outside for a breath of air.

Granny was brought firmly into the present and eyed him now with a mixture of anxiety, fondness, and exasperation. "Give me work for my hands," he'd urged her. "If my legs won't go yet, I can use my hands."

She had tried him at carding wool, but after an hour its tedium had sunk him into gloom. Hackling flax was not quite as bad, but she was afraid the exertion would irritate his wound. She let him help core and peel apples for drying and also hobble out to pick beans and break corn. The axe and hoe were forbidden him, though she'd seen where he'd hoed around the melons yesterday. She was relieved this morning when he found work in the barn mending harness.

"This is Rudi Näffels!" cried Granny in her spritely voice. "We found him robbed and hurt in the woods that day Robert's house was burnt. Come up, Rudi! Here's Mr. Richardson, a minister from the Waxhaws, and our neighbor, Aleck Fraser."

To the men on the porch he was simply an alien. He was dressed in old leather breeches too long for him and his own ragged shirt and moccasins. To Aleck Fraser he was not of their community, not of their kind. To William Richardson he was another of those souls without law or gospel.

Rudi mounted the steps slowly. The other men stood a head taller than he. Mr. Richardson extended his hand. Aleck did not. In his buckled shoes and shirt of good strong homespun, Aleck looked the epitome of respectability.

"It was God's mercy you were found," said the minister.

Rudi gestured toward the women. "I owe my life to them." Although he had not the strong accent of some Germans, it was there.

"What brought you to Indian Creek?" Aleck asked in a dry voice.

"I was going to Charlestown." He added somewhat unwillingly, "With a pack of deerskins. And for business."

They waited for him to say more.

"My horse, my rifle, all was stolen." Knife, powder horn, shot pouch, he could have added. Fifteen pounds in money. Even the little skillet Madle had given Eva, which he'd not wanted to leave for the vagrants who would rifle his cabin.

"Then you're a hunter," Aleck stated.

"I hunt. Yes."

"Do you have family here?" asked Mr. Richardson.

Rudi did not reply at once. "No."

Margaret listened with interest. Granny would not probe, and Margaret, after her bitter words that second day, had been ashamed to. It was ever her way to blurt out more than she meant. She'd rued it many a time.

Finally Aleck asked, "What will you do now?" To Margaret he sounded like Robert.

Granny said, "He must get well first. He's just now able to move about."

"When I can, I'll go. If I had a horse, I'd go now." Although the words were to Fraser and Richardson, Rudi glanced at Granny with a half-smiling apologetic look.

"He's welcome to stay as long as he needs to," said Margaret. "We'd be a sorry set if we couldn't take care of someone left half dead by robbers." Her eyes flashed. "I recollect the Scriptures speak of that!"

The men looked surprised, but Granny said, "That's so, Meggie!" She began to chuckle as if they were all her little children. "It makes us happy, indeed, it does, Mr. Richardson, when we can help one another. It helps our own feelings." She added quickly, "And I wouldn't doubt that Rudi won't turn out to be a help to us too."

"I'm little help to you now," said Rudi, but there was a curl of softness in his voice.

"Well, Jamie'll be here to help you tomorrow," said Aleck. "You can depend on him for wood and whatever's to do in the fields."

They resumed their seats. Rudi on the stool at Granny's indication. Margaret stood just inside the doorway. "How came you by Robert's horse?" she asked suddenly. She had waited long enough for that explanation.

"Now we've almost forgot the only good bit of news we have for you," answered the minister. "Your brother's horse was took up near the head of Duncan's Creek, loose in the woods, I'm told. His mark was recognized and I offered to return him."

"I made sure that's whose it was when I came up," said Margaret. "He must ha' got away somehow."

"See here," said Aleck, "if it would relieve you of care, I'll keep him for you till we're more settled hereabouts. If it would relieve you of extra trouble."

Granny and Margaret looked at each other. "A horse is not a great deal of trouble this time of year," ventured Granny.

"No, but with the possibility of these gangs—"

"I thought you were all going after them," said Margaret.

"To be sure, we are! But they won't be got rid of in a day. And with so many rovers and idlers about—"

"Would you like to take Molly too?" asked Margaret.

Aleck reddened. Rudi's face darkened.

"Maybe we'd best keep him," said Granny in her sweet, singing voice. "But I thank you, Aleck, for being so kind a neighbor. Frasers have ever a name for being stout, good neighbors, Mr. Richardson. You couldn't ask for better."

Aleck's mouth was clamped shut.

Finally the minister said, "You mentioned removal a while ago. Would you consent to remove for a time? Perhaps to a neighbor's house, till the country's more peaceful?"

Granny did not answer at once. "For myself I don't fear e'er a human soul, sir. My life's in God's hands. But I mustn't speak for my granddaughter."

Margaret tried to speak courteously. "Thank you, sir—and Aleck too for your concern. But I don't think I could see my way clear to walk off and leave my father's house to thieves."

"We ha' little of value here," said Granny. "They've left us alone so far. So we'll just be trusting the Lord for our keeping." Her voice was serene again.

Mr. Richardson felt a sudden lifting of the oppression that was with him everywhere nowadays. He felt as if he had come suddenly out of dark woods. Surely it was the Lord's mercy! And surely it was here all about him as it had ever been. Surely goodness and mercy shall follow me... He rose.

It was his custom to have prayer wherever he visited. At his bidding they stood. He prayed both generally and particularly: for God's glory, His will, His justice, and His peace to prevail; for the persons on the porch, even for Rudi's restoration to health and strength.

When he finished, Aleck and Rudi, on opening their eyes to the world of field, woods, and sky, looked directly at each other, then away. Aleck said to Granny, "I'll stable the horse for you."

While the minister said goodbye, Aleck took Dan to the barnlot. Noting the scant supply of grain and fodder, he sighed. Maybe something could yet be salvaged from Robert's fields. But what to do about those two lone women. As Robert's friend he couldn't help feeling responsible. But there could be nobody more stubborn than an Allen. And a cross-grained female

Allen at that. How Jamie ever thought he'd manage her—but he wasn't sure Jamie even wanted the managing of her.

One reason Margaret loved Granny so dearly was that Granny never scolded her. She corrected occasionally and sometimes instructed, but she never scolded. Margaret knew her mother would have expressed severe displeasure at her daughter's outspokenness on the porch this afternoon. Granny also disapproved of such forward speech, but she would not reprove her. Yet it was this loving forbearance that caused Margaret to feel guilty and to go about the rest of the day half-ashamed.

At their evening meal of stewed peas, johnnycake, and roasting ear corn Rudi said, "I can make you new good surcingles from the hide I see in your barn."

Granny said, "We'd be vastly obliged to you, Rudi. I know that old saddle girth's well nigh worn out."

"The saddle's not safe," said Rudi.

Margaret said, "Molly goes right well for me without a saddle."

"And for your Granny?"

It was the first time he had ever made free with her name for her grandmother and the first time he had ever implied that her judgment might not be perfect. Her anger kindled as she searched for a retort.

Rudi observed her under lowered eyelids. "I'll tend your gelding as long as I'm here. I'll see to his harness too." He paused. "I won't steal him."

Margaret turned upon him, her eyes flashing. But when she looked at Rudi, the glint in his brown eyes became contagious. She began to laugh too, a sound as low and fresh as the purl of creek water over rocks. Her face alight with laughter was like a sunlit clearing in deep woods.

Chapter Four

The coarse, strong scent of ripening corn Jamie always associated with the smell of a book because the end of harvest had meant resuming hours with Parson Craig. He could see again the shapely Virgilian lines, hear the rolling hexameters, *"Urbs antiqua fuit—"* and *Carthago, Tyrus, Ilium,* worlds before, would obliterate the rough walls of the schoolroom. Quicker, brighter than the other scholars, Jamie Fraser had leapt into *"Arma virumque cano"* and at thirteen, when the Frasers left the Shenandoah Vallely, he was mastering Greek verbs. He still said the paradigms to himself sometimes as he plowed a furrow or hoed between the stumps. *Luo, lueis, luei.* "I am loosing, thou art loosing, he is loosing."

To loose, to set free. The verb meant also "to break up," or "to destroy."

He broke the corn off the stalks. It was meant to be broken, set free. These nubbins piled in the basket to be shucked, shelled, their grains poured in a thick stream between stones or ground between the molars of living creatures, transmuted into—what?

"Except a corn of wheat fall into the ground and die, it abideth alone." Christ spoke of himself. But he spoke too of men. Jamie felt a surge of yearning. How can it be transmuted in me? What more for me than to eat, sleep, sweat? What words but *horse, hog, barn, field, cow? I come, I go, I own, I have gotten.*

I do not know. I cannot.

Ginomai. I come into being. I become.

I wish....

The September sun burned away the mist. The trees hung black-green against cloudless blue. From the Allens' house came the faint rhythm of a dasher plunging into a butter churn, from the fowlhouse a hen's high cackling. Butter and eggs. *Ginontai.* They become what they are meant to be.

I am not becoming. Except it fall into the ground and die, it abideth alone.

To marry Margaret Allen—a kind of death. A death to self. But would that self dying be transmuted? To life? Something of spirit yet undreamed of? Hard to believe it. He could hardly believe that the urgencies of flesh could accomplish the becoming he yearned for. No passion of the flesh, he believed, could touch the self that stood aloof, analytical. He could almost curse himself for its aloofness.

For he was so lonely sometimes he could have cried out to the oaks and hickories if such had been his way. Though at twenty-three he thought he should have learned how to bear loneliness.

James Fraser was the best-looking man of his family. He was tall, well-built, fair-haired, with a fresh, ruddy complexion unmarred by sickness. That he had not yet married and claimed his own land marked him as different from his kin and neighbors here. Back in Virginia there'd been talk of the College of New Jersey at Princeton for him.

"The lad has gifts to make him a rare scholar," Parson John Craig told John Fraser. But Fraser's desire for a securer place in spite of the Parson's exhortation to stay and last out the troubles had shut out that future for the boy.

Traveling in the same wagon down the same road that had brought John Fraser in 1740 out of Lancaster County, Pennsylvania, to the upper reaches of Beaver Run on the Middle Shenandoah, they had left that lovely valley which was terrifyingly open to Indians in 1758, and they did not stop till they reached the red clay lands west of the Enoree River in South Carolina. Here there was already a scattering of Virginia families along with a few Quakers and a German or two, but no meetinghouse, no minister. And hardly had they begun to clear fields when the same terror they had known in Virginia enveloped the South Carolina Piedmont.

Two years they existed in forts, half-starving much of the time, the men foraying out to shoot and be shot at. But 1761 brought their release and a heady freedom, a surge of energy to all of them. Seven of his brothers and sisters were now married, leaving only Jamie and two sisters at home. He was his father's mainstay, they said and were glad that he seemed content to remain so.

He was not content.

Sometimes when Mr. Richardson visited and gathered them under the trees, Jamie was stirred with a surging vision of his own. It was for an order, a pattern of beauty that transcended the short-lived fecundity of this natural world, that overarched the anxieties and toil and terror, the squalid failures of their own lives. He remembered the clear, straight gaze of Mr.

Craig, his warmth and authority. He saw himself too as a minister in a plain board meetinghouse, moving his hearers to his own vision, that splendor eternal in the heavens. He saw himself as a teacher.

"What is the chief end of man?"

The catechism answer: "Man's chief end is to glorify God and to enjoy him forever."

But alone? No. He grasped quite well that glorifying and enjoying God should be in concert with other men and women. Yet even in a large family, among neighbors like themselves, he knew himself alone.

He was too old now for schooling. Men his age had finished college and were already licensed and ordained. He could not be fourteen again.

When he went to the Allens' house for dinner, the Switzer was not there. Rudi had taken the old Queen Anne musket and some swanshot to the woods, Granny said. Again Jamie wondered how long before the man left for good. Except for his walking a bit stiffly, Jamie could see nothing wrong with him now, though to do him justice, one must admit he tried to make himself useful. Granny McGrew still fussed over him as if he might break. And Margaret—well, Margaret seemed to ignore him.

She was coming from the fowlhouse with an egg basket. He watched her cross the yard, the arch of her foot a part of the balance and flow of her movement. She walked with a queen's grace. *Regina ad templum forma pulcherrima Dido.* A queen of poultry and kine to her temple of square-cut logs.

"I do believe the hens are laying better, now they know their house is tight against weasels. This time of year they generally slack off, but ours seem to ha' taken a fresh start." A long speech for Margaret.

He could think of no answer. He waited on the steps. "Do you need fresh water?" he finally thought to ask.

"I'll see. No, here's a plenty. Granny must already ha' gone for it." She went inside.

The wooden pail was on a shelf by the door, its gourd dipper on a peg above it. He drank and splashed water on his hands at the edge of the porch. There being no towel, he dried his hands on his shirt.

The sweet, singing voice of Granny McGrew called, "Jamie, you must be famished! It's long past noon. Come in and sit down."

The room was dusky after the sunlight. He took a place on the bench at the long table and was asked to say grace.

They had boiled peas, fried corncakes and butter, and stewed apples with cream. A stone jug of peach brandy was on the end of the table. Later Granny and Margaret would drink sparingly, but would urge Jamie to partake more freely.

"If Rudi brings us back a mess of squirrels," Granny said, "it'll make a nice change."

"I don't see how he can hit a thing with that old piece," said Margaret.

"He is a skilled hunter," said Jamie.

"Somehow you never think of Germans as hunters," said Granny. "You think of 'em more as farmers."

After a few moments Jamie observed, "I've heard they're fine marksmen in Europe—the Swiss Germans."

"Aye, Rudi's a Switzer. I guess there may be a difference." Granny's voice held a question, but no one knew how to answer it.

Jamie wished he did. So many of them coming out of the complexities of older countries, but as ignorant of their past as new-hatched birds. His life had begun in a broad valley in the back parts of Virginia. Yet he knew now it had been shaped long before by events in the bogs of Ireland, the glens of Scotland, in the great halls of Edinburgh and London, perhaps even Paris and the papal courts of Rome. That dark-bearded man with the bitter line of mouth that sometimes curved into laughter, what had shaped his life?

Margaret rose. He watched her bend, lift, turn, move easily the big iron spider on the hearth and slip more corncakes onto the bread tray. It occurred to him that Margaret had no need to know of any shaping that made her what she was. It was as if she had sprung new-formed from these fields and woods. Or from Indian Creek? he mused. Or the Enoree? Smiling to himself, he pictured her rising out of some leaf-shaded pool beneath the willows. He met her eyes.

Grave, speculating.

His blood pounded. His face grew hot, his hands trembled. He looked at the cornbread soaking up broth on his plate. He felt tied to the bench, a misery of shame and panic. He tried desperately to order his thoughts, but with his senses rampant, he was powerless. As she placed the tray before him, her arm brushed his shoulder, and involuntarily he jerked back.

Then he knew. He must speak or act, do or say the irrevocable. Soon. For she expected it.

"Jamie, are you ready for a noggin of brandy? Meggie, fill his cup."

It was sour-sweet with the warmth of old banked fires. He longed to drink it fast and get away. Yet bravely he raised his eyes and looked at Margaret down the table across from him. Her hair pulled back made a raven's wing above her ear. He imagined touching it, smoothing its tangled mass down her back. She would not look at him again.

"I'll hitch up the wagon to bring in the corn this afternoon," he said hurriedly. "Since Henry's not broke to pull, you think I'd do better to use the mare or the gelding? I fear it'll be a light load."

"I knew that old field would make a scanty crop," said Granny. "It needs to be let grow over. But Robert, poor soul, he had his own newground to clear."

"Moll's gentler to handle," said Margaret. "Take Molly."

"I'll—I'll get to some clearing for you along in October."

Margaret looked up. "We couldn't let you do that, Jamie." Were her eyes troubled?

"Couldn't you?"

Granny rose, said lightly, "I hear one of my old cuddies cackling out there, and I think it's one that keeps trying to steal a nest. I need to go catch her so I can break her up from setting." She stood a moment with one hand on the table, steadying herself. In the doorway she paused again. "Oh, blessed Lord ha' mercy," they heard her say. Nowadays Granny often talked aloud to herself or to the Lord. She moved from their sight.

The dusky room was warm with the dying coals. The glow of the brandy was still in Jamie's throat.

He had never thought it would be like this—trenchers and empty bowls, the smells and fumes of meat and drink. He had envisioned a room with high-backed chairs and a small mahogany table perhaps, books and a candlestand. A lady with dressed hair and spreading skirts that would hide her small shod feet. A faceless lady. Madam, I beg the honor—   The face that looked back at him, he was shocked to see, held something he recognized. Fear. Courage. Will forcing itself to surrender to that loosing. Something to be broken. Self dying. For a moment he drew as near to her as he had ever been to anyone. He saw her wholly as individual, her fear and anxiety and perplexities. She was Margaret, no other, as he was James.

He said softly, "Mr. Richardson spoke of coming back in November. If we got word to him, he could publish banns for us then. What say you, Margaret?"

As she did not answer, he rose and went around the table, stood awkwardly above her. She did not move and he sat down sideways on the bench to face her, his legs away from the table.

When she looked up, he saw nothing he recognized. Her face was as inscrutable as that of a standing cow, a crouching cat—victim, predator—inscrutable as he imagined the face of some deity of the wild might be if there were such.

"Jamie, I'm not sure you really do want to marry me," she said low.

He blinked and drew back a little. "I'm offering myself to you," he said stiffly, "if you'll have me."

She looked past him. "Put it this way. I'll not say no, but give yourself a month more. Speak of it again in a month."

"Margaret, thinking's no good for me! Nor waiting either! I've waited too long already!"

At that she straightened her shoulders and he saw a glint in her eyes. Anger? She said, still in that distant voice, "Then give me the month. I've waited too and—I like you right well, James Fraser, but give me the bit more time."

Was he grateful or disappointed? Piqued? Or relieved?

He reached for her hand, raised it to his lips. It was strong, scratched, brown. He kissed its hard palm gently. Suddenly without warning he found himself catching her up and kissing her with rough abandon.

For a few moments she submitted. Then with her full strength she pushed him away, scrambled up from the bench, and ran out of the room.

He stood up breathing hard, wanting to curse and cry both.

Rudi saw Margaret running toward the pasture. Alarmed, he called, "What happened?"

She looked his way briefly as she caught Molly's halter and began leading her toward the mounting block. He dropped his bag of squirrels and started toward her, but suddenly she turned Molly loose and veered in the direction of the barnlot.

Seeing the look on her face, he paused. What a creature! One moment her face working with emotion; the next, closed. What was it? Or had he imagined it? Well, whether he had or not, she didn't want him. He went back to pick up his bag.

It held so little he was half-ashamed to show it. He blamed it mostly on the gun, but he felt it was due also to his own frustration. He had too many problems on his mind.

Where to go and what to do? Two months he'd stayed and he should have gone weeks ago. What kept him? At first it was the difficulty of going anywhere on foot. But he was healed enough now, he thought, to tramp wherever he wanted to, though not as when he'd been young and had roamed the woods like a wild thing. But by using moderation he was sure he could travel. Where? Back to Camping Creek? And what there? Though he'd hidden his tools, and the cabin might still be standing, without seed and stock the ground was all but useless to him. And he was still no more than a squatter on it anyhow.

A horse and a gun were his real needs. With them he could go anywhere, live as he'd been used to living. If he could get back to his cabin, get hold of his tools if they'd not been stolen, and take them somewhere to barter—a horse and any kind of old musket would do to start with. The tools ought to bring ten or fifteen pounds. Though how to pack plow-irons, hoes, and axes anywhere on foot he didn't know. And if he hadn't been such a fool as to leave the other house plunder out—why, skillets and kettles brought money too. Which was why they'd be gone. But only birds, he thought, could see the tools he'd drawn up into thick cedar branches and only beetles the plow-irons under the great rock. But from there?

Congarees was the best place to barter anything. But that meant Johannes Lienhardt because if Johannes heard of his visit, he'd be hurt if Rudi didn't come by. And Rudi shrank from seeing the Lienhardts. Nor did he want to face the other people at Congarees either, the fine folk with their wheatfields and buckled shoes and their big safe houses with furnishings brought up from Charlestown, folk like the Rieders, Gallmans, and Fridigs, who wore broadcloth coats on Sunday and rode fine horses. How could he go now among them, a tramping beggar, when once he'd cantered out as a new-married man with goods of his own and the prospect of more? Once he'd almost belonged to them, and they'd seemed to respect him. But he'd wanted something wider than that strip of farmland between the river and the sandhills. A world untrammeled by roads and manmade obligations.

And yet, and yet— He had other needs. To see respect in people's eyes. To spend a sociable hour, to tell a tale, to enjoy a meal that wasn't burnt or half-raw. To lift a child head-high and get his beard grabbed....

Joggi Lienhardt. That scamp would be nine years old in December. He remembered his first sight of the wizened little face that cold day before the fire. And Heiri almost seven. A couple of girls there too, no telling how many by now. He pictured the big clean room as he'd last seen it—fire-bright, alive with women's talk, children's prattle, all kinds of cheerful anticipation.

He closed his mind to it. It would be harder to go there than anywhere else he could think of. And yet Johannes Lienhardt, of all men, would most want to help him. His eyes darkened. Then where?

Little Granny caught sight of him as she fastened the fowlyard gate. "Come in the house and get you something to eat, Rudi! You've been gone since daybreak, you must be starved!"

He wanted to say he'd roasted meat in the woods, but one could not lie to Granny. He shook his head. "I brought little back to you." He showed her the bag. "No, I'll clean them," as she moved to take it.

She brightened. "I'll make up the fire."

He knew she didn't like cleaning game although she did it without hesitation. As for him, it was second nature to skin and gut anything he shot. But he'd seen the mourning in her eyes as she handled the small dark bodies, even though she always cooked and seasoned them into a delicious stew.

There was something about this very old woman that made him want to protect her. She made him think of a little holly tree, tender green, fiercely bright in winter.

As they went up the steps, the tall Irishman clattered down them.

Granny paused. "You better take you some rest, Jamie, afore you go out in that hot field again," she called after him.

The man muttered something about finishing early.

As Rudi and Granny entered the big room, Margaret came in from the adjoining one, which had its own outside door. So she'd come back in. She cleared the table while Granny got a clean plate.

But Rudi went to the open window and stood with his back to them. He saw the Irishman lead the mare from the barnlot.

"I must leave," Rudi said. "I'll go tomorrow."

The chinks and scrapes ceased.

"Come and sit down, Rudi," said Granny. "You need food right now."

He came to the table. He looked up as she set food in front of him. She had a crooked bit of smile on her face, but her eyes were filled.

Emotion deepened his voice. "It's not right I stay longer. And you have other help now."

Her sigh was the sound of wind-ruffled leaves. "I know you must go, Rudi Näffels. But coming when you did, it was like—well, you helped to take our minds off our sorrow." She cocked her head sideways. "And you'll come back, won't you? Sometime?"

"Where will you go?" asked Margaret.

"I'll go back to my old house if it still stands. I hid a few tools I can sell maybe. To get a horse."

"Where is your house?" They had not even known he had one.

"It's on Camping Creek. The north bank of Saludy."

"That's a far tramp," said Margaret. "About twenty-five or thirty miles? It'll take you how many days?"

"I can go in two days, I think."

"Woods are dampish at night," said Granny. "You must take you something from here for cover."

"And where will you take your goods to barter?" Margaret avoided her grandmother's eye.

"Now, Margaret—" came the mild reproof.

"How far will you have to take them?" Margaret persisted.

Rudi hardly knew how to answer. "Neighbors maybe will barter with me."

"Well, he's had enough of the woods for today. We'll let him eat his dinner in peace." From Granny this was rebuke.

Margaret poured hot water into a wooden basin and took the kettle outside to refill it. The sound of pouring, the clink of the lid, and she called, "Granny!"

"Eh? Did you call me, Margaret?" The old woman went out.

Rudi savored the buttery corncakes. He'd surely been spoiled these two months. Plain fare but well seasoned, well cooked. Different from now on. He relished the apples and thick cream.

Margaret and her grandmother came in to stand at the foot of the table.

"No, you tell him, child. I'll not take credit for your good thoughts."

Margaret stood turned in profile to him, her arched fingers on the table supporting her hand, a gesture of her grandmother's. Swiftly her glance brushed that of the man looking up. "We think you should take Dan,

Robert's horse. He'll be more trouble to us now fall's coming on, and besides," she continued in a rush, "we don't need him the way you do."

Rudi had no words.

"When you could see your way clear, when you could spare him, you could bring him back by maybe."

Now she met his look squarely, her eyes grave. She spoke in a halting voice. "I said words to you once—when you'd just come—I regretted. It was partly our—disturbance and grief at the time. But we'd like you to take Robert's horse, since your need is more than ours is now."

"I—I can't accept your goodness," he said thickly.

"Can't accept? Well, why not? You let us save your life, didn't you?" Her voice rose. "And after all our trouble, Granny's and mine, to drag you in and physic you, you think you can just go straggling off and maybe make it to wher'er it is you're going and maybe not? And Granny here worried to death about you and how in the world you'll manage!" Her voice rose angrily.

"But I can—"

"And you've sat here at this table and let her do for you! It's not as if you don't owe her anything!"

"But that horse is worth thirty pounds!"

"He's not doing us any good, child," coaxed Granny. "And he can do you much good. Take him now. You've been a good boy so far, and I've not been disappointed in you. Now do as I say."

Rudi drew a long breath of exasperation and frustration—that threatened to lift into exhilaration. He looked from one to the other, each willing him to submit. But it was not the light of battle in Margaret's eyes so much as the simple anxiety in Granny's that made him surrender.

"You are a pair," he said. "Both of you." His laugh was a deep chuckle. Whatever made people say the Irish and Dutch couldn't mingle?

The mist was rising as he rode along the path above Indian Creek next morning. His mood was sober. He had not liked leaving the two standing at the top of the steps—Granny's little figure light and still, Margaret silent behind her. He'd wanted to go back, to mount the steps, take each hand in his. He looked from one to the other, his look holding them. "I will not forget you," he cried, then turned the big gelding down the path.

Dew-wet leaves from a low-hanging branch of mockernut hickory brushed his face. He noted the thick fall of nuts in heavy grass. Hunting would be good this season as well as next. He saw deer tracks in the path. It felt good to have a horse under him, and his wound troubled him very little. They'd given him food enough for several days, enough to last all the way to the Congarees if he chose to go there.

His thoughts moved toward the sandy ridges above Savanna Hunt Creek. But large, floating above them, were the two figures on the high porch.

Chapter Five

Joggi Lienhardt raked his fingers through his wet hair to make it stand up and shook his head furiously in hopes of drying it quickly. The sun was already hidden behind reddening sweetgums and yellow-leafed poplars. He'd gone far down the creek, almost to the river. His slim body shivered in the rush of water about his knees. The air was cooler now. One moment he'd been squatting in sunlit shallows, playing with a little fluttermill he'd made, slipping into a deeper pool like a fish or a turtle; the next moment he was astonished to find sunlight gone.

He'd been very careful in taking off his clothes so there'd be no dampness or mud smear to show where he'd been. His fine silky hair usually dried fast and he'd intended to air-dry his body, dress and arrive home looking as if he'd just come from Pastor Theus's, where he was supposed to have spent the day in school. But so many things had caught his eye—the clay turrets of crayfish to lift and see if there was anybody home, all kinds of rocks and shells to cup and examine, whirly beetles to scatter, the bark of a river birch asking to be peeled off. Coming up the creek, he'd glimpsed a great white-billed woodpecker drumming on a dead pine, later a young deer resting in the bracken fern of a dry bank. And now, late as it was, there was no way he could arrive home dry. His code allowed him to mislead his parents but not to lie to them.

Anyhow Pastor Theus was sure to tell them later that he'd disappeared during dinner hour. The eight boys usually ate their baked potatoes and cornbread under the big old hackberry trees while the pastor took his nap in the house. Joggi knew he'd lose that privilege for quite a while now. Pastor Theus would whip him tomorrow. And Papa later. Oh well, he might as well go ahead and let Papa whip him tonight. It was not the whipping Joggi minded so much as his father's displeasure. Mama would have most to say, but Papa's mouth would get that grim, turned-down look that Joggi found most unpleasant.

Nevertheless, when he'd shaken out his neatly folded clothes and put them on, his body glowed with the feeling of warmth, a clean skin, and his inbreathing of crisp October air. He smelled fragrant smoke, though their chimney was hidden beyond the line of woods shielding their house from the road.

This road was one of the most important thoroughfares of the Province, part of the old Indian trading path that stretched from Charlestown up to the country of the Cherokees. Here, it ran along the west bank of the Congaree River. Joggi had come up from east of it, but the Lienhardts' land lay west of it. The white sandy ruts that ran straight north were bordered on the right by rich dense woods and on the left by his father's field, now harvested of corn, but not of peas and the ripening pumpkins. Back of the field stretched the dry strip of longleaf pines and blackjack oaks.

Joggi began to run up the road toward the turn-off. Even his shoes felt good on his feet. He leaped and twirled in the sweet, seed-scented air. He didn't care about any old whipping! He'd meet his trouble head-on, cry a little because he was supposed to, then eat supper. Suddenly he was ravenous. He hoped Mama had apple tarts.

Spinning, weaving dizzily, a black-haired sprite in a checked shirt, he might or might not have been seen by the men in the far woods beyond the field of stripped cornstalks. But Joggi saw them. Some were on horseback and some were dismounted. Why had they gotten off their horses? Joggi stood still. He couldn't see them at all clearly, but he sensed a darkness under their broad hats.

Some instinct, not really alarm or fear, simply caution, made him turn back toward the creek woods. Half-running, he slipped under dogwood, alder, and water oak toward home, not considering now from which direction his family might see him come.

On the other side of the line of the shielding woods that stretched at right angles to the creek, the familiar homeplace appeared—the tall little house of great square-hewn logs, with its fence palings, fowlhouse, cornhouse, barn, and barnlot. Joggi angled straight toward the barnlot in a trot.

Johannes looked around from his milking with a startled frown.

"Papa, I saw a bunch of men on horses! They were in the woods just standing there!"

"Where?"

Joggi pointed. "Over there. Near the Road. Near our field."

"Could you tell who any of them were?" Johannes set down his milkpail.

Joggi shook his head. "They were in the woods. It was too far."

"Where were you?" Johannes turned on his stool.

Joggi pointed. "Back there. Near the creek."

"I see." His father was silent.

"They had big hats on, some of 'em. Their faces were—I couldn't see 'em though." He did not know how to express the strangeness they impressed on him.

"Did they see you?" Johannes rose. He picked up the pail, covered it with a cloth, and set it carefully on a shelf built onto the barn wall.

Joggi shook his head. "I don't know. I went back and came along the creek."

"Where were you coming from when you saw them first? From the creek?"

Joggi looked down. "Yes, Papa."

"Well." His father just stood there. "Stay here. Wait."

Joggi supposed his father was going to get a switch, but when he looked up, he saw that he was letting the calf to the cow again, though the milk pail wasn't full. When his father returned, Joggi saw a very grim look indeed, but it was not for him. Johannes took his son by the shoulder, not grasping but guiding, and pushed him outside the lot gate, then stood with his hand on the boy's shoulder.

Johannes looked toward the house where Madle was cooking supper and Heiri was probably helping tend the baby, where the little girls were playing. He squatted down and drew the boy's slim body to him. "Joggi." His voice was quiet. "Could you go back—do you know how to go back through the woods to Pastor Theus and and let nobody see you?"

Joggi nodded.

"And tell Pastor Theus what you told me? About the men? Tell him I sent you."

"Yes sir."

"If he's not there, tell Frau Theus. Tell the big boys too. Don't wait. You understand me, Joggi?"

"Yes. Yes, I will, Papa."

"And don't stop at Theilers' or Busers'." Johannes paused. "The men might go there. I don't want you where the men might go."

Joggi looked speechlessly at his father.

"They might be bad men," Johannes said.

"Will they come here?"

"I don't know. But I can't leave Mama and the little ones. You understand that, don't you?"

Joggi gazed at his father. Why must I go? his look asked.

"If they're bad men, we'll need help wherever they go. Pastor Theus can send and get help. They won't go to his house, Joggi. That's why I send you there. You'll be all right if you go in the woods by the road and let no one see you. You can do that, can't you? I know you're not scared of the dark."

Johannes rose, guiding the boy before him until they reached the side gate to the yard. "Joggi." Johannes stopped and cupped the back of the damp head. "If a man like Rudi was here I'd send him. But there's no one else here—except you. Johannes felt Joggi's head jerk up and his back straighten. "We won't go in the house. I'll tell Mama later."

Joggi sagged suddenly and looked toward the house. He whispered, "Papa."

"What is it?"

"I'm so hungry!"

"What am I thinking about? You wait here."

Inside the fence the old dog Bläss came toward Johannes, swishing his tail. The windows by the chimney were on this side the house, and if Madle looked out, she'd see Joggi. Johannes thought, how'll I ever get food for the boy without her suspecting something?

The big room was warm and fragrant with supper. Heiri sat by the cradle rocking it and talking to Hansli, and Cathri and Babeli played on a bench near the open front door.

Johannes put the pail on the table. "Will you strain it for me, Madle? Joggi's helping me. We'll be late. You and the children go ahead and eat, don't wait for us."

Madle turned quickly, dusting her floured hands. "What's happened? What is it?"

Johannes went to the fireplace, kept his back to her, said hurriedly, impatiently, "I've got to move that black heifer and the calf and make changes in the lot. How about a tart for him and me both since we'll be late?" Not waiting for her answer, he picked up two of the big tarts heaped on a platter.

"You'll burn yourself, Johannes! Here, wait, take this cloth. You'll spoil his supper too! Where has he been so long?"

"He's with me. I've got something for him to do now, so have pity on him and on me too." He turned with a quick smile, then surreptitiously, he thought, folded another tart in the cloth and clumped out.

The face at the gate seemed small and pale. It brightened at the sight of the napkin. Johannes led his son around the fence toward the front of the house.

"Joggi, I'd go back the way I came, down that way." Johannes motioned toward the creek. He hesitated. He wanted to say, "If the men are gone when you get to the road, if you don't hear or see any sign of them, come back."

But there'd be danger for some other man's house and family. "Are you sure you couldn't see their faces? How did they look?"

"They—they looked dark. Their hats were down. They looked—it wasn't anybody we know."

Johannes still held the boy loosely. Decent men wouldn't harm his son. As for others—well, Joggi was smart enough to keep out of their sight. Still, it was a long way this time of day for a boy so young.

"Where'd you go today? To the river? Down the bluff?"

Joggi looked up and smiled that so familiar smile of his mother's that had beguiled Johannes all his life. "Not quite." His eyes had brightened considerably with food. "You're not going to whip me, are you, Papa?"

"No. Tell Pastor Theus I said not to either, this time. No, you can have all three. I'll take the cloth. Eat as you go, but don't eat too fast. And, Squirrel, don't run. But just—don't lose time anywhere."

Johannes watched the dark head, the checked shirt disappear down the gentle slope into the trees, then hurried to the barn, where, indeed, he had much to do.

Joggi looked both ways up and down the road and crossed it where it dipped toward the creek. From here the rise of land kept him from seeing where the men had been. He slipped along east of the road through the trees. It was still light, but as he drew near the woods where they'd been on the other side, he couldn't see anyone. Yet he seemed to sense a withdrawn presence, to hear distantly a snuffling, a jingling of horsegear. He sensed a dense waiting mass drawn farther back among the oaks and pines.

Joggi moved deeper among the heavier trees to the east. It was a long way to go, but he knew it well enough to go almost in black dark. He moved in a light half-trot as he finished his third apple tart.

For at least the fourth time Madle peered out the back door. Once she'd called and Johannes had answered amid moving shapes. Now all was still. She called again, "Johannes!" She descended the steps. "Johannes!"

She turned toward the doorway. "Heiri, watch Cathri and Babeli! Keep them away from the fire!" She began running toward the lot. At thirty Madle did not run so lightly as once she had run across a Toggenburg meadow, but her active life kept her trim and she still moved quickly.

The lot was completely empty of beasts. The door of the cornhouse stood ajar. She looked inside. Emptied. And the shed empty of the wagon. Only for a moment was she mystified. Not Indians this time, no. He'd taken the livestock and grain up the creek because some outlaw gang was near. Men had gone out against the outlaws with burnings and whippings, and already they'd heard how the gangs were retaliating. She stood with her hands twisting in her apron.

The dusk was mysteriously sweet. The light from the doorway was a dim rose that cradled the brightness and trust of child flesh.

She ran to fling open the barn door and saw in the gloom its familiar barrels, hoes, rakes, farm gear, all the new-stored fodder. "Jo-han-nes!" she called long, loudly, then caught a faint answering hail.

She ran toward the house, and even as she scanned the sky, a glow rose over the woods to the northeast. "Oh Lord God, protect us! Lord, save us!" she cried.

She paused on the steps to control her face, looked back toward the creek woods. Let them come in! she cried. Joggi! Come inside the house!

The room was rich and full. Their possessions gleamed. The homeliest stone jar had a beauty of shape, every stool and chair an intimacy that made it precious. For her children it would be as much a part of their security as her own flesh, she thought, as the will and strength of their father.

She closed and latched the two small windows on each side of the fireplace, looked at the baby's stubborn little mouth crimped in sleep, then went to shut the heavy front door. "Move, Cathri." The little girls were already in their nightgowns. She slid the bar in place.

"Mama, when's Joggi coming inside?" Heiri lay stomach down across a bench, idly rolling a wooden-wheeled toy cart back and forth.

"He's with Papa. They'll be here soon."

Heavy feet pounded up the back steps. Johannes stood breathing heavily in the doorway. "Madle, forgive me staying out so long." His eyes took in the room. "The damned wagon got hung up. I was trying to secure it from the horses. Though what's corn, God knows, compared to— "

"Where's Joggi?" she interrupted. "I know what it is. Where's Joggi?"

Heiri and the little girls ran up and stood big-eyed in front of him.

"Joggi's at Pastor Theus's ... or should be almost there by now."

Madle's face whitened. She gripped her hands together. "You sent him?"

He nodded. He shut the back door and put the bar in place.

"Four miles?" she whispered. "In the night alone?"

"It's less than four miles, Madle," he answered low. "He walks it every day. It was good light when he left. He knows the way."

"But in broad daylight," her voice broke, "with older boys— Heiri, take Babeli and Cathri into the other room—"

"Wait, Madle. I don't know." He drew her away from the children, said low "I'm thinking—you could take them up to where I hid the wagon. I know you'd be safe there and it would be shelter for you."

"What about you."

He shook his head.

She moved to pick up Cathri. "I'll put them to bed. Get your supper," she said tightly. "Heiri, you come too. Babeli."

But Babeli stood looking up at her father. "Papa, why did you send Joggi to Pastor Theus?" She was five years old and resembled her oldest brother.

"Because—" Johannes bent stiffly, took her head between his hands and kissed her forehead, "Joggi's a big boy. He took a message. Go with Mama now."

Plump Cathri in Madle's arms held out her hands to her father also before her mother took her out.

Johannes stared into the dimness. He was in an agony of self-blame. He'd seen that yellow glare. Theiler's house or barn, maybe both. They'd gone northeast, the very direction he'd sent Joggi. Surely, surely Joggi would have kept away from them! But men on horseback moved fast. Or what if he'd gone too deep in the woods, got lost in the dark, fallen in some slough? ...But wait now. Surely Joggi would have passed Theiler's before they got there. And the boy was far more at home in the woods than he himself was and clever enough to evade anyone.

But what a conscienceless fool he'd been, leaving Madle alone while he looked after livestock! It was only by the mercy of God they hadn't come here with him outside. Though he'd tried to listen and keep a lookout, and he'd thought if the animals and grain were destroyed.... But him out like a fool with no gun! He hadn't wanted to alarm her by coming to get it, have to tell her about Joggi.

She'd take the children and hide only if he downright ordered her to, and then probably only if he went with them. But he could not, he would not leave his house to be plundered and burned. He'd left for the Cherokees, yes, but for white scoundrels, no! Yet oughtn't he to be headed toward Theiler's right now with his gun?

Fool, he told himself, think! A couple of men against fifteen or twenty? Think straight!

But what can you do here? Put a musket ball in one or two. ...And Madle, the children, the house burned down over their heads? ... Would white men go so far?

They'd go far enough. They'd raped many a woman and girl-child with the rest of the family bound helpless, if not murdered....

Stop. Get your mind straight. Others have seen that fire, he told himself. The gang won't linger now. What they're doing is pure revenge, hit and run. They'll clear this neighborhood in a hurry. Oh my God, why did I send Joggi out?

Johannes was only half aware of Madle's low singing to the children in the other room. He took food from a pot, sat down to it, but in five minutes was up again. He kept turning between table and door, door and hearth. He unlatched one small window by the chimney and peered out. He heard Bläss give a low growl. Suddenly the dog sang out.

Madle stood in the doorway of the other room, Heiri behind her. Johannes went to her.

He was a sturdy man slightly under middle height, still clean-shaven, but his face was burned dark by eleven years of South Carolina sun. He put his whole strength into his voice. "No one will come inside this house, Madle. They can do what they will outside, but they'll not come in this house."

She just stood there with drawn face.

"Is the window in that room shut?" he asked.

She nodded. They strained their ears for sounds above the dog's raging.

Johannes pulled up a bench to the front wall to lift down the rifle and the musket with the powder and shot he kept hanging there, high above the reach of children. He handed the rifle to Madle, who stepped back, while he got down the musket, powder and bullets. He tapped a little powder into the musket's flashpan, poured more powder down the barrel, rammed the bullet in.

"Madle, take the children upstairs, all four. Heiri," he called, "get your sisters up." His voice allowed no remonstrance. "Lead them up the steps. Now. All of you."

He heard them moving, whimpering in the other room, her low voice and their stumbling steps on the stairway.

He removed the plug from a square hole near the front door, a hole big enough for his eye and a gun barrel. He saw no light through the screening line of trees and heard no sounds above the dog's barking.

"Hey, Lienhardt!" came a sudden bawl in German, close out of the darkness. "Call off your cur dog, will you?"

"Who is it?" called Johannes. "What do you want?"

"I need to talk with you. Either you come out or let me come in, one. I can't talk with that racket."

"You tell me what you want," said Johannes. "I hear you all right. Who are you?"

"It's Bastian Zingler. Remember me? We marched up to Prince George six years ago. I'm looking for a stray horse, and I heard—"

"Yes, I remember you," broke in Johannes. The dog's white paws against the fence showed where the man stood.

"How about letting me in then? Call off your cur!"

"Men don't come looking for strayed horses this time of night! No!" The white paws jumped back, then forward at the gate. "You come inside that fence and you'll get a musket ball in you!"

The man whooped, laughing. "Hey, boys!" he yelled in English. "This nest got to be smoked out too!"

Johannes whistled sharply to Bläss to hush him. "Wait!" he called. "Listen, Zingler. Tell them! You can burn me out. You can try to. But the ones that come in here, there'll be a couple won't leave!"

"I never heard how one man could stop a troop!" Zingler yelled. "You think that over!"

And he was right. There was no way, Johannes knew, that he could stop them from burning his barn and his outbuildings. But the house was stout. They'd find it hard to break in here. Unless they decided to fire it too. Yet, villainous as they were, he'd never heard of their burning a house down with people in it. Their way was to get inside first or entice the people out. But many a house they *had* burned.... Oh, for another pair of hands! Somewhat against her will, he'd taught Madle how to load and shoot the musket; yet everything within him recoiled at having her down here with him.

Lights from a half dozen torches appeared out of the woods. "Bläss!" called Johannes, turning quickly to lift the bar and open the door a crack. "Come, Bläss!" he called low. The old dog was too faithful, too much loved by the children to be sacrificed. Johannes whistled sharply, but the dog merely ranged closer to the house, still barking furiously. Johannes cursed, slipped out on the porch and called more urgently, and this time the dog dashed to his hand. Johannes lunged, caught his collar, and dragged him inside, then slammed and barred the door. "You damned scoundrel, you want to stay out there and get your head blown off? Madle! Heiri!" he shouted. "Come drag Bläss upstairs and keep him quiet!"

Bläss did not like the steps, so Johannes lifted him bodily up to Heiri, who pulled him the rest of the way.

Back by the door, Johannes saw pineknot torches and shapes of men and horses milling about at the front fence.

"Come on out, Switzer!" one yelled. "What's the use to hide in the house?"

It was less than fifty yards. The musket would do at this range. He slid the barrel through the hole, sighted a man holding up a torch, and fired. The torch fell as someone screamed amid a roar of yelling and cursing. He took up the rifle, tried to aim for one figure, and shot again. More yells as Johannes plugged the lookhole. Bullets hit the wall under the porch roof.

Swiftly Johannes reloaded the musket. He looked out again. Some of the riders had scattered toward the woods, but he saw torches streaming around to the side of the house. The musket was no good for that range. Johannes' fingers fumbled as he reloaded the rifle. He needed more light. He edged open a shutter by the chimney.

The smell of lightwood smoke floated in the air. The creak and jingle of harness told him more horses were passing outside the fence. He lifted his rifle, lowered it. A shot at random. Don't waste it. He longed to open the backdoor and shoot, but someone could be waiting to rush him, maybe a half dozen. He cursed himself for never having cut a lookhole at the back. But if he could slip out the window of the other room, run to the corner of the house, get a few good shots from there—

He closed the door between the two rooms to keep out light that might silhouette his body, ran between the big bed and the trundle, hit his knee on Madle's chest, cursed, and unbarred the shutter. This window was larger than those by the chimney, but he could see nothing against the northward rise of the orchard. Johannes had pushed the shutter half open when he heard the stamp of a horse reined in. He fired into the darkness and slammed the shutter to.

Too many. He couldn't venture out without risk of their getting in. The best he could do was warn them away with gunfire. The back with no opening but the door was where they were. Soon the growing din in the barnlot made him know what they were doing.

In the loft room Madle saw light flickering on the underside of eaves through the space between wall and roof left open for ventilation in warm weather. She heard shouts and yells, the crackle of pine logs, and saw the glare.

She thought of the fowls shut up on their roosts. The fowlhouse was not in a direct line to the lot, and she prayed it might be missed in the dark. How thankful she was that Johannes had taken off the other poor creatures.

She crouched on a low bed with the baby in her lap. Cathri and Babeli huddled on each side of her but Heiri sat at the foot of the bed. She reached now for one child, now for the other. She reached into that emptiness where the oldest should have been. She thought she could endure it all if only he were here. She tried not to be angry with Johannes. She'd known early that separation would come. But, God, not tonight, she begged, oh, not tonight! Oh God, let me keep him longer! She raised little Hans to her bosom, moving her cheek against his. Oh Heiri darling, she cried silently, come closer! But he sat apart, his bare feet in Bläss's fur.

Heiri thought if Joggi were here, he wouldn't be so scared. He was afraid not only of the fire and yelling outside, but even more of what could happen to his father—he'd seen crusted blood at a bullet hole and dead eyes in an animal—and of the terrible things that *were* happening now, his father shouting and cursing and shooting too. The sulphuric stink crept into the loft, overpowering the scent of dried fruit hung in bags from the rafters, the new-cut apples laid on sheets beneath the eaves. He and Joggi slept here, close by the chimney when it was cold. Joggi would tell him about giant foxes in the woods and deer you could ride on. Joggi was in the dark woods now. Or maybe already at Pastor Theus's. Heiri twisted his bare feet in Bläss's fur, trying to see Joggi and Pastor Theus a long way off. They too were in the dark. But Bläss's fur was under his feet. He was glad Papa had brought Blass inside.

Earlier, looking back, Joggi had seen the riders stream out of the western woods as he cut across Theiler's cornfield east of the road. He'd begun to run. Shapes were still clear in the evening light, but if the riders noticed him, they paid no attention, for they crossed the road into the woods through which he'd just come.

Joggi ran till he was breathless. When he gained the cover of trees, he looked behind him but saw no one. Were they going to Theiler's? He was glad Papa had told him not to go there.

It seemed a long long way to go yet, longer than ever it was to school. Papa used to take him on horseback and sometimes he let him ride the mare, especially if it was cold, but since there were usually other boys for company and the mare was needed for work, Joggi walked most days.

You couldn't go fast on a horse through the woods, not in the dark. Besides, if he'd been on a horse, the men might have seen him.

His legs hurt. It was not like when you could stop and eat persimmons or sit down and watch a yellowhammer dig out a hole. He needed to get where he was going. But he was already so tired.

Joggi didn't listen much to grown people's talk. The big boys talked of old Govey Black and old Winslow Driggers and the Moon and the Tyrrel brothers, though Jim Tyrrel was dead now, Willi Rieder said. They were heads of gangs that stole horses and burned people's houses down. Yet even though people said, "Watch out for strangers," all the talk seemed to Joggi about things a long way off. He'd seen Papa take down the rifle and load it one day last summer, only to hang it up again, though for two or three weeks his father had not left the place.

Later, after coming back from the Congarees, Papa talked to Mama about men who were going to "regulate" things. "If Charlestown won't give us officials to regulate the country, we'll have to do it ourselves." Joggi did not know exactly what that meant Something to do with the outlaws, he gathered.

Yet here were these dark men in his own woods, riding among the hawtrees and sparkleberries, and trampling over rabbit and possum tracks in the white sand in *his* woods. It unsettled him deeply. He wanted to run far from the road. There were places you could go near the river and no one could ever get you, where horses couldn't go because of guts and sloughs and the thick cane. In the dark there'd be no sounds but those of hunting owls and maybe foxes.

He held his course. Go to Pastor Theus. Tell about the men.

He came to another broad field and was nearer the road than he'd realized. There was still light in the western sky but it was dark over the river woods. He could go faster in the road. He'd take to the woods on the other side if he saw someone.

He angled toward the road, looked up and down it, continued his half-trot, avoiding sandbeds. Several times he looked back. Only Buser's field he was passing. He was only halfway there. White sand glimmered on and on before him. He was covering the same ground over and over, his feet beating the earth in a dream.

The horseman was coming toward him before he realized it. Joggi leaped for the trees. But the horseman was not coming fast. It was too dark to see who it was. An outlaw? Or just a traveler? Maybe somebody he knew. But Papa said not to waste time, go as fast he could, and only to Pastor Theus's. Joggi slipped through the trees but stayed close enough to the road to observe the horseman.

The rider came on at a leisurely pace. He wore no hat. Then as the open field attracted the last light from the west, Joggi saw the man clearly. He hurtled out of the woods, screamed, "Rudi!" and went flying toward the rider, who drew rein sharply.

"Wait a minute! Whoa! Hold on, hold on!"

"Rudi! Rudi! Oh Rudi, I'm so glad it's you!"

"Joggi Lienhardt! I thought it was a Choctaw! Wait now—"

"Rudi, I thought you'd *never* come back! Oh Rudi, listen!"

His words poured out. Rudi dismounted and listened.

"All right, it's to Theus's we'll go!" He swung himself into the saddle and helped Joggi up behind him. They turned and this time the big gelding went at no leisurely gait. Joggi floated in wonder. A dream or real? In ten minutes they were turning off the road and galloping toward the dim light under the hackberry trees.

While Rudi talked to the minister, Christian Theus, to George Kelsinger, who happened to be be there, and to Theus's son, Peter, Joggi tried to keep behind Rudi. The pastor's eye had impaled him at once.

"Peter, you'll ride up to Rieder's and Gallman's," Theus said.

"But not beyond," said George. "They'll have others to send beyond the Congarees."

"Bachman and Steg and Murff, don't forget Murff."

They would spread and gather men as they went, hoping to meet at Tom's Creek in no more than an hour.

"Look there!" cried Rudi. They stood outside the house. Peter had already run to saddle horses. George was mounted. They saw a glow in the sky to the south.

Rudi said, "I'll go that way. I'll go on to Lienhardt's now."

The others didn't speak. Theus said, "Wouldn't it be wiser to wait till there are more of you?"

An hour? "No. I'd feel better to go on now. I'll call out to Köhler on the way. And Buser. If I can." For they might already have been called to in a different way.

He was on his horse. "Where's Joggi?" Rudi looked about. He'd thought Joggi was with them. "Well, I know you'll keep him safe, Herr Pastor."

"I'll keep him," said Pastor Theus firmly.

But at a turning three hundred yards from the house, a shrill voice called and Rudi drew rein. A small figure was at his stirrup.

"Joggi, you can't go with me!"

"Please, Rudi! Please let me! I've just got to get back! To Mama and Papa and all! Please!"

Rudi knew it was wrong. Yet the boy's intensity cut through his reason. "Get up then. But if something happens to you, God knows how I'll ever look your Papa and your Mama in the face."

Glare lighted the field all the way to the creekside trees. Johannes stood helplessly at the small window, unable to see the blaze, only its light. His dawn-to-dark work destroyed in less than an hour. The first fruits of his labor in the prime of his youth and strength. It had been a passion inside him, the shaping and building of his fields and house and barn, almost indistinguishable from his passion for his young wife and their unborn child. In less than an hour these strangers were destroying what he'd felled to the ground those first late winter days in the new country, what he and Rudi had heaved into place the following autumn in Wine-month. It was some of himself they were razing. His sense of maiming was unbearable.

Like Madle he thought of the fowlhouse and its trapped creatures. And what if a floating spark caught the cedar shingles above? The air seemed still; yet from time to time bright flecks floated above the yard.

"Madle," he called. He went to the stair. He wanted to cry, "Watch for any sign of sparks catching the roof." He called, "Are you all right?"

"Yes," came her low answer.

He returned to the window. The distant roar intensified. Through the narrow opening he saw a man on horseback drawn off to watch. So he himself had watched a fire once in the Toggenburg when he was young. For a brief space he was one with that man, a spectator watching a fire. He raised his rifle. The man was in good clear range. Yet Johannes did not fire.

A confusion of misery overwhelmed him. Was it because he had not killed the man, or because he had almost killed him? He did not know. It was one thing to kill a man when he threatened you face to face, another as he stood unaware. The rider moved, gestured toward the house and rode out of sight. Lord God, if they tried anything more from the back, what would he do?

He heard a shot. North of the house? There'd been no shooting now for twenty minutes or more. Hope lurched up. Then more shots from the barnlot and back of the house.

"Johannes, let me in!" came an urgent voice from the porch. "Rudi Näffels! Let me in!"

Johannes bounded to the front door, heaved up the bar, and a fierce bearded man pushed in. For a moment Johannes thought he'd made a terrible mistake. Then they grasped each other without words. It had been three years.

Rudi looked about him. In the dim glow from the hearth the familiar things in the room seemed dream shapes. Reality was the crackling and flames outside, the beast shapes ramping about in the glare.

"Rudi, I'm up against that wall at the back," Johannes was saying, "with no way to see out but to open the door. And Madle and the four little ones upstairs."

"And you down here alone."

Both men were silent; yet Johannes felt a great wash of hope. He felt his force more than doubled. "Rudi, if you can just help me stand 'em off from the house, that's as much as I'll hope for! But how in God's name did you get here?"

"I'll tell you later. Listen. Let's do this."

Rudi said he'd crept down through the orchard and shot a man standing sentinel at the northwest corner of the house, but no one was at the front. What if he slipped out the front and around to the south? Johannes could cover him from the little windows as he made for creek trees and took a few shots from there? That would draw them off until—

"It's too risky," interrupted Johannes. "What if they caught you? No. Listen, just having you inside is enough. We can give 'em plenty from inside.

Madle heard the voices below. In a minute or so she knew who it was and began to weep soundlessly. "Who is it, Mama?" whispered Heiri.

Was it five minutes or thirty before they heard the thud of hoofs to the front of the house and a bellowing voice. They heard a great confusion of movement and shouting at the back fence.

One voice rose above the clamor. "Listen, you dumb Dutch coward hiding in there! Next time it won't be just your barn and your little old sheds! It'll be your house and you and your young'uns too maybe! You remember that next time you go to scratch your mark on some paper!"

"And friends of Bill Hoddy'll maybe have something for you before then!" yelled another.

"Hear me!" roared Johannes in the darkness. "Next time it won't be near my house or my children either. It'll be in daylight but not in this place!" And I don't scratch my mark, he would have called. I write my own name!

"Their lookout's warned 'em," said Rudi at his elbow. "Men are coming from Congarees."

"What? They are?"

"Yes, and they've made good time. I'd've been here sooner if it hadn't taken me so long to get down through your orchard."

"How did you know to come that way? The fire?"

"That and your boy. I met him just about dark."

Johannes was conscious for the first time of hot emotion breaking up inside him. He was glad his wet face couldn't be seen in the dark. "He got there safe then," he asked hoarsely, "where he was going?"

"Oh yes. Though you'll want to kill me, Johannes. He's up in the woods now with my horse. I threatened him every way I could think of if he moved an inch from guarding my horse."

"Well, don't tell his mother," said Johannes. "Just go get him."

Even though the sounds of the cavalcade had receded, Rudi left by the north window. Five minutes later George Kelsinger called from outside, "Johannes! You all right?" He waited for the answer, then said, "They've gone toward Sandy Run. There are about fifteen of us and we're going to trail after 'em and try to keep 'em from any more devilment tonight."

"Wait! I'll come too!"

"I can't wait, Johannes. I've got to catch up with the rest. We don't need you tonight. You just come up to Congarees tomorrow morning. We're meeting at Rieder's."

Johannes remembered his horse was up the branch. He was going to ask about the Theilers when George called back, his voice fading, "You sent us your boy. That was enough."

And fifteen minutes later amid the ecstatic yelps of Bläss, that boy's voice was heard at the front gate.

And now to Johannes his barn seemed of small account. All he could do was look at his son. He wanted to pick him up like a baby, hold him high over his head. At last he drew the boy loosely to him, gave his shoulder a hard shake. Joggi was weak-eyed with weariness. Yet beneath his drooping lids there was still a glimmer of brightness.

He had not looked once at his mother. Her heart was breaking with pride and pain. Now he turned to her and smiled. Of his own will he went to her. "Mama, you know Rudi's come? Look, Mama, it's Rudi!" He leaned his head against her and let her smooth back his hair.

Heiri said, "Joggi brought you, didn't he, Rudi? I'm sure glad Joggi went and got you!"

Chapter Six

In the gray light Johannes looked at the ashes. Wisps of smoke were low and sullen in the damp air. Wooden parts could be refitted on iron tools if they were not cracked or twisted. But all the fodder was gone. And the new barrels. Why hadn't he removed his flax seed and hemp seed? he asked in anguish. A half-burned trough sagged at an angle. So much to do over. Prongs of forks and rakes, all handles to be carved again. And the body-breaking work of hewing beams.

But it was the ruins of young wheat that brought his grimmest anger, the tender blades ground underfoot in the churned-up field. He swung his gaze toward the house. Well, God be thanked the fowlhouse was spared. And the beehives near the orchard. In the dark they'd missed things. The house untouched. But it looked tall and naked without its partner. Be thankful, you fool, he told himself. Madle came out of the house. Get down on your knees and thank God.

He was unprepared for her storm of grief at the sight of it all. He put his arm around her heaving shoulders. "Hush, hush now. The children—you don't want to wake them up yet, do you?"

She threw her apron over her face.

"We'll build back!" he said vehemently. "I wanted a bigger one anyhow, farther from the house!"

"Oh no, no, no! It was our own that you worked so hard on! It can't be built back!" It was his voice ringing across the stumps in spring sunshine with *"Mir Senne heil's lustig!"* his bright face coming into the kitchen when she was just beginning to love him, his face still fresh with some light of joy from high alpine places. When he was building something of his own cleanness of life here.

"...just a barn!"

So let it go, her mind answered wearily. You can't hold on to barns and houses any more than to youth itself. ... Yet what right has anyone to invade and violate our lives!

No right. But it had nothing to do with right, only hatred. It was their malevolence that hurt more than anything else, hurt more than lightning or

54

storm, that will to stamp out their good. "What have we done that they should hate us so much?"

No answer. At last he said heavily, "That's all some men know, Madle."

"I can't understand such people!"

"I'll be going up to Congarees this morning. You want to come? It might be for the biggest part of the day."

She was silent. "I'm not prepared," she said finally. She had not the food ready that she'd need to take.

"Those vandals have cleared out of these parts by now, but we can't just let them get away. You know that, don't you?"

"I know." She saw how haggard he was in the chill of the overcast day.

"You understand what it'll mean?"

She nodded. It was the difference six years had made. She knew now it was not for his pleasure that he rode with other men.

Rudi Näffels came down the back steps. If she had not known who he was, she would never have recognized this bearded, wary-eyed man. She thought he looked ten years older than when she'd last seen him.

She tried to smile. "Rudi, you've been so long coming to us, I wish we weren't in such plight." She dabbed at her eyes with the corner of her apron.

He looked about him. "Yes. It's too bad." He gazed at the ashes and charred foundation beams.

She remembered that August Sunday when he'd come down the ridge with leaves and pine needles in his ragged clothes. There'd been no barn here then either, only the unroofed house. Madle went to Rudi, put her hands on his shoulders and swiftly drew his head down to kiss him. "I never greeted you properly last night." She smelled his familiar smell of horse and the woods. "Thank God you've come safely." And he did wear a decent shirt this time, even if he was without a jacket.

He regarded her with relief. Much had changed but she had not. Though her face was as worn as that of most women her age, it still had its own look—a blending of reticence and warmth, of cool detachment and confiding eagerness. His own face worked into a smile. "I've missed you, both of you." He added in a low voice, "I've been too ashamed to come."

"Ah no!" And why should *you* be ashamed? she wanted to ask. She reached again to touch his arm. "Joggi prays every night, 'God bless Rudi,' and Heiri does too because Joggi does. They'll both be standing on their heads this morning. You can be glad they're still asleep. Were you able to sleep?" She and Johannes had tossed and turned till daybreak.

"Yes," he lied. He could not tell her that there had been too many emotions beating him this way and that in the shadowy room, too much memory and regret.

Johannes was looking at him. Rudi shifted his gaze. That hard line of his jaw, Rudi thought, I never noticed it before. He's angry. Well, he's got a right to be.

Johannes thought, He's had more than one hag on his back since I saw him last. "I'd better go see to the stock," he said brusquely. "You want to come?" He turned away, added, "It's not too far up the creek."

As they followed the path by the edge of the woods, both men thought how last night it was as if there'd never been a break in their old camaraderie. But now this sunless morning the years lay between them.

Johannes tried to bridge them. "Remember that rise over there with those big oaks? If I'm not mistaken, that's where you shot us a ten-point buck one afternoon. Along about this time of year it was too."

"When was it? Fifty-nine? That first time I stayed here?"

"Fifty-eight. Just before Joggi was born. The autumn of fifty-eight."

Rudi was silent. I was wild as a buck myself then, he thought. But prime game. It was here that, rootless, homeless, he'd first been enticed within stalking distance by rooftree, bed, and cradle. And later shot down.

"How's the season shaping up for you?" Johannes asked. They'd heard how Rudi had abandoned his land after his wife left him. From time to time they'd gotten word of him from up the country.

"It looks to be a good one. I'll need it."

"That's a big strong horse you're riding."

"He's not mine."

"Oh?"

"I got cleaned out last summer, Johannes. Came close to being finished for good and all."

They were approaching the cattlepen which extended into the creek. Johannes stopped. "What happened?"

They stood still as Rudi told briefly of his last three months. "When I finally got back to Camping Creek, I was able to gather up enough of the farm gear I'd hidden—somebody'd burned down the cabin—and I traded it for a fair rifle. I've got a few pelts now to trade for what I'll need this winter."

Johannes was silent awhile, trying to take it all in. "You say it was Irish people tended you?"

Rudi nodded.

Johannes whistled. "And lent you that horse too."

"Ulster Irish they call themselves. You know the country's full of 'em up beyond the Deadfall Line. On the Enoree and the Tyger. Up the Broad and all through the Waxhaws."

Johannes nodded. "Scotch-Irish, some people call 'em. You remember Jesse McGowan? Helped me out six years ago? It's what he is. Came from Scotland before they went to Ireland, he told me." The cattle crowded at the bars. "As for me, I don't care what they call 'em, but I say this, I'd rather have a man like Jesse McGowan on my side than a few Switzers I could name you. Rough in some ways maybe, but he'd not back away in trouble." Johannes spoke with unaccustomed force as he let down the bars. "And yet some people around here want no more to do with 'em than with a Cherokee Indian."

"They're different in some ways," said Rudi. "You can't get around that."

"Well, I tell you, Rudi," said Johannes vigorously, "it was a God's mercy the ones that found you. When you think of the kinds that *could* have found you. Or not have found you at all."

They let the cattle out—four cows, six yearlings, and three heifers. "Wait, I'm about to forget the bells." He had taken the bells off last evening to silence them. Rudi helped bell two of the cows. "I'll come back for the wagon and everything else after breakfast." He had gotten the horses late last night.

"I tell you, man," Johannes said as they moved the little herd into the path, "there are things in this life we do well to heed. We're so blind. Sometimes we get knocked in the head and we still can't see it."

"What do you mean?" Rudi's voice sounded wary.

Johannes tried to think how to say it. He didn't want to sound pious. Yet it was truth he'd long perceived and he thought Rudi ought to see it too. "A pattern maybe. We can't understand it at the time. But looking back, we see—" He groped for the right words.

Rudi waited.

"Looking back, haven't you sometimes had the feeling—someone was with you or behind you? Letting you go your own way, and yet—turning you a certain way, and you not knowing it then? But looking back, you could see the goodness of it all?"

"Looking back, it's the goodness of that old woman I see. And the girl's. She was the one found me."

Johannes was silent awhile. "Not everybody's found by people like that, Rudi."

"No. I can't forget them. I feel much obliged to them."

I'm glad, Johannes thought. Or I am if they're all he says they are. "You say a man up there was murdered?"

"Yes, by some of that same gang that was here last night. Oh, they keep busy!"

"Listen, Rudi." Johannes' voice hardened. "We're meeting this morning at Congarees. I don't know what'll come of it, but we've got to do more than just chase out after those villains twenty or thirty miles. You want to come with me?"

Rudi almost said, "I've got my own business to tend to, Johannes." And besides, do I even belong here now? But he thought how selfish it would sound. Where was the obligation he'd spoken of? If not here, where did he belong? Not with Frasers. "I'll think about it. I'll see."

Johannes glanced at him oddly. He felt uncomfortable.

The milch cows moved ahead by habit to the barnlot while the rest of the herd strayed to browse. The dingling must have been heard at the house, for before they were in sight of it, two small figures came flying to meet them, leaping over stumps, then stopped, suddenly shy, though there had been nothing shy about them last night.

"Just look at those sprigs," said Johannes. "They're what keep me humping. And you can't take your eye off either of 'em for thirty seconds." But his voice was warm.

Rudi thought suddenly that if he'd had anything in the world of his own, he'd give it all for one boy just like them, either one of them.

Johannes need not have worried about being late for the meeting. It was early afternoon before most men arrived, tired-eyed from lack of sleep. Their tempers were not genial.

"If there'd been more of us, we could have kept on after 'em and maybe cut some down right then and there," they grumbled. "But that's our trouble. We're always too few and too late."

"We can't get enough to go!"

"Act like they're scared they're going to get lost."

"Hell, scared of lead's what they're scared of."

They were gathered in the long front room of Hans Jacob Rieder's two-story plantation house at the Congarees, where for twenty years, passing Indians and other travelers had been served rum punch and savory stew. Although the house had never been licensed as a tavern, Hermann Rieder, Hans Jacob's father had been quick to take advantage of his location, probably had it in mind when he built here. But now with licensed taverns between the landing at the fort and Friday's Ferry a mile farther up the river, and fewer Indians passing than formerly, the Rieders enjoyed little custom. Hans Jacob's wife, Maria, was glad, but his mother, Elsbeth, was not. She grumbled endlessly.

"It's those low taverns that give us our bad name here at the Congarees. Oh, I've told Pastor Theus and I've told others, many a time I've said it, it's more than meat and drink they offer in such places, and it's no wonder we're overrun with rogues and riffraff, when day or night, any time you set foot in one of those dirty sheds, you'll see a dozen of the lazy, no-good scum slouched over tables, gaming, dicing, sloshing about and worse than that in other rooms I wouldn't even talk about! I've told Hans Jacob and I've told Maria, I tell everyone, *never* will I allow such behavior under this roof, nor would his father have either. Plain meat and drink is what anybody gets here but good as you'll find anywhere in this settlement. And good West India spirits brought up from Charlestown at fifteen shillings a gallon...."

Right now, however, there would be no spirits. Not that some of the men weren't ready for a dram, but everyone knew better than to begin refreshing themselves before the meeting. Some thirty-five were crowded onto the scarred benches and rush-bottomed chairs, with a few leaning against the wall and in the doorway. The fire smoldered low and the doors were open.

"Well, we can sit back and be scared, but as long as we do, nothing's safe. We ought to know that."

"Who's scared?" demanded Hans Jacob, who had not gone out last night. "It'll take more than riding off half-cocked and shooting up the woods to get rid of what we've got to contend with. What's the use of chasing out if you don't know where you're going and what you're going to do when you get there? We've got to have some planning, some organization!"

In the silence tempers began to rise.

"If some of us hadn't gone out last night," growled Benedict Köhler, "there are houses might not be standing today."

Johannes stirred. "I didn't go last night because my horse wasn't to hand and George said you couldn't wait. But I'm obliged to those who did go. If you hadn't come my way, my house might not be standing this morning." He paused. "What I say is, we mustn't fall out over what's been done or not done. We all know something more has got to be done. If we didn't think so, we wouldn't be here." Johannes seldom spoke at a meeting, never this forcefully.

There was a stir of agreement, some easing and settling back.

"Well, getting to the main question," said Heinrich Gallman, an older man, their accepted leader, "who's willing to give service? We must know who we can depend on before we know what we can do."

"We've already been through this once! We signed our names two months ago and what have we accomplished? I still say what we need is—"

"Nobody disagrees with you, Hans Jacob," interrupted George Kelsinger, "but as Johannes says, no use to keep talking about what we've done or not done. Let's get on with what's to do tomorrow. Some of us didn't sign up before. Captain Gallman, why don't you take a poll? Go around the room and let each man give his word if he's a mind to act and you write him down."

"That sounds fair," answered Gallman. "All agreed? Let each man say if he's willing to act. Heiri," to his son, "how about you?"

"I'm willing."

"Hans Jacob?"

After a slight hesitation, "Yes, I'm willing."

"I'm willing," each man replied when his name was called.

Then one answered, "I got to know when and what we're talking about before I can say."

"That's right," another called loudly. "What are we saying yes to? You mean regular patrols the way it was during the Cherokee War?"

"Looks to me like that's a job for the Rangers."

"Lord God," exploded George Kelsinger, "two years we've been sitting reared back on our hind ends waiting for the Rangers and everybody else to do our job for us. Haven't we all learned by now it's up to us to protect our own selves? Charlestown's not going to do it. That handful of soldiers at the fort can't do it. And those puny magistrates and bailiffs are about as much use as a bunch of sheep."

"What have you got in mind, George?"

"I'd say an organized expedition. One that'll go prepared to fight a pitched battle."

Several men looked away but others called, "I'm willing!" "Yes, I'm willing, write me down!" The calls became a chorus.

"Wait now. Let's be orderly. Johann Geiger, how about you? ... Gaspar?" The poll continued around the room.

Rudi Näffels stood just inside the door, leaning against the wall. Gallman did not call his name.

"How about Rudi?" injected Johannes. "You skipped Rudi Näffels!"

Gallman seemed not to hear Johannes but continued calling out other names.

Johannes wondered uneasily if he'd overlooked Rudi on purpose. Men had not greeted Rudi with the warmth Johannes expected. Had they forgotten his service during the Indian War? Rudi had gone to church here and been married here, though the girl was from up the country. It was Hans Jacob Rieder, who, at the instigation of his mother, Elbeth, had most effectively cleared him of entanglement with that wicked old man down Orangeburg way. They'd accepted Rudi eight years ago. Why cold-shoulder him now? Because he hadn't settled among them? They could be such a clannish, suspicious lot.

Johannes glanced at Rudi worriedly, saw a peculiar look on Rudi's face.

Gallman finished his poll. "Now if you'll hear my opinion," he said, "I believe our best hope is to join with men from other parts. We're still too few to attempt much by ourselves. I propose we send messengers this afternoon, this very afternoon," to sounds of impatience, "up Broad River to Cedar Creek and as far as Crim's Creek maybe, and then over to Godfrey Dreher's, say four men, two each way, and acquaint them with our proceedings, tell what we propose."

Some felt they were merely temporizing.

"But it's not just thirty or forty of these thieves we've got to deal with," answered Gallman. "It's more like two or three hundred."

"Yes, they may ride in small bands, but they're linked up all over the Province," agreed another.

"And if we're not strong enough to wipe out the whole operation, it's no use going out. All we do is stir up more devilment."

"And I'll tell you something else that's got to be dealt with too. These houses, these nests where they harbor, they've got to be burned out too."

Someone objected that that was too much like what the gangs did.

"Well, I say we've been outraged and plundered long enough," answered another. "We better learn to fight fire with fire."

"I agree. We've got to deal with them that support the thieves. Listen, all through this country there're hundreds and hundreds of damned idlers too lazy to do a lick of honest work for themselves. They'll lie out in the woods all summer long, raise a little corn in some clearing they're too sorry to get legal claim to, raise just enough to keep off downright starvation, maybe hunt a little, and they're good for nothing but to fiddle and fight and beget young ones in some open-sided shanty. And this country's getting so filled up with such riffraff if we don't do something, we're going to keep having the same problem year after year!"

"Are you talking about poor people just come into the country?" asked an older man. "You're bound to have poor people anywhere. It's not a sin to be poor and unfortunate."

"In the old country maybe not. But in this country you make your own fortune. Everybody knows that. People too lazy to work like the rest of us, we don't want. Let 'em go elsewhere."

"And God knows anybody that's had genuine misfortune we've always helped."

"I just don't know," came the slow, meditative voice. "It's not our place to start telling other people how to live, is it? I mean if a man's content to live a certain way, content with what he has as long as he harms—"

"Well, we'd better start telling 'em they can't live by thievery and plunder!"

Johannes rose to stand by the wall near Rudi, but Rudi was gone. Johannes pushed out onto the veranda and saw the big gelding trotting down the road. He felt sick inside. He wanted to go after Rudi, yet asked himself, To what purpose?

Inside, they were deciding who would go to Dreher's and who would go to Cedar Creek and Crim's.

At least, Johannes thought, he's headed down home—I hope. Surely he won't leave yet. He remembered uncomfortably the growing complaints against hunters. Some claimed the way they left skinned carcasses in the woods caused predators to multiply and prey on people's stock. They were beginning to class hunters with vagrants. Did Rudi think they'd been talking about him? Had they?

Joggi hoped in vain Herr Pastor wouldn't keep school today because of last night's excitement. However, though Theus appreciated the distractions to which his scholars had been subjected, he believed in doing his duty, which, in addition to instructing them in principles of religion, was to get at least the rudiments of reading and ciphering into their bullet heads. Sometimes he tried to impart a little knowledge of the world beyond these creek bottoms. If only young Jacob Lienhardt was as interested in the geography of Europe as in that of Tom's Creek.

Theus was grateful for the hibernation of frogs. However, the season of persimmon seeds was at hand, and a fistful of these or a pocketful of acorns hurled stealthily across the room made a rattling diversion. The young faces revealed no guilt. Theus thought he would have to resort to keeping them an hour longer. That was more effective than a dozen whippings. The trouble was it took its toll on him too. And he ran into objections from parents because the boys weren't home to do chores.

Inwardly Theus sighed, and as an exercise in more rigorous mental discipline, he began to catechize them. One after another he called on them for the answers in which he had been drilling them for the last three days.

"'Which is the sum of what God commands thee in the six commandments of the second table?'" he asked.

He asked it again and again, met only vacant looks, dropped heads, or stumbling garbled answers

He strove for patience. "Jacob Lienhardt!" he called.

"'That I love my neighbor as myself: on these two commandments hang the whole law and the prophets,'" Joggi answered promptly.

"'Canst thou keep all these things perfectly?'" Theus asked quickly.

"'In no wise: for I am prone by nature to hate God and my neighbor; and to transgress the commandments of God in thought, word, and deed.'"

"'Hath God created thee naturally so wicked and perverse?'" The teacher held his breath.

"'By no means: but he created me good and after his own image, in the true knowledge of God ...'"

Question after question, the boy's answers were flawless. And this in spite of yesterday's truancy!

Theus looked into the clear-eyed face, and his own relaxed in pleasure. Not a thing wrong with that boy's ability to learn! he thought triumphantly. That boy was ready for Latin! Dare he attempt to introduce the rudiments of the Latin language to Jacob Lienhardt? What would his father say?

He thought Johannes would be pleased. Johannes was an unassuming kind of man, with no more than a common education, but as sound as a rock in his principles. Johannes would want education as much as goods and land for his children.

An impressed silence followed Joggi's performance. Theus was aware that the young face looked at him hopefully. "Well done, Jacob! Well done!" he said loudly, then found himself saying, "You deserve a reward. What shall it be?"

The words came in a rush. "Please, Herr Pastor, Rudi's home, and he may go again before I can show him—" he paused, "what I've learned." Let Herr Pastor think he was referring to the Heidelberg Catechism if he wanted to. "Please may I go home after—" he paused again to consider tact, "after Scripture?" Besides the Pastor might read one of the more interesting stories from the Bible in the afternoon.

Theus considered in turn. More likely he wished to show that vagabond cousin of his how he'd learned to hang by his heels from the barn rafters or show him some squirrel he'd tamed. Theus sighed again. Well, if he let him go, it would be easier to drill the others. And after all the boy had learned the section perfectly. Theus permitted himself a smile and nodded. "Request granted, Jacob. After Scripture."

Joggi flushed with pleasure. He and Herr Pastor regarded each other for a moment as friends. Virtue did bring reward. Or a good memory did.

"Just don't catch cold in the creek," said the Pastor dryly.

Again Rudi and Joggi met on the road. Overtaking the boy as he was about to angle off through the woods, Rudi called him and dismounted.

Joggi dashed back to the road and together they walked toward the turn-off.

"Where's Papa?"

"He's still at the meeting."

Rudi was glad the boy didn't ask more, for he wouldn't have known what to say. He only knew he didn't belong there, was not even wanted.

"When are they going after the thieves?"

"I don't know. ...Where are the other boys? I thought you'd still be in school."

"Herr Pastor let me go." Answering Rudi's skeptical look, he said, "The other's didn't know their lessons."

"And you did?"

But Joggi had drifted to the side of the road. "Look what a bunch of possum tracks, Rudi!"

"They've been after these haws." They stepped under the low-growing trees. "See those fox tracks? Those are a gray fox. You don't often see them around here."

They squatted to look and Rudi explained how the signs and habits of gray and red foxes differed, the gray fox being much more wary of people. They noticed snake tracks and talked of rattlers and spreading adders. "You want to be careful around old wood and dead logs," said Rudi.

"I know. Heiri almost stepped on a black snake one time. It didn't hurt him though."

"No, they won't hurt you. ... When's Heiri going to school?"

"Papa says soon. Soon as Mama can spare him from minding Babeli and Cathri. I wish he could go already. He's seven and I started before I was seven." Rudi thought it strange they should keep the younger boy home, until Joggi continued, "Heiri got chills and fever, but I didn't, so Mama said she'd go on teaching him. He can read better already than Willi Rieder. But he can't do sums."

Rudi could do sums but he couldn't read. He'd learned to work sums by himself, but he'd never had anyone teach him to read or write. He was by no means the only man in the country who made his mark for his signature, but whenever he had to, he thought what a satisfying thing it would be to write his name himself, always correctly.

But what did it matter how they spelled it, when there was no other soul of his name in the whole country? Who cared about his name? He could be Jack Smith for all it mattered.

As they walked on, Joggi chattered. "Willi Rieder said his Papa's going to take him to Charlestown and buy him a Sunday coat with silver buttons and a gold-headed cane, but I said, 'Who cares about such trumpery? I'd rather have a big horse and a fringed shirt and leather leggings.' I'd rather go up the country with you than to Charlestown." He looked up longingly. "But Papa wouldn't ever let me, would he?"

"Wait a few years, Joggi," Rudi smiled down at him. "Papa might. Though I don't know about Mama." He roughened the black silky hair. "But you'll be such a scholar by then, you might look down on an old woods-rover like me."

For a moment Joggi was wordless. "Why—you're the learnedest man I know! I'm not going to be a scholar. I'm going to be like you!"

"Like me!" Rudi laughed. "Why in the world would you want to be like me?"

"Because you can do anything you want to! I mean—you can do all the things I want to do—"

Like what? Live like a possum or a fox, I guess he means. Or like a rattler or a black snake. Prey and keep from being preyed on is about it. He doesn't know how it gets to be after a while.

...Am I meant only to be a gray fox?

They're disappearing in this country.

Then go somewhere else too. You're not wanted here. At least not by men. Just children.

He looked down at the bright eyes, his heart twisting with the cramp of love. What would this child be? Would he ever do more than hoe corn, defend his own den? Or would he trot across a clearing in the moonlight and yearn under a winter sky?

The high cackle of a hen came faintly. Joggi stopped and tugged at Rudi's arm. "Wait. Come see this place, Rudi, it rocks and some trees around it that make it like a little room!"

The Lienhardt rooftop and chimney were visible through the thinning trees.

"What about Dan?"

"We can take him partway and hitch him to something. Rudi, it's a place you can stay in even in the rain and it won't even rain on you. Or not till it rains hard. Come on. It's a place not even Heiri's been to."

Boy, man, and horse turned into the deep woods toward the river.

Chapter Seven

Sleet danced on the fence rails. The cattle moved gladly under shelter although it was only mid-afternoon. Margaret's old plaid shawl blended with the dun shades of the byre and the creatures as she measured out grain for Bess and gathered up shucks for the others. They could not forage for themselves today. Only one cow was milking. They were all getting gaunt, for with the fear of thievery she did not allow them to stray very far. She estimated their store of grain and knew it would never bring them through the winter, not with weather like this. They did not feed grain to cattle or even to milkers unless it was absolutely necessary. But it was necessary now, if old Bess was to continue giving. And she and Granny needed all Bess had to give.

She took Molly a scant pail of bran mixed with corn. The little horse whickered and nuzzled under her arm, and Margaret reached into her pocket for a piece of dried apple. She rested her arm along the mare's neck, stroking her in distracted affection.

It was a hard time they were having. Granny'd had a painful pleurisy for a month, following some kind of chest infection, and although her fever was gone, she still had that hacking cough and was beginning to complain of shortness of breath. She'd rubbed and dosed herself and done everything she knew to do. "I'll just have to wear it out, child." But it was slow wearing. She had not been out of the house since November.

The work was almost more than Margaret could manage alone. Their neighbors had not forgotten them in such matters as gathering firewood and butchering a hog, or an occasional offering of other fresh meat or game, but there was no one to help with the everyday drudgery. Nor would Margaret's pride allow her to tell anyone how scanty their provisions were. If only some cattle had been sold last fall when they were fat and at least one yearling butchered and the meat salted and dried. It was the kind of thing Robert would have seen to. She had thought Jamie might offer. She knew now she should have seen to it herself. Granny gave few directions anymore.

Margaret stared bleak-eyed into freezing rain and sleet. The ground was

67

whitening. The fowls huddled in their coops and would need grain with the ground like this. She didn't know what she and Granny would do without milk and eggs. They still had dried fruit and a fair store of dried beans and banked potatoes, some bacon and ham so they weren't on starvation, but it was the scantiness of bread corn she worried about, and they lacked dried beef. They'd been out of salt for two weeks. Coffee and sugar were absent luxuries.

Her brother David had come in October, but she thought Jamie Fraser's being about the place had disguised their need. Though she was noncommittal about Jamie, she knew her brother assumed more than he should have. He rode off thinking them provided for. Not wanting interference, Margaret was glad to let him think so.

What a fool I've been, she thought. Why under heaven didn't I take Jamie Fraser when he offered? Handsome face, fine form, what more could any woman ask for, much less expect? And not only fine-looking, but gentle-mannered and learned as well. Where else in this whole backcountry would you find another single man like him? And from a respected, settled family. Not a woman in the country but would be glad to catch him. Who was I to be turning him down?

...Though I didn't really. But I might as well have. I hurt his feelings—or his pride. But just as I thought, he didn't love me enough. Oh, he halfway wanted me maybe for a time. But the month passed and two months, three, four, and he'd never said another word. Her mouth twisted.

...Oh, he's shy, he's proud, afraid of being turned down again! ...No, she answered herself quietly after a time, he's like me. He doesn't know how to give himself. He doesn't want to. Call it selfishness, she thought. Give it its right name.

Yet he'd kept coming and helping with one thing and another all through the fall. Not wanting anybody to think he'd been rejected? Or not wanting her to think it mattered? But since that day in September he'd held distant. As have I. How could we ever marry? ...Oh, but why can't I love him and him love me? If only one of us could begin.

Well, *he* was willing to begin, she told herself soberly. And if he offered now I'd take him in a minute, just to have somebody to help me with Granny! Yet a corner of her mind said again, And how much good would he be to you? Jamie doesn't belong here.

But she thought that if she were to see him come riding out of this bitter wind, she would run to meet him. Let him come, she cried, and I'd run gladly! ...But how would he greet you?

She stooped to get a turn of wood to take to the porch, thankful she'd chopped a good pile this morning. The sleet rolled into the folds of her shawl as she stacked wood on her arm. Rising, pausing to balance, she saw how low the sky was. Ice was forming on the trunk of the white oak back of the house. This rain mixed with sleet would have everything coated by dark.

She gazed east across a stubbled field. Two rows of native red cedars grew along what had been intended for an approach to the front of the house, although no one ever came that way. Visitors coming by the creekside trail always rode up to the high porch on the western side and entered the big room where they cooked and ate and sat. The other room was called the front chamber, but it had no chimney, for it had been added later. There they slept and in the warm months spun and wove. To the girls of the family, stepping back and forth at the spinning wheel by the window, the cedars they saw through the front doorway suggested callers moving formally toward the house. As a child, Margaret's sister named the first comers "Polly," "Anne," and "Jenny"; their husbands were "Samuel," "Abraham," and "Archibald." Jeannie made up stories about these mannerly ladies and gentlemen walking up so neat and proper, and her mother had smiled to listen.

Now the cedars were unshapely in the streaked gray air, their coated limbs separated and drooping. They were derelict trees like those at Robert's place.

Ice pellets stung her face. Her hands were numb. She'd better go inside or Granny would start to worry. On the high porch she looked toward the veiled gray woods by the creek. *Jeannie, Robert, David* — names whispered thinly in her mind.

Dan must know where he is, thought Rudi. The gelding was picking up his feet with energy, and he sniffed the air. Five or six more miles maybe.

The storm was growing worse. Rudi dismounted to lead Dan as well as the new horse, for the path was getting treacherous, the rocks and roots glazed. Dan packed four fine quarters of venison, and Rudi's horse Stony carried the other gear. Overhead the trees creaked in the wind. The only other sound was the light rattling of sleet on trunks and frozen leaves. All wild creatures were crouched, burrowed, and hidden.

Rudi looked up through the straining limbs. Why do trees look taller in winter? It must be the emptiness of those high spaces, no leaves to hide the heights and lower the limbs. The poplars and sweet gums soared a hundred feet or more, the oaks, hickories and chestnuts almost as high. The limbs of a massive sycamore spread white upward and outward. Yet for all their bareness they were his cover. They were the furniture of his house. These last three months in the woods had eased him.

Still, with the rising wind and accumulation of ice, he thought he ought to get out from under the trees. No other creature had so little sense as to be out this afternoon. Or he could find a good hollow and back up into it. Why not? Unsure as he was of where he was going, or at least what he'd find when he got there, he might as well find or rig up some kind of shelter. He'd lain out in the worse weather. Come now, he told himself, you might as well.

But Dan was stepping along so eagerly it would be downright mean to deprive him of better shelter on a night like this. No, something said, push on. Besides, there was the meat. Why else had he let himself get caught out in such weather except for the chance at that buck and the time it took to dress him. He didn't want to arrive empty-handed, especially since he'd waited so long to come back.

He had stayed a week with the Lienhardts in October, but his visit never again attained the satisfaction of its beginning. Johannes was kind, Madle was gracious, but with so many more of them now, he felt himself one too many. The house was too full. Also Johannes was much taken up with the plans of the Regulators, as they called themselves. They expected action in November. Both men were embarrassed over Rudi's leaving the meeting at the Congarees. Neither knew how to discuss it, so they didn't.

Rudi's best time was the day he'd helped Johannes fell logs for the new barn, though he'd been dismayed to find the hewing and lifting were harder because of his recent injury. When Johannes realized it, he put a stop to the work. Depressed, Rudi left two days later. He sensed their sadness as he rode away.

He did not stop at the Congarees. The faces there had seemed to him closed, uncommunicative. What's come over me? he asked himself miserably. Once I could make friends wherever I chose. When they felled me on that path, what else did they take besides my goods?

He'd headed for the backcountry, moving over into Georgia, straying occasionally into Cherokee lands. It had been a good season so far. Already he'd taken thirty-five deerskins and seven beaver. At fifteen shillings for a deerskin and twenty-five for a beaver, he'd realized thirty-five pounds from the trader at Augusta, which had enabled him to buy this sturdy young horse for twenty. Now he felt like himself again.

His thoughts moved ahead to Indian Creek. He should have gone by there long before, he told himself worriedly. It was now the middle of January, almost four months since he'd left. Was the tall Irishman still coming? Or fixed there permanently? Rudi never consciously admitted it was this possibility that kept him away. He must not return as destitute as when he'd left, he kept telling himself.

But perhaps by now the Irishman had taken them elsewhere. What if the house was empty? Or worse still, in ashes?

Urgency tore through him. How monstrous he'd stayed away so long! He saw Granny's face, lightened with her hidden merriment. And Margaret's, the clear blue eyes, the wonder of her unexpected smile. Oh, what if some mischance had struck her! He saw her through the mists of that autumn morning, looking down from the porch, removed, smaller and smaller as he rode away. That girl's face, almost yet never quite hidden by the meshing of twigs and his campfire smoke.

Rudi quickened his pace. But he was beginning to feel pain in his groin. Weariness from the path seeped into him.

He had been approaching in a general northeastern direction, for he'd come up from Augusta by way of Ninety Six. He'd crossed Saluda's Little River, Bush River, and an upper branch of Indian Creek. Now he turned east and slightly south. Soon he should find himself on the north bank of Indian Creek itself, he thought. But the lay of the land looked odd. It was rising where it shouldn't with high ground to his right. He halted. Was he even on the path? He thought he saw it winding down the slope.

Thirty minutes later he came out upon an immense canebrake and knew he had missed his way. Strange how that thin white covering could make the familiar seem unfamiliar. In front of him the wind rattled a wide stretch of house-high cane. Normally the horses would have approached it eagerly, but not today. Dan kept turning his head southward. He'd tugged at the reins a time or two farther back, Rudi remembered. "I overshot it, didn't I?"

He'd come too far north. This must be a branch of Duncan's Creek.

The sky was thicker than ever. What a time to lose his bearings. "Dan, which way?" He dropped the reins, gave the wet-blackened shoulder a slap. "Well, you take me there. Don't you know the way home?" Slowly he turned the big gelding, slapped his haunch, then dropped the reins again.

Both horses stood, heads lifted, their breath white, fine sleet whipping their sides. Dan lowered his head, picked up his feet and moved back through the woods, the man at his side, and the packhorse following.

Twenty minutes later Rudi said, "I'm afraid you'll have to carry me awhile, old fellow." They angled southeast over the ridge they had just crossed. How much more daylight? It seemed they'd been coming for hours in the same gray wind.

The wind had died. The ground was white. The shining encasement on the thick-twigged limbs weighted them down.

Margaret took a deep breath. The twilight was light after the close-shuttered darkness of the house. She'd tried to keep a big fire all afternoon so the damp and chill couldn't creep close to Granny. It worried her that Granny sat so huddled and quiet. Margaret prattled on about one thing and another just to keep the sound of her voice in Granny's ears, but the old woman did not often answer.

Oh God, God! she cried suddenly. Help her to get better! Please help her! Overcome by sudden dread, she went down the steps, almost forgetting why she'd come out, and walked away from the house.

More wood, much more to pile on the porch. She must keep fire all night.

The milking was done. What else was it? Oh yes, a stout log pushed against that back side of the fowlhouse where something had been trying to dig under it. Cold as it was, this was the kind of night foxes were most apt to try to get at the fowls because their wild prey would be hidden. She'd have to drag a log out from under the house. Years ago her father had stored there a number of squared logs left over from building the front room. Only three were left, resting on rocks where the house was high off the ground. But first to bring up more wood.

The sound of her axe rang sharp in the still air. She already had enough for tonight, but in case it snowed, she wanted plenty for tomorrow. And hard work seemed to move back her dread. With the blunt side of the axe she knocked apart the hickory and oak poles frozen together, cut length after length, carried armful after armful up the steps till there was no more room on the porch.

Now to get out that log. If she could. She wore old woolen mittens, but the snagged one was unraveling, and she thought, Everything on this place, inside and out, going to rack and ruin! Oh, she ought to go in and catch up the yarn right now, but light would be gone if she did. She stooped and crept under the house. She felt for the big dry poplar beams her father and the boys had put there five years ago. It took her whole strength to dislodge one, for it was much heavier than she'd thought. Pull it down. Thud. Drag it out. Just two left. Hard, solid wood, well-seasoned. Too good really for her purpose. But she had to protect the fowls. A stone pillar was in the way. She came out from under the house to straighten her back and stand awhile. She noticed blood on her hand, then bent again under the house, tugged and pulled, now at one end, now at the other, till finally the big log was free and out. She tumbled it over several times in the yard and discovered she could slide it on the icy ground. She moved one end, then the other around in a half circle and stopped again to rest.

She gazed about for a moment.

Posts and tree trunks rose clean and black above the white glaze which gave a luminous clarity to the blue air. She moved away from the shadow of the house. In the western sky the cloud blanket had lifted a bit and the gray had a faint pink undertint. Even as she watched, a glint to the south struck a twig in its frozen entanglement. But across the wasteland to the east, the line of woods was dull. She saw the cedars more rough and disheveled than ever, wings weighted down with ice, great drooping birds.

Then at the end of that forlorn avenue, coming down from the northeast corner of an old fallow field, a clumped formation appeared, two beasts and a man.

She felt an instant of fear, but then the weary gait of the horses and the bent figure of the rider told her she had nothing to be afraid of. He saw her and hallooed. She recognized the horse he rode and stood to watch them coming.

Rain-darkened between the misshapen silver-gray cedars he came, the first visitor in her memory to approach down that avenue. The breathing of the horses was white, their plodding and creaking clear in the twilight air.

Larger and larger they loomed between the cedars.

Margaret stood locked still, waiting. Then something broke loose, something set free, and she found herself moving toward him.

Rudi slipped out of the stirrups, stiff enough to fall, but he did not. The beauty of this girl was like the beauty of all he had come through this day and all seasons—hard, hurting, wild—and it twisted deep in his vitals with a wound from which he knew he would not recover.

More naturally than she had ever sought anyone, Margaret went to him and put her hands on his shoulders, lifting her face. There was nothing to say but his name.

He said, "I missed the way. It's God's mercy I got here tonight."

"God's mercy," she breathed.

Shyness and longing fought in him. He kissed her very gently.

Her hands dropped from his shoulders. She felt the convulsive reach in him, quickly restrained, and love swung out to meet him even as she stepped back.

"Come in now out of the cold. You must be perishing cold."

He gathered up the reins to lead the horses, and she walked beside him around the house. "Let me put up the creatures while you go inside," she urged.

"I've meat here. We'd best unload it now."

She stood by him while he unstrapped the venison haunches and she helped him take them on the porch. "I must see to the horses first," he said. "They've come a cruel way." He stopped, took a deep breath. "Granny? Your Granny, is she—" He could not finish.

"Oh, come speak to her! Just come please speak to her first! It'll do her the world of good to know you're here!"

"Yes. Oh yes." But he kept his gaze on her face, the eyes that did not look away. Why was it all so joyously familiar in this half-dark?

He remembered that little fellow come flying out on the road to meet him.

When they pushed open the heavy door, the old woman already stood trembling and holding to her chair. Rudi could barely see her face in the dusky room, but with her he knew no shyness at all. He did not hesitate to rush and catch her up. As he held her, frail and trembling, his cheeks were wet.

The blazing fire drove back the cold. Though their store of candles was small, Margaret lit one, and their eyes were soft and bright in candlelight. Granny, as warm as if she were sunk into down feathers, felt a loosening of the tightness in her chest. She ate her supper with more appetite than she'd had in weeks.

"I've always relished a nice collop of venison," she said. "Meggie, you've done these to a turn."

"Aye, it's prime meat. The best we've tasted in many a day." The pride that would have forbidden the admission earlier was gone; she had only the desire to give him pleasure.

Rudi thought, What if I hadn't pushed on?

Margaret brought out the muscadine wine with its tang of summer. As she poured the cup for Rudi, she poured for him her lightness among the branches of the chestnut oak. He received it with wonder. How can it be? he kept asking himself.

...Jane Gordon, as she'd once been, remembering, stood young in April dusk with John McGrew on a rock bridge that overarched the River Roe. Behind them, moorland stretched up toward the dark peaks of the Sperrin Mountains. Linnets twittered in the hedgerows and a blackbird whistled in the heather and whins. "You're the one for me, lass, no other in this world," and his arms folded her life into his with the water flowing beneath their feet up into the sea water of Lough Foyle. It did not matter then that no woman ever in all this world could give him his heart's craving. His hands spanning her waist made her feel as comely as a flowering maytree.

...And Meggie's taken off her old brown shawl and donned her mother's of crimson wool with its sweet spice smell. Like the woodbine that crimsons in May, clambers up the branches of trees. But this Rudi, this gaunt-eyed lad, he's no great oak or lordly poplar either. He's not a one to come striding down the glens and claim the ground as his own. Well, rarely does woodbine climb such trees. More like to climb some low-growing, stunted variety. She'd seen the old scars when she'd salved and soothed him. Gently, Meggie. Be gentle.

Rudi said, "You give me a—home feeling." He looked at them earnestly, then away, looked again into Granny's soft, blurred face. "You're more to me than friends." He could hardly bear to look at Margaret's for fear its flashing beauty would die like the hearth-rose in the night. Yet he did not miss her thinness or the signs of anxious toil. "If I can serve you any way."

Granny said, "Then will you bide awhile with us? At least through the cold?"

"Not because you can serve us," said Margaret quickly. "Though God knows you can do that too. But I'd not have you think it's for your service."

Rudi waited. Let her say the word. What word I do not know. But when she says it, I'll know.

"When we found you on that path—when I found you," she corrected herself, "we did not know what we were doing, or who you were." She paused. Her next words were very clear. "I know you now. You bide here awhile, Rudi Näffels."

There was no pleading in her voice or eyes, not even what might be called invitation. It was merely a bidding as when one said, "Come to dinner." It was as natural as if close kin had bid him come.

"Yes, I'll stay," he said.

They sat only a short while after supper, for it had been a hard, long day.

"You can help me to bed now, Meggie. Rudi, it's like to be perishing cold in that loft room up there. Bring down the fleeces and make ye up a good bed here by the hearth. Meggie, come get him to drag out that little flock mattress in the front chamber."

After he'd gotten the fleece and the other bedding, Rudi went outside. The night was still except for the barking of foxes. They'd come nearer as the night wore on. He heard wolves in the distance. He'd helped Margaret secure the fowlhouse, amazed that she'd gotten out that heavy beam by herself. The sky was clear now, and a new moon was low in the west. Out from under the trees the smooth ground was luminous. He wished she were here with him. Though she would not come out. She was not one to follow after a man. Would she have gone already to bed? It was partly to give them a chance to undress by the fire that he'd come outside.

When he went in, the room was empty. He brought in more wood, and firelight leaped against the walls. As he arranged his bed, he thought it was wrong that he should have the warmer room and they the cold one. But they had each other, a warmth stronger than any from oak and hickory. When they admitted him into the front chamber to get the bedding, a room he'd never entered, he felt they were admitting him into their lives for good and all.

He looked at their closed door. No, she wouldn't come out again. She wouldn't taunt and tease; she was not that kind. He sat down heavily, his face in his hands, for the second time that day a wetness on it.

No, God be thanked, not that kind. Then strangely he thought of Johannes and his words that morning when they'd gone up the creek to get the cows. "A pattern maybe. We can't understand it. But looking back, you see."

Chapter Eight

Ice was solid in the pails on the porch. The light was hard and cold as a hammer. Rudi brought the pails in to set them on the hearth.

Margaret, hearing his movements, dressed quickly. "Stay abed now, Granny, till the room's warmer." In the dark of the shuttered chamber, she combed her roughened hair.

The big room was empty but fire blazed high. She opened the outside door to solid cold.

The sky was beginning to pink with sunrise, but the trees and earth were locked in ice. She heard noise in the barnlot. Ah, he'd be seeing to the creatures.

She closed the door against the wall of cold and moved to the hearth. He must have kept up the fire all night, for the pail on the table had only a skim of ice. She began to prepare breakfast.

Thought could not cope with emotion. She might try to speak reasonably with herself, but feelings pelted her in warm turbulence. What is it about him? Why? she might ask in mirthful dismay, but there answered only this delicious sense of being wholly alive. She saw him among the beasts so near at hand, and all outdoors was full of him. She longed to rush out with her milk pail. Are you turned wanton? She accused herself, smiling. Shame on you for your boldness!

She heard the thump and scrape of footsteps. She swung out the crane, stirred the big pot vigorously, and swung it back over the fire.

Light came into the room, his head uncovered, briefly a shape against the light, every curve and grace known instantly, then the bulk of him advancing out of the gloom from the shut door.

"Be careful when you go out," he said, "the ice is slick as glass." In his voice a laughingness like the running of summer. That was it, she thought quickly, the laughingness.

"It'll be a fair day, do you not think?"

He paused halfway into the room as if in some way uncertain.

"Come up to the fire. Warm your hands, Rudi." Again she'd said his name. Why had it ever been hard to say?

78

She stooped swiftly and lifted the cakes of cornbread in the spider to see if they needed turning. To their sputtering in hot grease she rose. He had spread his hands to the warmth, still in his heavy coat, but with her rising he turned.

Without thought they moved together, the warm cheek against the cold one, their ardor blending and blazing. They drew back a little, Margaret breathless. "Rudi, I—" She looked into his dark-fringed eyes, sighed deeply, and once again wove her hands behind his head, amazed at the naturalness of all she did. She was someone other than she'd known she was. And yet, she thought, she was more herself than ever she had been in her life. I never dreamed it would be so. As natural as breathing.

It was her gentleness that moved him most and her sweetness. Angular and sharp as she sometimes seemed, who would have thought she'd have this wildflower sweetness? Carefully he held her face between his hands. "Why?"

She smiled, echoed, "Why?"

"You know me, Margaret?"

I know your gladness and need. And your loyalty. "Are you not a true-hearted man, Rudi Näffels?"

"I try to be," he murmured. "But I'm nothing much else."

"You are you." She spoke with a hint of fierceness. She whispered, "And you love me too."

He drew back a little, spoke almost in a groan. "Aye-God, I do, Margaret."

He dropped his hands. "Listen. I had a wife once. I must tell you. But she was not true-hearted." His heavy voice seemed to come from some place of tumble and dark. "I did not think to love any woman again. I did not want to. I must tell you that. But—" he shook his head, unsmiling, "now I do."

She too had drawn back, but he caught her hands and held them at his breast. "Listen. I have a friend. He says goodness comes to us. All my life—it's been sometimes hard and sometimes I've been a fool, careless in my ways, and yet—I think much has been given me. When I was left half dead. You and your Granny. You are the best ever come to me, Margaret. But I'm not—good like you."

"Your wife. You said you had a wife." She was turned away. Her face was pale.

"She ran off." He let go her hands.

Margaret waited, taut.

At last he sighed heavily. "She's dead."

Still she did not move or speak.

"I did nothing to harm her before or after. I never found her or the man either. Word came later she was dead. You see—" again he sighed heavily, "I've knocked about so, I'm not the man maybe for a young girl like you."

"I knew," she said huskily. "Times I knew there'd been some bad loss. I have not the sight some have, I think Granny has, but times I seemed to know about you—even afore you came back here last night." She looked past him into the shadows. "And you have no child," she added.

"No."

Once more she moved to him, holding him with strength as she'd held him, fallen on the forest floor, when she and Granny were trying to save him. "You're my joy," she said and thought, If we have e'er a child, that gift too will be mine.

"How old are you?" he asked. "You're younger than I once thought."

"How old you think?" she whispered.

It was the smell of burning cornbread that called them back into the morning. "And oh Granny dear! I must see to her!"

The early hours brought special clarity to Jane McGrew. She lay in bed knowing that her grandchild and that alien young man—not alien either but strangely loved as any child she'd ever tended—that they were finding themselves in one another. Ah, but it's a hard way they'll go, she thought. Who knows what straits they'll endure?

And years gone by, I'd have opposed such a one for mine. "Not of our kind," she mocked. "Not of our kirk or kin." Not even our tongue does he speak with ease. And no lettering that I can tell. Yet I warrant, she addressed her unseen hearers, there are better things in the world than these outer fashions. At least for this child. They two fit together like halves of a nutshell with goodness at the center. They'll make a rare wholeness.

And now I'll die the easier he's come, and I'll trust Thee, Lord, to bring them fast together. ...I must say a word to these Lairds and Frasers. Let some of 'em come soon.

She moved and pain tore her chest. How long, Lord? she gasped. I did not know it would take so long. In the deeps of hard cold? Many a one will go in this cold. Her thoughts slowed. Seventeen and sixty-eight the year I've come to. Oh Lord, ha' mercy, to ha' lived so long and come so far....

He'll may be here when I go. Let love be with me, Lord. Ah, to think a young man would love a one as old as me. A rare gift. Is that why I'd have him for her? Oh Lord, I'm a poor old selfish creature still.

...No, it's the tender heart in him. Not many have that tender-heartedness. Now James Fraser's a fine, upright young man, but he has not now the lovingkindness I'd ask for Meggie. Aye, he may love her. But not with kindness.

Though she might live without it. But I'd not have her be the proud, harsh woman she'd be if starved of the lovingkindness. She might never know the blessedness that comes out of hurt and grief.

Lord? Oh dear, dear Lord! The old woman, thanking God for the blessedness, but not moving lest the pain tear her again, heard a door open and close, and drifted into sleep.

Time doubled back. In its cold depths she was making her way across murky, rush-grown ground, was trying in the gloom to sight the walls of their cottage with its inner hearthfire and her mother's dresser of glinting delftware, but she kept finding herself by sedgy pools, then among mazy streams that were seeking some great lough.

Now the open sea was before her, walls of water moving in across the land, wastes and wastes of rolling cold gray water. Oh, where was home? Despairingly she kept moving backward for some purchase of ground, but all behind her were bog and pool and before her the vast and moving water. Terror cried in her throat.

And she woke, thankfully still, waiting for the smell of turf fire and her mother's voice.

The grind of a heavy door opening.

"Granny, are you awake? Let's wrap you up good now. Come and I'll help you get up. You must dress by the fire. No, wait, say your prayers by the fire. It's solid ice outside."

Her limbs were solid ice until the will to move brought life and pain.

The milking and feeding done, shortened for Margaret today—she marveled that one's man help could make such a difference—and livened by a laughing interval of sliding down on the ice and being helped up and slipping again and pulling Rudi down with her—how long since she'd played on ice?—the two paused before going into the house. The world was brilliant. Two hours of sunshine had started the steady drop and break of crystal.

"First job is to cut cane for the cattle till you're ready to let 'em out," he said.

"I'd be afraid to let any out today. One might slip and founder."

"I'll take Stony and Dan. They're careful-footed. We'll bring back plenty of cane."

"Will you take the sledge?"

"No, that's too heavy. I'll make something light to drag on."

"Come in now and get a warm dram inside you first."

"Wait." He touched her arm. "Granny. She's not the same as when I left here."

Margaret's face sobered. "No. She says it's a thing she'll have to wear out. But I don't know." She looked down and spoke low. "I'm afraid for her. The thing that frights me most, it's not just the pain I see, she's had that other times, but it's—she's given all over to me, the managing of things. She was never used to do that." Margaret looked away.

They stood in silence with all around them the tinkle and shatter of ice.

Rudi said, "I'll not leave you again. At least not till—not till spring. I'll not leave you alone."

She glanced at him swiftly. And what then? she wanted to ask, but it was not the time. "Come in now. You've done her the world of good already. It may be she'll rally if we can have a good long warm spell."

In the evening the three sat again before the fire, Margaret knitting and Rudi cutting deerhide strips for binding poles. In addition to dragging up bales of cane, he had cut and hauled more wood, and late that afternoon he had shot two wood ducks.

"I'll go for more salt one day next week," he said. "With salt you can let cattle rove more free."

"Aye, they'll always come home for salt," Margaret agreed.

Granny sat wrapped in a quilt, her knotted hands slowly drawing wool across one bristly card with another. She was long past her spinning days, but she could still comb wool and flax. "What news of the country do you bring, Rudi?" she asked.

"A month gone," said Margaret, "we heard a great band was riding out after the thieves, but we've not heard e'er a word since."

"It's two companies of Rangers," said Rudi, "Regulator men deputized as Rangers. Two companies."

"How many would that be?"

"Fifty-four men. Twenty-five men and two officers to a troop. Last I heard they'd gathered somewhere up Wateree River above Pine Tree."

"Will it be enough, you think? Just fifty-four men?" asked Margaret.

"If they're determined, it will be. If they don't turn back. The gangs will scatter. They'll go up into North Carolina, I think. They have mountain places they go. Some go to Virginia." Rudi paused, asked sharply, "None have been here since September, have they?"

"Not close, not to my knowledge. Men from here have scouted through the country. I've heard of skirmishes some places. What they've done mostly is to burn out houses where they think the thieves harbor." She'd heard how some, thought to be in with the outlaws, had been dragged out, tied to trees and flogged, but she didn't wish to speak of it. "Aleck Fraser told how over one thousand men ha' taken oath to clear the country."

"One thousand ought to do it," said Rudi. "If they don't go too far."

"You mean go too far up in Virginny?"

"No, I mean punish other kinds of people. Ones that aren't thieves."

Margaret was silent. The ones that aided and abetted evildoers deserved punishment, she thought, the cowardly scavengers who came after the thieves. Finally she said, "I wouldn't want anybody innocent punished."

"You can't always tell who's innocent." He let his work rest. Arms on knees, his look was brooding. "I have as much cause to hate thieves as anyone. You know that, don't you?" He glanced at the women. "I wished to ride with the decent men myself. But I'm not a—settled man. If you're not a settled man, they don't want you."

"They lack understanding," said Granny.

"They're a narrow-minded lot," flashed Margaret, "whoever they be!"

"No, I understand them. They think if you have no land and goods, they can't trust you. Still—because I'm not a settled man, it gives no one the right to put me in with the thieves."

"Ah, dear honey," mourned Granny, "people can be cruel-blind."

Margaret's face was somber. And so I might have judged you once.

"Some think if you don't live by the hoe and plow," he continued, "you're no better than a savage. As if there's no other way to live than grub all day with a hoe." As he'd been driven to it by that old slavemaster Bruger, he could have said.

"Oh aye, indeed," agreed Granny, "many other ways."

"I know well what's in this country. I've gone ten years back and forth in it, and I know about the jail-castouts and runaways and the poor souls made orphan by Shawnee hatchets maybe, no one now to care if they live or die. Yes, they might steal your shoes. But one might share a johnnycake with you too."

"And if we had the courts here, there'd be no need for all this private judging of one another," said Margaret vehemently. "Let's have courts here to give us justice, I've been hearing that for years—instead of down in Charlestown, where they don't know or care about our condition here!"

Rudi looked up. "Yes, I've heard others say the same." But would a court in Orangeburg have given me justice ten years ago? I don't know.

"And it was for giving evidence in Charlestown against one of those gang members they later turned loose, it was because of that, my brother was shot. And poor little Janet, dear soul, driven to take her own life."

Granny's face crumpled. "Oh blessed Lord," she keened softly.

"Ohh there, now see what I've done," Margaret whispered. "Granny dear, I'm sorry! I don't know what came over me to be talking so! Oh, I shouldn't ha' been talking so!"

Granny swallowed and wiped her eyes hard. "It's my weakness, child. I can't seem to stand things anymore. But I know she's where no hurt can come to her now. And Robert too. And others back through the years. But it's how it all came about that makes such sorrow. ...And I ha' not the strength to contemplate it." She picked up the cards and stroked the wool fiercely.

After a while Margaret said, "Granny saw bad days in Virginny and Pennsylvany too, didn't you, Granny, and even in Ireland where she came from. Tell about old days, Granny. But tell us some good things you remember from bygone days. Remember when you used to tell how it was in County Derry, old Derry where you came from? Tell Rudi how it was there."

Granny knew Margaret was only trying to turn her mind from grief. But it was woven together, the bright and dark, and more of the dark than bright. Yet let them see the bright when they could. She drew one card more slowly across the other. Rudi picked up his work; Margaret's needles clicked. The cards and wool rested in the old woman's lap.

"Ah well now," and her tongue took on more than usual the brogue of northern Ireland, "the green of it all is what stays most in my mind, that and the softness of rain. We had fine flax fields and such green grass for bleaching grounds as you'd never see here, so much mist and rain as it was. ...A rock house we had and you could see to the next one when you stood at your window, a leaded window ye could see through. The houses all whitewashed and maybe green grass growing on the old thatch. The thatch would be different colors from the different times it was patched.

"...And sheep. My father aye kept sheep, though the wool was no longer profitable, he claimed. Many a time I've helped bring in a yoe that was to drop a yeanling and later played with the wee thing as if 'twere a babe. Lambs in spring is a thing I miss most in this wilderness. A lamb will follow you and look to you like a human child.

"...But there were wolves too in the mountains. Men would go out in winter and hunt wolves. They paid men there too to kill off wolves.

"...But another thing now, Rudi, you might like to hear about, we had salmon in the rivers that would swim up from the sea. They'd commence to come in January, so thick you could not see between 'em, great fish sometimes the twenty pound or more. So curious, to think how the young would move far out to sea, yet fight their way back, it's said, to the very burn they were spawned in." Her voice stopped. Up the Foyle and up the Roe. Up the Susquehanna. Shenandoah. A long way from the ocean. How they could find their way and go so far. Enoree. Ah well. Man does not seek his way back. Maybe it's because his last home is somewhere other than a river of earth.

"Meggie, I'm ready to lie down now. I get so stiff when I sit up long you'll have to help me."

Margaret disentangled her from the quilt and shawls and wool, but it was Rudi who supported her.

"I did ever like a strong lad's hand under my arm." She stood very still a moment, head bent, so they could not see her face. Margaret observed her anxiously, but when the old woman looked up, her countenance was clear. "Ah thank you, dear lad, you've got a strong grip to you." Her voice took on a mischievous note. "I'll not trouble you to come to bed wi' me now, Meggie, but mind you don't sit up too late. The front chamber gets awful lonely after a while."

Margaret's heart lightened at the brightness in Granny's voice.

Aleck and Jamie Fraser hailed and rode up the next morning. Rudi laid down his axe at the woodpile as Margaret came out and welcomed them. Rudi nodded and touched his hat. The men returned his salute without speaking and climbed the steps. Rudi returned to his work.

When the Frasers entered the house, they were surprised to see how shrunken old Mrs. McGrew was. Nor did she rise to greet them or direct her granddaughter in dispensing hospitality as she usually did.

"I'm sorry we ha' nothing better to offer you than this poor brandy," Margaret said half guiltily, not looking at Granny. There were only two or three gills of whiskey left, which she decided quickly must be saved for a greater need.

And who'd been drinking up their whiskey, Aleck thought, but that German!

"We're sorry not to ha' come sooner, treacherous as this weather's been. And how have you fared through it all?"

Margaret waited for her grandmother to answer but, when she did not, said, "Well enough."

"We'd thought to come and haul up wood, but we see you've other help now."

Jamie thought, Why must he use that dry, sarcastic tone when it was his concern that brought us here?

When Margaret did not reply, Granny said, "Rudi Näffels came the evening of the ice storm. He brought us a pack-load of venison."

"And did he bring back Robert's gelding?" asked Aleck.

"Aye. He has his own horse now."

The men were silent. Aleck was about to remark, "But he's not paid you horse-hire, has he?" when Jamie interposed, "Well, I'm glad he came. I'm glad to know someone was with you in the storm and ice."

Aleck glanced at his brother in exasperation. And what kind of man are you, James Fraser? You see what the fellow's up to, don't you?

Margaret's look was as direct as her words. "Rudi Näffels is an upright man. He has gratitude for our help last summer. And he has much regard for my grandmother." To her dismay she felt herself flushing as the two men looked at her, their unspoken words a shout.

Again, to prevent Aleck from speaking, Jamie observed, "He's given no cause to doubt his honesty, I'm sure." But the words sounded falsely smooth even to his own ears.

Granny exerted herself. "It's great generosity and kindness he's shown us at a time when Meggie's sore needed it."

Margaret rose. "Shall I ask him to see to your horses? You'll stay and take dinner with us?"

Aleck would have accepted out of an angry kind of concern, but Jamie answered quickly, "No, we have not that much time."

His brother said gloomily as he felt in his coat pocket, "Here's a small bag of West India coffee Mary sent you, which she hopes you'll do her the favor to accept. And some gallipot here of some kind of balm or such. She said you'd know the use of it." There was a loaf of pumpkin bread too in the saddlebag which he'd offer later.

"Ah, you must tell dear Mary we're vastly indebted to her," said Granny. "Aye, she has a skillful hand with anything. She'd not to be outmatched by anyone."

And no one could outmatch Granny's civility either, Margaret thought, as her grandmother proceeded to inquire after every Fraser and family connection by name. How could she ever make shift to live without the balm of Granny's good manners?

"What news of the country do you bring?" she asked, an impersonal question which she hoped her grandmother approved of. But they had nothing to tell except mention of some trees the ice had split.

"I don't like it at all," said Aleck as they rode away. Jamie did not answer.

Aleck continued, "It's not right, a loose, roving fellow like that in the same house with two lone females, and one a young unmarried one at that."

"I doubt he'd be there if they'd not invited him," Jamie observed.

"Aye, true," Aleck admitted begrudgingly. "And why the devil had they got to invite him?" he asked pointedly.

"As Margaret's Granny allowed, she needed help," Jamie answered lightly.

Aleck could not read his brother's face. Oh, what he'd like to say to him! But it would mean a quarrel, probably a fierce one, and it might end up with Jamie's knocking him down. Nobody knew better than Aleck how very fierce Jamie could be when once he was roused. No poor shilly-shally about him that way.

"Ah man, I don't understand you at all," he said finally. "Why did you keep going back there all fall if you decided you wanted none of her?"

"What makes you think I decided that?"

Aleck snorted. "You don't mean to tell me *she* decided!"

Jamie did not answer.

"Well, if it's you that's not made up your mind, you'd best do it soon or that black-jawed German'll make it unnecessary. If he's not done so already."

Jamie sighed to himself, No doubt he had. And how much did it matter after all?

"Though if he has," said Aleck, "there may be some of us hereabouts will have a word to say about it."

But what if she has a word? Jamie wondered.

More alluring than ever the flowing suppleness of her seemed to him today, the grace of her hands, and the high lift of her head. Ah, Margaret, what is it holds me back from you? And what is it holds me to you? Ten minutes and I'm like wax or water around you, and yet I can forget you a week at a time and not seem to care at all about your struggles here alone. ...And if you took me, what would it be for? A man to plow corn and hew your wood? For both of us, what more than for our coupling?

"Aye indeed," Aleck was saying, "some of the rest of us might just have a word to say about that."

Chapter Nine

There were two weeks of spring in February. The hens sang and their combs reddened. The cattle came home late. Rudi broke up the garden for Margaret to sow cabbage, turnips, carrots and beets. He spoke of plowing the cornfield, but she said to wait and he went hunting instead.

She sprinkled earth over the last row of fine seed and smoothed it with the palm of her hand. She could smell smoke from miles away. From now until mid-March the air would often be gray with smoke because Indians and settlers alike would be burning off the woods for a good crop of grass and wild peavine. It took skill to burn woods properly. How will we do it this year? had been her question yesterday. What about spring planting? But today there was no room for anything in her thought but the bloodstains on Granny's bedclothes.

Margaret had supported the racked body, eased it into a chair by the fire, and done the little she knew to do for relief and comfort, and all the while heard herself talking normally, while a corner of her mind was amazed that her anguish was contained.

When at last the look of suffering left the white face empty, Granny said, "You must put seed in the ground today, Margaret. You've got your rows laid out. Make haste now. I'll be all right." So the tiny seeds were planted in the sign of those great red stains.

Margaret framed a note in her mind. "Dear Mistress Laird, if you can spare the time, I beg you will come as soon as convenient. I fear my Grandmother has a terrible ill in her chest. If you can come, I will be greatly obliged to you. I am your respectful friend—"

She must try to make ink and get out quill and paper without Granny noticing. If he returned tonight, she'd ask Rudi to take the note tomorrow.

Rudi did not want to take the note himself. He would rather have stayed with Granny and let Margaret go if he could have done it with a clear conscience. But since he could not, he accepted without comment her directions and the leather packet with its folded page.

"You may find Mistress Laird somewhat sharpspoken, but there's none hereabouts more skilled to deal with sickness." Except Granny, Margaret could have added.

As they stood at the foot of the steps, Rudi observed her rigid shoulders and the grip of her hands. The weather had changed in the night. The sky was overcast and soon it would drizzle. The damp in the air caused her hair to thicken about her face.

If only he had the right words. "I'll go and come back quick," he said.

As he rode through the woods, he noted hard buds on the hickories, lichen gray-green on wet trunks, a cocoon on a twig. One part of him was intent on serving to his utmost, but another part wanted desperately to ford Indian Creek and ride west toward Saluda and on to the Savannah and across it, lose himself among the gorges of north Georgia.

What can I do to stay her life one minute? I want to remember her when she was brisk and able in the sunlight. Why must I watch her die? he cried.

Animals went off by themselves. As far as he knew, only humans felt they must stay with one another to the end. That was what it meant to be human.

Oh God, would either of them have left me alone? he groaned.

Martha Laird was a big-framed woman in her forties. She had lost most of her teeth so that her mouth was pursed inward with hard creases, but the planes of her face were still handsome and waving red-gold hair showed from under her cap. She received the note in silence.

When she looked up, her face showed no softening. "Can you understand English?"

"Yes, I understand English."

"Tell Margaret Allen I'll be there afore night."

"You'll not come alone, will you? I'll wait if you—"

"One of my sons will come with me. You go ahead and give her my message."

He'd thought she might ask for particulars about the sickness.

"I ha' things to do here. You can go now. I've given you my message."

As he rode away, he mused on her manner, vaguely hurt, but as he neared the Allen place, he dismissed it for the larger trouble.

When Margaret told Granny she'd sent for Martha Laird, Granny said,

"Well," and was silent awhile. "It may be you've done right. It's my opinion she'll not be needed yet awhile. Still it's in my mind you've done right."

In the drizzling dusk Martha came with her seventeen-year-old son. "Looks as if it's set in for a rainy spell. I wouldn't doubt there'll be downpours by morning."

She was right. It rained heavily in the night, and they breakfasted to a drumming on the roof and sweeping gusts against the house.

"Best wait till it clears, Davie, afore you go back," Martha told her son.

But Rudi could have told her that it would not clear that day. Heavy clouds would keep moving in from the west for days.

The five people in the house seemed a crowd even though there were no problems about sleeping arrangements. Martha Laird had a bed to herself in the front chamber with its two beds and the trundle. Rudi slept on one of the three beds in the wide loftroom, the Laird boy on another.

During his previous stay, when he'd gotten well enough to move about, Rudi had offered to sleep in the barn, but Granny said, "Rudi, if we cannot offer house shelter to a fellow creature, I've come farther into savage country than I thought." This winter after the severe cold abated, she'd again instructed him to sleep upstairs. Knowing the two were below had given him the warm feeling that they were indeed under his care. But sometimes he had other feelings in the loftroom, contradictory feelings, that caused him to steal downstairs and go outside for an hour or so. Sometimes he thought he'd do better in the barn.

After breakfast he stayed outside as much as possible. He'd learned to milk, for somewhat amusedly Margaret had taught him, and this morning he offered to do it for her. Later he'd find other work in the barn, the cleaning of horsegear and such.

Restless indoors with three women, young Laird rode home in the rain.

Martha talked with Granny about what she'd been taking. "You've tried cherry bark, I know. What about mullein?"

"I've tried it. I thought it helped at the time."

"It's a pity we ha' no coltsfoot here. It's a sure remedy for lung complaints. But I brought you some horehound. We'll make strong tea with a little sweetening and some spirits. Where do you keep the whiskey, Margaret?"

As Martha prepared the tea, she said little. Last night she and Margaret had had some slight conversation about Granny's condition.

Later when Martha brought the infusion, Granny said, "I thank you kindly, Marthy. This has the true horehound flavor to it. It's been many a year since I've tasted horehound." She sipped very slowly but soon began to cough and blood appeared on her lips.

Both women moved swiftly, Margaret holding and lifting, Martha with basin and cloth.

When the hemorrhage was over, Granny lay back in her chair breathing heavily. At last she whispered, "I'm a deal better now, Marthy. I can breathe now it's out." She opened her eyes, smiled tremulously. "Meggie dear, don't fret. The pain's gone."

Out of Granny's hearing, Margaret and Martha consulted. They decided to move a bed from the front chamber into the big room. They tried to work quietly, but it was rough work taking down the bed. When Granny realized what they were doing, she cried with strength, "No! I'm better to sit up when I can! And when I can't, I'll not lie out in the common room with all manner of coming and going and men about me!"

"It's the warmth we're thinking of, Granny dear!"

"My bedchamber's warm enough. When was a featherbed not warm enough for an Ulsterwoman?"

"Oh Granny dear!" Margaret crooned, kneeling at her side, caressing her hand.

"Now be my good dear honey and do as I tell you, Meg. Marthy," the tremble was back in her voice, "this afternoon I'll be better still and we'll talk a bit."

Outside, beneath the beat of rain on the porch roof, Margaret said, "Oh, Mistress Laird," but could ask no question.

And silence was her answer.

Finally the older woman said, "You cannot tell. Let's pray it will not be long."

Margaret turned away, gripped the porch rail, her eyes shut tight, no heaving commotion but only the ache and the ooze of tears. She felt the other woman's arm laid awkwardly about her shoulders. Neither spoke. The arm fell away.

"You must remember your Granny's had well over fourscore years. Not many have that long."

"She's so good," whispered Margaret.

"Aye, she's good. And it's why she deserves far better than this world can give her now."

Margaret ran down the steps in the rain, not toward the barn or orchard but toward the line of woods southwest of the house. She half-ran and stumbled till she came to the leaning chestnut oak, grasped its trunk, felt its ridges grind into her forehead.

In the afternoon Granny rallied as she'd said she would. She ate a bowl of samp without coughing and her color was better. She sipped a cup of weak horehound tea.

Margaret, quiet-faced and tired-eyed, her wet hair combed tightly back, moved slowly about, clearing, cleaning, doing all she could think of to keep busy.

After a while Granny said, "Meggie, I know you've not slept for two nights. Go take you some rest now. I must talk with Marthy. So go in the front chamber, my dear. And lie down." She held out her hand, beckoning Margaret. "Do it to please me, my dear."

In the dim bedchamber with the door closed, Margaret heard only the sound of running water. She saw darkness on the wall where rain had blown in through the sagging shutter. She lay on top of the coverlet with only a shawl over her. It felt so strange to lie here, for when had she ever lain down in the daytime if she was not sick abed?

She gazed at the coverlet, woven years ago in the Valley of Virginia, its pattern Wheel of Fortune. How long had it taken Granny and her mother to weave it?

How long? Her pattern finished. "Pray God it will not be long."

Many a time when Margaret was younger and was out of the house with some chore, she had thought, What if I should go in and find her dead? It was the way old people went sometimes. Many a time she had thought of it, because she knew it would not happen then, and thus considered herself prepared for it.

But when it *was* happening, it was different. She was not prepared for dissolution, only for the quick break. It had been quick with Robert and her father and almost so with her mother. But Granny had ever been there for strength and comfort. How will it be with her gone? she cried. All of them gone. Yet under her cry, the secret intimation—Ah, but there'll be yet his presence and later others. There'll be change.

Oh, change! If only it could change easy, with her here to bless all changes! With her gone how can there ever be ease and gentleness again?

And who are you to expect ease? someone asked her. When did she ever know ease? Aren't you ready yet to face the hard that all endure?

But I've already faced hard!

No, not as she did.

Margaret thought about what she knew of her grandmother's life, more of the very young years that Granny sometimes talked of than her later ones. Granny, married at eighteen, had lost six babies in Ireland and in Pennsylvania. Had lost a daughter in her teens to smallpox, a grown son during the Indian troubles in Pennsylvania. Margaret had never known her grandfather, but she knew he'd been a hard-drinking man, prone to violence in his young days, stern with his children, yet having great energy and a store of wit and humor that made him good company and a good drinking companion. He'd moved his family three times in Pennsylvania. It wasn't till after she was widowed that Granny came with her daughter and John Allen to Virginia, where Margaret was born. Granny had never known a settled home—except this one in South Carolina, if you could call it that, and not even here as mistress till John Allen's second wife left. Yet no one, Margaret thought, could give you more of a "home feeling," as Rudi called it, than Granny did. Will home go when she does?

Oh, she left her home and kin. Early she left it. And many a time later she left whatever of home she had, but always she brought some with her. Oh my dear Granny, what has life been that you've gone through so much so long and had ever yet some good for others?

This leaving— Oh God, how can I do without her to see my goings and my ways?

You'll go and you'll do. Same as she did.

"It's in my mind I'll see spring, Marthy. Though I know it's as He wills."

Martha said low, "I could wish you'd not to have to suffer so."

Granny was silent awhile. "It's the debt we all must pay. I'm thankful I'll not have a greater."

"I hope Mr. Richardson or some other minister of the gospel will come here soon."

"He will. Other years he's come in March. I'll pray to God to send him."

They were sitting side by side before the fire. Martha Laird was knitting, but Granny's hands lay still.

"About the burying. Let there be plenty of Scripture. I want Psalm One Hundred and Three. And Romans Eight. That's alongside what'er else the minister chooses. If you'll get the Bible off the shelf, we'll mark it. And hand me down my old Psalmbook too. If you please."

Martha marked the passages in the Bible with broomstraws between the pages and a prick of her needle at the head of each Scripture. "I want 'The Lord's my Shepherd,' of course. And be sure you sing 'Old Hundredth.' Mark that too, if you please."

They talked of times and of those near enough to be summoned. "Maybe you'd best let David and Jean know afterward. With spring planting and all, they're too far away to pick up and come—any time soon."

"I doubt not they'll come later for Margaret."

"There's another thing. I wish you most particular to understand it. And I'll trust you, Martha, to make it plain to all. This young man here, Rudi Näffels. He's been a son to me these last months. Give him all respect. And let him be one of the bearers."

Martha did not answer at once. She was sitting slightly in front of Granny, who could not see her mouth stiffen. "I'll tell them. Who else would you have?"

They spoke of this one and that one. Granny said, "Marthy, I'm glad you've come while I still ha' my wits. I'm glad to ha' had this good chance to make things clear to my neighbors. About Margaret. She's a good lass. But she's country-born and somewhat more outspoken than I would ha' been at her age. This country makes young ones more strong-notioned somehow. But she's a faithful child for all her manner. When I'm gone she'll know her own way. And it might not be a way you'd choose. Or her own parents either. But I'm satisfied about it. And I hope all will bear it in mind."

"I would ha' thought she'd be wed to James Fraser by now."

"Aye, Jamie's a fine lad. But he's maybe not the man for her."

Martha could not quite find it in her heart to say what she wanted to, so she compressed her lips again. She'd say her thoughts to Margaret later.

"Well, we'll see no harm comes to her."

Granny sighed. "You must not misjudge. Either her harm or her good."

Rudi sat on an upturned keg in the barn, his elbows on his knees, turning the snaffle bit over and over in his hands, feeling its smoothness and joints and edges. His thoughts were as orderless as the fragments of leather and straw at his feet.

If Granny died—or when she died, he made himself say—what must he do? Leave Margaret at once? Stay? Not till they'd stood before a minister. What minister? Would one of her kind even marry them? And where after that?

They'd talked vaguely of the where. He'd spoken once of new land on a lower branch of Reedy River, but she'd said, "I must bide here with Granny, Rudi, as long as she lives. I couldn't endure to move her again."

The land on Indian Creek was to have been divided between Robert and David, who'd agreed that Margaret and Granny might live there as long as they wished or till Margaret married. Robert had planned to buy out David's portion if it was agreeable and consolidate his own holdings. But with no will, Robert's property was in the limbo of proceedings yet to be put in motion.

Rudi asked what he'd asked fifty times. Where could he take her? Would she go with him? Could he live here? Not without the brother's consent, he couldn't. He wouldn't.

He sensed the suspicion of these Irish people and could not understand it. What did they think he was? That he was out to defraud someone?

Another part of the difficulty was that he and Margaret had not talked openly. Fear and dread had kept them from it. He'd vaguely hoped that if Granny got through the winter, he could go out in early March to finish the hunting season, acquire a few more worldly goods, and then they might marry when the minister came. But although they seemed to understand each another, the word "marry" had never actually been spoken. Somehow he'd not been able to say it. He knew he loved her as he'd never loved Eva, loved her not only with passion but with the tenderness he'd not known was in him. Why then was it so hard to make certain steps clear? He'd never do anything to harm her; never would he suffer a hair of her head to be harmed.

...So he must face the fact of leaving—either alone or with her. But where could he take her? Yet how could he leave her to struggle here unprotected while he got a place ready? But where else could she go? He thought of Johannes and Madle, but the idea seemed incongruous.

Oh, if only he had some friend among these people! Never could he talk to that cold-eyed Aleck Fraser. His brother? He'd as soon take his problem to some high-nosed Englishman.

Her own brother now. He held the snaffle bit still. No blood kin of Granny's could be wholly unfeeling.

He rubbed his forehead. I'm so dumb. Her own brother, he'll surely help her. I'll go to him soon, he's the one to speak to. David Allen lived beyond Ninety Six on the headwaters of Little River on Savannah. I must trust to her brother's good understanding, he told himself.

...Yet a man that doesn't know me, what will he see? Some good-for-nothing vagabond? But I must talk to him soon. And speak clear words to Margaret.

But as February ended and March began, Granny's worsening kept Rudi away from the Savannah River valley. After three weeks at home, Martha Laird returned.

There were more drenching rains in March. Creeks and rivers rose; swamps were flooded; cattle and hogs drowned. Wild plum blossom fell rain-bruised, and shadblow and the lovely pinkster. But bloodroot bloomed crisply close to the ground. The little purple flowers of wild ginger hid under their heart-shaped leaves on hillsides, and pale blue bird's-foot violets made a lightness in open clearings. But they were not gathered by Margaret.

Granny sat or lay, her feedings and eliminations attended to, parts of her body still working their functions as they had for eighty-four years.

In the long nights, the endless afternoons she would try to think back to days of light, gathering them to hold as you'd hold pretty things in your hand, examining them singly, turning each one this way and that. ...That second spring in the Cumberland Valley when they planted their garden. The afternoon she and John knelt by Isabelle's cradle, knowing the child would live. A far, far winter evening when she'd run and danced down the moor in a new kersey gown, singing out to the world. Days in the Shenandoah Valley a half century later, when she'd rocked and sung to wee Margaret. A day of birdsong last spring. The night young Rudi returned.

But other times she had no will to think back, times in the pain and stench of her decay that she endured only by holding herself flattened as it were to the cross-stretched figure above her, palm to palm, breath to breath.

In the evenings Margaret would read Scripture to her. Often Rudi would lift her. "Once a man and twice a child," she'd say. She would want the window and the door wide open, "so I can breathe," although the air was heavy with damp.

In the end she fought for life breath. Margaret was by her in her last struggle. Why must it be so hard for her? Margaret cried over and over. Why must her death be so hard?

Because she's strong. It's the weak who give way easy. Because her life was of value. It's not to be let go easy.

"The last enemy that shall be destroyed is death!" cried the sunken-eyed minister by her grave, by the mound of damp earth, red clay with rocks in it. Hard digging it had been, to the north of the rows of cedars, by the other graves with fieldstone slabs.

The time of her burial was a lovely afternoon with blue sky and the feathery greening of trees all around. Birdflight shadowed the ground with the comings and goings of nestbuilding.

Margaret had not much feeling now. She was glad it was a fair day, that the struggle was over. She could not sing with the others, "'Him serve with mirth, His praise forth tell,'" but she was glad they were singing it, for nothing could be more fitting at Granny's funeral. "'His mercy is forever sure,'" they sang. The minister had read it in Scripture again and again, and Granny herself had said it scores of times, but it was a thing that Margaret did not now feel.

"'Time like an ever-rolling stream bears all its sons away.'" The voices were high, strong, yet thin too beneath the vast spring sky. "'They fly forgotten as a dream dies at the opening day.'"

No! cried Rudi Näffels, Not her!

He had his place in the two rows of men. His shoulders bore part of the last lifting of her.

Margaret turned away as the clods fell.

Some forty people had come. Many of them had sat in the house last night, hearing the shrillings and boomings of night creatures. Martha Laird had been there ten days, Mary Fraser, Aleck's wife, for three.

Much of the food for the funeral feast was provided by Granny herself, for almost a month ago she had given Rudi two gold English sovereigns no one knew she had and sent him to Robert Goudey's store at Ninety Six. Buy wheat flour, spices, coffee, rice, loaf sugar, and any delicacy such as pickles or chocolate to be found there, she'd told him. "And bring back two kegs of good spirits. I want nothing scanty here when people come."

Nor was there scantiness. A long table was set up under the white oak with platters of fowl, beef, pork, and venison; plates of cakes, pies, and pastries; bowls of puddings and stews; and three kinds of drink—Malaga wine, whiskey, and peach brandy.

Men and women had eaten quietly at midday with solemn faces, and they would eat again in the late afternoon. As time drew on, notes of everyday cheerfulness crept in. Men gathered in groups while women worked with food or sat in the house nursing babies. Mr. Richardson had already gone, for he said he hoped to be well on his way to Crowder's Creek by dark. He looked more pale and weary than ever. Rudi Näffels had disappeared.

The younger men talked of the activities of the Ranger-Regulators in North Carolina and Virginia.

"I hear they hung sixteen in North Carolina."

"And a goodly number brought back to Charlestown for trials."

"I believe they'll let convictions stand this time."

"Brought back over a hundred horses, I heard."

"How would you go about making claim if you thought yours might be amongst 'em?"

"And brought back thirty-five of young females they'd carried off."

No one spoke for a while. They thought of the young female from Indian Creek who would not return.

"Well, to be sure, it sounds as if the country's been cleared of the worst."

"Aye. The job's well over half done."

There was another silence.

The same speaker said, "The rest of it's up to us."

His hearers nodded.

It was near dusk when the last horses left. Margaret was beginning to feel frantic because Rudi had not reappeared. Martha Laird, her youngest son, and one of the Fraser girls were staying the night.

Martha said, "Tomorrow we'll help you clear and straighten here, Margaret. Then I want you to come home with me."

Everything in Margaret wanted to cry, "Please, just leave me alone! It's only here I can get back what she gave me!" But she did not say it because she knew she must rouse as little opposition as possible. "What can I do about the creatures?"

"You can take along the horses and your milkers. The other cattle, someone can ride over once a week and put out salt for. The fowls—well, we can come back and get them too. My Davie'll ride over ever so often to see to things. David Allen no doubt will be here in a week or two."

"That's so," said Margaret. "Rudi Näffels has offered to take him word straightway."

Martha cleared her throat. "Well now, I'll tell you, Margaret, Aleck Fraser has settled it he'll set out for David Allen's tomorrow afore daylight."

"Mistress Laird—" Margaret's voice broke. She began to tremble and cry as she had not cried since the onset of her grandmother's illness.

"Oh, my dear!" The older woman tried to put her arm around the girl's shoulder, "You've borne up so well so long! Do try to hold up now," but Margaret moved away and ran out on the porch, stood there a moment before running down the steps.

A man was coming up from the creek bottom leading a horse. Martha stood in the doorway and watched as Margaret went to meet him, not running now, yet each approaching the other swiftly. She watched them embrace.

"I go now, Margaret," he said gently because he saw she'd been crying. "You understand why I go."

"Oh, come back soon, Rudi! Please come back soon!"

"Oh yes, I'll come back. We'll know better then how to do."

They stood awhile in silence. He said, "I thought once to speak to your minister today. But it was not the time."

"No, it wouldn't ha' been fitting."

He looked toward the porch where the Laird woman stood. "You'll go with them awhile?"

"I don't want to."

"You go with them. Your Granny would say that. It will be too hard here alone."

"Well. I'll see." She rested her head on his shoulder. "If only you wouldn't go off in the night."

"Sooner I go, sooner I'll be back."

"You won't ride all night, will you?"

"Oh no. But with the moon so bright it's hard to sleep. I'll stop when it goes down."

"I was afraid you'd already gone. That somebody'd said something."

"No one said anything." And that was just it. They hadn't said anything. Not one friendly word. "I wanted to be by myself. I need sometimes to be by myself."

"Oh, I know. ...You've got the letter?"

"I've got it."

"Then I wish you Godspeed, my dear. I'll look to see you and David in maybe a week."

She stood a long time looking after him as he rode west along the edge of the woods, stood looking even after he had merged into their dusk. When she turned, the house was black against a mauve sky, its open doorway a dim yellow square. Passing figures darkened it.

Not a one of mine left.

A loneliness bleaker than any she had ever known descended. That empty house. She dreaded to go inside to the talk, to the emptiness. She stiffened and mounted the steps.

The whiteness of moonlight hung on leaf and blade, the light sky alive with it. Night breezes fluttered the leaves. A hunting owl swept low across Rudi's path.

The woods were alive with the fragrance of bloom and sap and unfurling leaves. He came out into an old clearing, rode on. More and more distance between himself and the house on Indian Creek. If he got far enough away, the house might become again what it had been. A hearth at the heart of it. Tending hands, a small white head, and a chuckling voice that prattled on about herbs and garden things. She might be there yet, the brightness and sweet, strong merriment of her fixed there. Like long ago by the window.

...No more. Only the ache and taste of a white spring night.

Chapter Ten

The second morning of his journey Rudi reached the trading center of Ninety Six. There he recognized a black horse with white hind feet as belonging to one Gabe Gambrell, a hunter like himself, whom he had not seen since they'd run up on each other a year ago above the Pacolet River. But sure enough, at the far end of the veranda fronting Goudey's Store, there was Gambrell lounging on a bench with a noggin in his hand.

"Hello, Gabe!" called Rudi. "Man, how are you?"

Gambrell was a large, brown-faced young fellow with gray eyes and ragged blond hair cued in bear's gut. He wore moccasins, leather breeches, and a fringed shirt. His face lit up as he shouted, "Old Bull Shoulders! Ain't seen you in a long time! Where the devil you been to?"

Rudi laughed. "Here. There. How about you?"

They gripped hands and pounded backs. "What you doing here? You just in time! Got us a jug here nearly 'bout full!" Gambrell reached under the bench.

"I'll go in first and tend to business," said Rudi. "It won't take long."

He had not intended to stop by Ninety Six, but then he'd suddenly decided he might as well dispose of his few pelts since the season was over. You could never get as much here as at Charlestown or even Augusta, but his pack was too light to take all the way to Augusta, much less to Charlestown.

Twenty minutes later he emerged from the store with seven pounds for his skins. Goudey was fair. You'd have to say that. Close but fair.

The trader's place was unusually empty for this time of year. Only two men were inside talking. A halfbreed child playing at the other end of the veranda jumped off as Rudi came out.

Rudi sat down and accepted a short pull from Gabe's jug. "No thank you, Gabe," he answered the other's remonstrance. "I got a ways to go yet. I can't afford to get lost. What you doing here?"

"Fixing to leave, for one thing."

"Where to?"

"North Caroliny."

Rudi looked at the young man. "What you got yourself into?"

"You've not heard what's been happening around here to the likes of you and me?"

"What you mean?"

"Stay awhile and you'll find out."

"Tell me what you talking about, man."

"Whereabouts you been, Rudi? You've not heard about that law some of these dirt-grubbers are trying to get passed? Don't want a man to hunt no more'n seven miles from where he stays."

"Well, I don't," said Rudi, laughing. "I hardly ever go more than five miles from where I stay. Where I sleep, that is."

"You know what they mean. From your place of resi-dence," Gambrell mocked.

"And if you got no place of resi-dence?"

"Then you're not welcome in this province."

Neither spoke for a while. Gambrell said, "I'm thankful to God there do be other places."

"You think it's different in North Carolina?"

"If you go far enough back, it is."

"If you go far enough back, it is, anywhere. But then you know who you got to contend with *there*."

"Hell, I'd rather contend with them than these damned bogtrotters and woolbritches—"

"Hold on now—"

"—come into this country ten years ago, barelegged as you and me—"

"They're not barelegged now."

"No, but they're not about to tell me I can't go that way if I choose to. Go buck naked if I choose to."

"Why you think they got anything to say about that?"

"Don't tell me you've not heard about this mob calls their selves the 'Regulators'? They're trying to regulate all of us."

Rudi was silent awhile. "I hear they got rid of the thieves for us. That was a good job."

"Sure, if they'd stop with that."

"They haven't?"

"Man, where you been?"

"Tell me what you know."

"Look here. In every settlement just about, they've set their selves up to be law. Dragging out people they don't like, tying 'em to trees, flogging 'em. Just 'cause somebody's living 'irregular,' they say. Irregular, hell, they respect nobody. They even flogged a magistrate down on Horse Creek, Jacob Summeral. Tied up a magistrate and whipped him."

"What for?"

"Some kind of a brangle a few years back. Grudge work." Gabe spat in the dust. "You've heard of John Musgrove. Major John Musgrove on Saludy. They're even out to get him. Brother of Edward, I know you've heard of *him*, and would you believe they're out after him too? They're out after anybody opposes 'em.

Rudi whistled. The Musgroves were big men, especially Edward Musgrove, who had been a deputy surveyor, a militia captain in the Cherokee War, a justice of the peace, and a large landowner for years. His mill on the Enoree was only fifteen miles from the Allen place. Strange he'd heard nothing. But then—not strange. "Sounds like it *is* getting out of hand. ...Yes, I did hear something once. That is, I heard enough to wonder." He remembered the meeting last fall at the Congarees. "Who's in it over here."

"Just about everybody, one way or another. You got to live far back up the creek not to be. It's why I'm leaving."

"Now, Gabe, don't tell me *you* got enemies."

"I'm a hunter. Some people don't love a hunter."

"That's not new."

"When somebody starts telling me I can't be one, it is."

Rudi let the words hang there awhile, then said strongly, "It's not right. Decent men won't go along with it."

"How many decent men you know?"

Rudi gazed at the line of greening trees beyond the outbuildings and fields of Goudey's establishment. I've gone up and down these trails for ten years, he thought in rising anger. Rode for two years to help make it safe for others too. Run me out? Tell me I got no right to be here? We'll see about that!

He turned on the bench, faced away from the building. "I'll not be run out by a parcel of turkeycock, purseproud farmers!" he said loudly. "I got as much right here as anybody!" He stood up, leaned his arm on the veranda post, and looked down the well-trodden road.

He turned to the man on the bench. "I got to be on my way," he said abruptly. "Tell me something. You ever hear of a David Allen lives up the Little River beyond Long Canes?"

Gabe thought he might have but wasn't sure. "The country's getting so damned filled up, you don't know who lives anywhere now."

Rudi went inside for more information. When he came out, Gabe was tightening the saddle girth of his black horse. The jug was slung onto the harness of his packhorse. "Sure you don't want to go 'long with me? I could wait a couple of days if your business didn't take too long."

"It's like to keep me here a long time, Gabe," said Rudi quietly. "Well," raising his voice, "you look out now! You watch the path!"

They parted, riding in opposite directions.

Early next morning Rudi's way led him near the four-year-old French settlement of New Bordeaux, where Long Canes Creek branched off from Little River. Rudi observed it from across the river with interest—the frame houses they'd built instead of log ones, their gardens and vineyards and the young mulberry trees they'd planted for silkworms. How could you ever get cloth from a worm? he mused. But then wasps and hornets made paper. No better wadding anywhere to seat small shot than a piece of hornet nest.

The little town was laid out square and very neat, a big plain log building in its center. A church? It didn't look like one. ...Huguenots. They were very religious people, he'd heard, and they'd been used to worshipping out of doors and in hidden places in the old country, so maybe they didn't need a churchly building. Folks said they'd known terrible mistreatment. Do these men too look hard on poor fellow creatures not like them? Are they different from other Carolina people? Their homes, though in some ways like, looked different. It might be the vines and the mulberry trees as well as the planed wood.

But David Allen's house, which Rudi sighted shortly after midday, was like a thousand others in the back country. Built on a rise some three hundred yards above the banks of the little creek that for years to come would be called Allen's Creek, it stood in sloping fields cleared of every bush and tree except for one young shade tree. Rudi approved of the clearing. If I lived this close to Creeks and Cherokees, I'd get rid of everything around my dwelling house too, he thought. Near the almost windowless house were a roughly fenced garden and the usual outbuildings.

Most of the stumps were gone from the fields, which looked well tended with a good stand of sharp-pronged corn four or five inches high, but beyond the planted fields was a band of burned stumps. Someone was working in the upper field. Rudi hailed and dogs barked.

A bonneted woman came from the garden and quieted the dogs. Three small children followed her, but the person in the field did not leave his work.

To Rudi's inquiry the woman answered that this was indeed David Allen's place. "But he's not to home now." She was young and so deep-bonneted her face was in shadow. She had a pleasant voice, Rudi thought.

"I come from his sister Margaret. I bring a letter."

"Oh, it's not some trouble, I hope!"

Rudi hesitated. It had not occurred to him that he would have to speak to anyone but Allen. "Their grandmother is dead, Mistress Jane McGrew. She was buried on the twenty-ninth day of March."

"Ah," said the woman softly, "that's sad news, indeed. Sorry will he be to hear it. ...And how is Margaret? He's long been anxious to hear from her."

"She's well enough." He was silent a moment, perplexed. "Will your husband come back soon? I must give him her letter."

"Not for four days or more. He left sunup this morning, left for Augusty. I'd say you might go after him, but I fear you'd not overtake him now. He aimed to travel fast as he could, for it's no good time to be gone."

Rudi's dismay showed.

"I don't know what to advise you. If you'd want to leave the letter with me," she said gently, "I'd make sure he got it."

The children clustering at her skirts were a dark-haired girl about five years old and two younger tow-headed boys. Rudi saw she was expecting another child. She felt for the youngest head at her knee. While Rudi hesitated, she said, "Will you not light down and take refreshment?"

Rudi dismounted heavily and began to open up his saddlebag. "I'll give you the letter then." He motioned toward the figure working in the upper field. "Is that one of your kin?"

"He's a lad stays here to work for us. David felt better to go off with him here."

Hired or bondslave? Rudi wondered. He drew out the leather packet, unopened since Margaret had handed it to him. He didn't know what she'd said or how she'd said it. The fact that he couldn't have read it even if he'd looked at it added to his feeling of disadvantage. "If you'll give it to him soon as he comes back, please. It's important to her. And to me."

The little silence told him she might understand the import of his last three words. She said encouragingly, "I'll take good care of it for you. Time he returns, I'll give it to him. I'd best go put it up right now. You can hitch your horse at that rail if you will."

Rudi accepted standing the milk and scones she brought him. As he tasted the scones' buttery crispness, he was insensibly cheered. When she took off her bonnet and fanned her face, he saw she was quite young and very fair-skinned with a scattering of freckles. "My name is Rudi Näffels," he ventured.

"Nancy I'm called. Nancy Caldwell, that was."

"You have fine fields here."

Her face brightened. "I'm proud to hear you say so. Dave works awfully hard. He hated to leave this morning, but he's had so much mischance with stock loss and one thing and another, he felt obliged to go down there to make purchases he'd not thought to make, and there was so much high water through here all spring he was delayed in starting."

"The water's down now," said Rudi. "He'll travel easy if we don't have more rain."

The sky was certainly cloudless, and the April air was alive with humming and singing. Again Rudi looked at the tilled earth spread out about them, then down at the small faces gazing up. Suddenly he squatted down in front of the little girl. "What's your name?"

"Isabelle," she said bravely.

"We named her for Dave's mother. She takes after Dave's side."

And so she does, thought Rudi, with those clear blue eyes. Less brave, the little boys went behind their mother's skirts.

Rudi stood up. "I'm sorry I missed your husband, Mistress Nancy. If I thought I might meet him on the way back—" He broke off.

"Well now, it's possible. You might."

"But then if I missed him—and if I didn't he'd still have to come back here. No, I must trust you to give him the letter. That's best." He handed her the empty cup. "That was indeed tasty," he said, using Granny's words. "I thank you indeed." He unlooped Stony's reins. "I think I must ride back now the way I came."

"I'm sorry as can be he's not here," she said earnestly. "And so sorry for Margaret's loss. I was never around Dave's Granny much, but I know she was dear to him. To all of them."

"She was dear to me too," said Rudi.

When he had mounted Stony, he observed the still group, the woman and three children. In a few moments they would recede smaller and smaller as he turned from them. Then he happened to think of something he'd picked up on a creek bank, a perfect snail shell, delicate and pearly smooth. He sometimes picked up such things just to keep for a while. He took it from his pocket and leaned down a little hesitantly to hold it out. "Here's something the little girl might like."

"Oh how pretty!" cried Nancy as the child looked up at him. "Issy, bow the way Mammy taught you," she said low, "and say thank you."

As Rudi rode away, he looked back once to see the three children waving. Nancy too lifted her hand and now the two little boys ran far in front of her to wave goodbye.

If I'd stayed longer, he thought, I might have found myself telling her many things. But that wouldn't have been good.

In spite of his disappointment, Rudi left David Allen's place feeling better than when he had arrived. He had braced himself for suspicion, maybe even hostility, but he had met simple acceptance and an unguarded openness that were as refreshing as the milk and scones. But she ought not to have been so quick to tell me how long he'd be gone, he thought. I could have been anybody for all she knew. Maybe somebody come to do harm ... though I wasn't. Could she tell that about me? Or was it just her way?

Now Margaret would have been different. But Margaret's smarter. Which way's better? No matter, no matter—smart, quick-tempered, the tart makes it all the sweeter underneath. ...Meggie. I'll call her that one day and see how she likes it. Soon I'll begin to talk like an Irishman. "Commence" to talk like one, as they'd say. He amused himself recalling their expressions.

Yes, he'd speak English in his home. He'd been picking it up for over ten years now, and his German wasn't that good anyway. Madle sometimes corrected him. ...Their *home*. The word bloomed out for him. A true home he'd have as he'd never had that he could remember, or as only in the dark of memory. A good strong house, wider than the one he'd seen today, a wide hearth, at least two broad rooms with hospitality for all comers. He'd build bigger than Johannes even, with more of vines and fruit trees than the Irish. And children? Just such a little girl as the one back there with maybe her eyes. And sons! He shut his eyes with that excitement. No more wandering up and down these creek valleys then! He'd stay *close* to home! And work? Oh, how he'd work! If he could just get established.

Why not? He was only twenty-seven. He had strength of body and skill of hand. There was still plenty of good land for workers and doers here, almost for the asking. All it took was purpose, determination! Face it. That was what he'd lacked. No reason before to live any other way than how he'd always lived.

He must close his mind to former wrongs. Oh yes, he'd known that Eva had deliberately done a thing to make herself miscarry. No more such ways! no more even of remembering them! ...Well, he was not without fault himself, he said soberly. What more had he looked for in a woman than a certain shape and feel and promise?

...But I did want more, he thought quietly, after it was too late. So, dumb as I was, maybe I deserved her. I do not deserve Margaret.

He rode beneath the new-leafed branches of winged maple, box elder, sycamore, and tulip poplar, through the fragrance of wild crabapple and clouds of dogwood and floatings of redbud. Great tiger-striped butterflies flitted across the path. The woods were alive with birdsong. He heard the soft trilling of bluebirds. Do I deserve such a day? he laughed. Yet here it is.

He glimpsed the white scut of a deer leaping away. "Come back, friend!" he called. "I'll not shoot you today! Stay! Wait! I'd not shoot you today for anything!"

April continued cloudless. The weather was so fine he traveled at a more leisurely pace than he had, coming, especially since he had no word from David, no reason to hurry, he thought. Margaret needed time to herself, time for her grief, not pressured by their own problem. But he mustn't cause her anxiety. "Come back soon," she'd begged.

On the fourth day he pushed hard and so arrived at the farmstead on Indian Creek with the sun still an hour above the trees.

How still it seemed. For the first time he saw the chimney smokeless. No hens about the dooryard, no geese in the orchard. He went up on the porch, knocked, tried the latch. Well, he wouldn't have wanted to enter that emptiness anyhow.

The barnyard too was empty, though the ground was heavily trampled. He noticed someone had recently put out salt. He stood uncertain. She was probably at the Lairds. Should he push on over there now? It would be almost dark by the time he got there and it might cause awkwardness for her, his coming at dusk. He wanted plenty of time to talk. No, best to go in the morning. He'd sleep in the barn.

He rode Stony slowly up the creek to graze on new cane and hobbled him loosely so he couldn't stray. On his way back Rudi saw a couple of browsing cows that raised their heads in recognition. He stopped at the garden and looked at the rows of cabbages, beets, and young peas white with bloom. They needed working. He went to the barn for a hoe.

Someone else besides the cows saw Rudi. The Laird boy, who had just put out salt, saw Rudi ride up and stayed awhile to watch what he'd do. He even followed him up the creek and was about to turn away, when he saw Rudi dismount to return. He watched from his covert of trees till Rudi disappeared into the barn. He did not see the man begin hoeing the garden, for he was riding down the creek toward Frasers'.

Although he was tired, Rudi could not sleep. He lay awake hearing without hearing, the booming of bullfrogs, the shrilling of spring peepers, the call of a chuck-will's-widow. He could not throw off his feelings as he had during the journey. He could not help remembering that little gray-bonneted head you could see just above the paling when she bent over her hoe. And Molly under the apple trees. That other swift-moving figure, strong as a young-leafed willow withe, fair-hued as apple bloom pearled on the branches.

Moonlight barred the place where he lay. He turned this way and that in his blanket, could not get comfortable. At last he rose to stand in the open doorway of the barn. He gazed east at the moon riding high above the dark chimney. Foxes barked across the creek. He shut the door, lay down again and finally drifted into sleep to the mingling of night cries, and he kept riding through creek bottoms or clambering along rocky hillsides.

He was awakened suddenly by the sounds of horses, by torchlight cutting through the gaps between the logs. He heard a murmur of voices, couldn't catch words. More than two or three voices. He got up quickly, edged the door open.

Horsemen were clustered in the dooryard. The shock of it turned him cold. Oh God, not thieves again!

"He went in the barn, I tell you!" came a high, excited voice. "Look there!"

Anger, consternation turned his cold to hot, made his blood sing trembling through his veins.

He flung open the door even as a voice inside him said, Slip away in the dark.

"You want me?" he shouted. "Here I am if you look for me! Rudi Näffels, if you look for me!"

Eight men on horseback turned toward him. Dismounting swiftly, they spread out and came toward the barn.

"Näffel'! cried one, "you don't leave us a choice! If you'd gone on about your business and stayed clear of here like the upright man you claim to be, we'd have no call to meddle wi' you. But sneaking back here to trespass and plunder, you don't leave us a choice!"

"Sneak!" cried Rudi. "I come in broad daylight. Any man could see me. Yes, you saw me, didn't you?" he shouted to the unknown talebearer. He emerged from the doorway and moved to his right. "And why not speak to me then? Why do you wait for night and come like a gang of thieves yourself?"

But two men had already flanked him, now laid hold of him, one on each side. Rudi jerked away and knocked one down, kneed the other, crying a curse, but his cry was cut short as the other men toppled him, pinioned his arms and legs, and throttled him from behind. He was no match for six men.

They dragged him struggling and cursing toward the great white oak tree. "It's too dark under that tree," called one. "Use that post!"

"No, it's not high enough and he might pull it down! Light more torches! We'll make it light!"

Rudi stopped struggling and stilled himself. He tried to look at his captors. Two were men he had stood by at Granny's grave.

"You, Fraser! You think you serve that woman who died here?"

"She's beyond any need of my service and beyond any cozening of yours now too!" cried Aleck. "As for the other one, she may well thank us one day!"

"Strip his shirt off!"

Again Rudi jerked, lunged, tried to kick and elbow, but in the end the panting men had torn his shirt off and stretched him bound tight, his breast to the trunk of the tree, against which he ground his face in sobbing rage.

"From the looks of him, I'd say he's had a few doses of this medicine afore now."

They drew away, breathing hard.

"All right!" shouted one. "How many?" The cowhide whip trailed across the ground.

"Ten each."

"No more than ten?"

"No, but make 'em hard."

"Wait now before we start," came a dry older voice. "We ought to make it plain. Tell him why."

"Well, you tell him, Arch Logan. You tell him."

In the quiet, with only a jingle and creak as a horse moved, the booming and shrilling of night creatures sounded far away.

"Listen, you German, Switzer, whatever you be! It's to clear this country of vagabonds, men of no known habitation we do this! You can tell all others! We're tired of the disorder you and your kind bring here! And in your case—though in fairness I'll say there was some disagreement on this point—we ha' good reason to believe you've taken mean advantage of unprotected females—"

The harsh voice rang in Rudi's ears without meaning. The oak bark bit into his shoulders. He shut his eyes against the light.

"—defenseless females we hold ourselves responsible for—"

A man interrupted, "Wait a minute. Somebody's—"

"Then where were you after they killed my brother and dragged off his wife?" shrilled a breathless voice, crying up the hill. "Where were you when they came back and burned his house? You saw the smoke! Days and days afore e'er a one of you came about us that time!"

Margaret slipped off her winded mare and rushed among them. "Shame, shame on you for the pack of cowards you be!" In the glare of light she saw the tree. "Oh, and you'd do such a thing—" she came closer, caught her breath, "and him that's worked for us, helped us, come back when he'd no call to and stayed on and cared for my dear Granny as if she'd been his own—" Her voice broke high.

She looked at the surrounding men, her eyes a glitter in the torchlight. When she spoke again, her voice was low and deadly quiet. "Aye, you cowardly, canting hypocrites, think of her now in all her loving, gentle ways that you knew right well. Think of her there in that grave, and think if you'd ha' dared to bring this wickedness here while she lived!"

The men seemed stupefied. They looked at one another. Who would speak?

"Margaret Allen," said Aleck, breaking the silence, "we know you've been beguiled half out of your senses. But I'd not ha' thought you so shameless as this!"

"Shameless!" Her eyes blazed. "You to talk of shame? You that stood here eight days ago, bowed your head before Almighty God, spoke meeching, sorrowful words to me! Tell me this, Aleck Fraser, was it my brother David sent you to do this business?"

"I told you, I didn't see him!"

"Then get off his land!" She took a step forward. "Get off his property, you vandals and trespassers!"

"Margaret, get away!" Aleck entreated. "We've come here to do a needful thing and you make it harder!"

"Hard for you! How many did it take, all seven or eight of you to seize one man and tie him up—because he's not of your sneaking, baleful kind?"

"Drag her off," one muttered.

No one moved.

"Come away, Margaret!" called a strong voice from beyond the light. "They'll release him!"

"Jamie!" Aleck turned sharply.

"I'm sorry not to ha' got here sooner, Margaret. I'd have spared you this if—yet I don't know either. I'll not forget you now, and I'll wager some others won't either."

"Well, what have *you* come for, James Fraser?" asked a man. "I thought you said you'd ha' naught to do with it."

"So I did. And I'm ashamed of it. For if I couldn't stop you, I could at least have got here soon enough to warn the man what he could expect from such upright Christian Presbyterians as we are. Listen, you men, you listen to me! I tell you—though not with the fine scorn she's shown because in some ways I'm guilty too—but I tell you this: what you're here for tonight is sin! It's sin before Almighty God. And you can be sure of this! He will have none of it!"

Jamie came out of the darkness with power. "Look you here!" He moved into the light. "Do decent men, do Christian men ride out to lay hold of another in the night and punish him as you're about to do? And for what? What has he done? I've never heard yet one crime laid to him save that he doesn't live here! What kind of justice *is* it you're dealing in? In the black of night!" He paused. "A crowd of you going out to lay hold of one man in the black of night!"

His words reverberated in the silence.

Jamie said more quietly, "About the only crime I can accuse him of is gratitude. And caring about two people I wish before God I'd had the Christian grace to do more for. God have mercy on us, it appears to me we could all learn something from this man."

There was absolute silence. Borne down by the sheer authority of Jamie's voice, an appalling conviction fell upon them in the still air.

Someone moved quickly behind the tree and cut the thongs. Rudi half fell, stumbled, righted himself. Margaret put her hand on his arm for an instant, but he moved out of the light. Someone offered him his torn shirt.

Arch Logan cleared his throat. "Well—" he began, "well," he cleared his throat again. "It's possible you could have the right of it, James Fraser," he said heavily. "God knows there's not a one of us can't err in his way." He hemmed a third time. "If so, I'll ask forgiveness."

Again there was silence.

A man sighed deeply. "Aye. In such case we might ha' been too hasty." He added gloomily, "Aye, might well ha' been led to misjudge," and sighed again.

Someone blew his nose. "Well, no more to be said, James, if that's how the rest of you think."

No one spoke.

Finally one said, "We'd best go our ways."

Somberly the men turned and got on their horses without another word. They left not in a group but most went their separate ways.

Margaret moved out from under the shadow of the tree, Jamie following her.

"Margaret, my dear, I beg you, forgive me that I—"

"Rudi!" called Margaret. "Rudi, where are you?" She picked up one of the torches still smoldering and called again.

No answer anywhere.

She called again. Jamie added his voice. Eventually the chuck-will's-widow added hers but received no answer either. Rudi was almost beyond hearing as he stumbled through the shadows to find Stony.

Chapter Eleven

Jamie crossed the fallow field with its rose-blue haze of sheep sorrel and toadflax growing up among old cornstalks, the blue of the toadflax fragile and delicately scented but with no charm for Jamie.

This field should have been plowed and seed gotten into it weeks ago, he told himself. So why did you not come to plant it? Too fine to callous your hands when you saw no reward? ... No, it had not been the lack of reward. It had been a lack in himself, an impotence. A week ago he had not been able to give or lend himself with no expectation of return. No wonder, he thought now, no wonder!

He caught a whiff of smoke from the house. Well, thank God! he breathed deeply.

In the white moonlight last night he had finally left off trying to comfort or advise her.

"Get away! I want naught to do with e'er a one of you! Can't you see what you've all done? Get away from me!"

As she wept on the steps, he stood in the dark until her sobs checked when she realized his presence and she cried out, "Are you still there, James Fraser? Before God I beg you, go home! I want none of you here!"

A quarter of an hour later he stole back to hear her groping at the house door, to hear her shut it. He was relieved to know she was still inside. The great moon touched the far trees as he left, in his heart a mixture of pain and strange exhilaration.

Now with the sun an hour high, he rode again into the trampled yard and called, "Oh Margaret! It's me, Jamie!"

He heard no sound in the house or yard.

He climbed the steps, rapped, called again, "Margaret!" He knocked hard.

He edged open the door but saw only the shapes of benches and table in the gloom and some live coals in the fireplace.

Boldly he went in and opened a shutter. His arm brushed a washworn bonnet on a peg, and a breath of something elusive, as of herbs and balm, pervaded the room. He seemed to hear the soft fluttering of fowls outside,

117

a musical, "Come along, old cuddies," ... a dove in a cedar tree.

"And what do you here to make so free of my house?" the harsh voice demanded.

He had not heard her bare feet on the steps.

"Oh Margaret, I crave pardon. It's just I've been so distressed for you!" Yet even to himself his words sounded mincing and effeminate.

"You can save all such for yourself. I'll thank you not to come in here like this again."

Her hair was disordered and there were stains under her eyes. He saw twigs and last year's dried leaves on her dew-wet skirts.

She threw down the bridle she carried. "You think I'd go out trailing and tracking a man" Her lips were compressed. She reached for an empty waterpail hanging on the wall.

"You saw no sign of him?" Jamie persisted.

"Oh, aye, he's taken to horse and gone. You've run him off, the pack of you, so now your job's done. Tell that to your brother and be satisfied."

Jamie was silent.

"My horse is fresh," he said at last tentatively. "I've no doubt I can follow him. Would you like me to—"

"What, meddle more in my affairs? See if you can meddle more and tangle 'em up the more for me?"

"And would you rather I'd not meddled last night?" he cried.

"I only know," she whirled to him, "if you'd left us alone, all of you, if you'd had the decency and forbearance to—"

"But, Margaret, I was not one of them! You know that!"

"Then why did you not stop it sooner or give warning?"

"Margaret, I do blame myself. You're right. It's ever my way to think too long and be too slow—you know how I—" He broke off. He knew the scorn his next words would bring. "But I say this to you," he continued firmly, for he knew at last the weight of what he was going to say, "I care about you."

His words hung awhile, dropped to the floor.

In the doorway she had turned to look out as if she could see beyond the branch where buzzards wheeled above the April woods. Now her face was as bare of feeling as the porch and its walls were bare of the paraphernalia of daily life that she'd taken inside when the house was shut up.

He went out too, wanting to stand near her. He saw a hoe leaning against the garden paling. "You've been working in the garden?"

"No. He did yesterday." Her rough voice broke and her eyes filled, her face darkened.

And Jamie saw a man go up and down the rows, having ridden up from the south with hope in his eyes. "Come up, Rudi!" called in his memory a sweet-singing voice.

"Margaret, whether you want me or not," he said softly, "I'll come here every day as long as you're alone. No, wait, I'll not trouble you with words, but whatever's to be done—"

"Are you deaf?" she hissed vehemently. "I've told you I want none of your help!"

"—I'll try to do, and I'll see to it no one else troubles you either. I mean from hereabouts, till you know your way clear."

She dropped the pail with a clatter and went inside.

Jamie called after her, "It's in my mind he'll be back!"

He heard her shut the door between the two rooms. He stood irresolutely, then picked up the pail.

Returning, he set the bucket quietly on its shelf. "I'll be here in the morning," he called loudly. He stood a moment. He heard a scraping, dragging sound inside.

As he mounted his horse, she appeared in the doorway.

"Then see if you can help me to get my things back from those Lairds. Get all my things together and brought back here so I'll not have to scald my eyes with the sight of such people again."

David Allen came the fifth of May and stayed three days. He arrived at dusk, and when Jamie saw the strange horse there the next morning, thinking it might be the Switzer's, he felt a sinking desolation, and yet almost at once, as Allen came out, along with his relief he knew a curious disappointment. Is it for her? he wondered. Do I feel even her disappointment?

Allen was a tall, lean-jawed, dark-browed man, his hands big-knuckled from hard work, yet with the same clean line from forehead to chin that Margaret had.

"I'm obliged to you for your service here," he told Jamie. "I'm sorry it's not in my power to give recompense."

"It's not for recompense I serve," said Jamie. And he believed it was true. He had caught and brought back fowls, endured the questions and comments of Martha Laird and of his own mother, had planted corn, pumpkins, and peas in the field near the house, cut firewood, laid off garden rows for beans and squash, later plowed the corn and attempted to hoe the garden—although he was a clumsy workman there and hoed up some parsley by mistake. Margaret seemed to accept his work indifferently.

But he discovered that no drudgery was too much if he could do it for her. Whether she ever loved him or not, at last he knew this soaring into life that he had never experienced before. Sometimes he felt strong enough to gather up this whole world of hill, creek, and forest and shape it into some Eden-garden for her to walk in. It was not that he wanted anything from her, he told himself; it was what he wanted to give her that mattered—an order, a peace, an ease of soul and spirit. And yet he labored dumb, putting his feeling sometimes into old lines of verse.

> "...love is not love
> Which alters when it alteration finds
> Or bends with the remover to remove.
> Oh no! it is an ever-fixed mark..."

And I wondered if I loved her before, he marveled. God be thanked he's given me to know this.

He did not return while her brother was there, for he did not wish to seem to curry favor with him and so bring pressure on her.

But before Allen left Indian Creek, he rode over to the Frasers', to express formal appreciation to Jamie.

Allen said, "Meg tells me it's her wish to stay here till frost. After that she'll make some change."

Jamie did not know how to answer.

Allen continued, "There's legal entanglement to be cleared up about the property. I'll get to it in the fall." He paused. "I've told her I'd be willing to settle this place in her name when all's clear."

Jamie said, "That seems fair."

"Robert's place added to this one would make a good middling sort of plantation. I'd make it easy for the man she wedded to acquire it."

"No matter who he was?" asked Jamie.

Allen didn't answer at once. "Aye, no matter who," he said gloomily. "You can guess my wishes. But I doubt," he added dryly, "my wishes'll be of any consequence."

Jamie was tempted to agree but didn't comment. "She'll do well enough here, I think, the summer." Aside from her terrible aloneness, he thought.

"There's been no visitation of rogues hereabouts lately?"

"No. All's quiet in this neighborhood."

"I believe we ha' things under control now. Though I hear some reprobates are trying to get up lawsuits against us."

"Against Regulators?"

"Aye. They're being backed up by some of these crooked magistrates, but I doubt they'll be able to get warrants served."

Jamie did not answer. Both men appeared to contemplate two blue jays attacking something along a fence rail. Likely a snake after guinea eggs.

"Well," Allen sighed at last, "it's what happens when you've got no courts, or none worth speaking of." He beat his hat against his leg. "If we could only get proper courts!"

"Yes, courts," said Jamie with sudden force. "And schools. And religion. What we want here is more than corn and cattle."

Allen glanced at the big, fair-haired young man. "Aye, to be sure. I'll want my young ones to have at least the chances I had in Virginny." He paused. "But it takes corn and cattle to buy goods. And to frame up a meetinghouse and pay a parson. A book now costs how much? Not to mention the expense of traveling somewhere to get it."

"And yet we might do more with what we already have, it seems to me. We have the Book we brought here. We have good minds. Nobody keeps us from reading and thinking. We brought some knowledge into these parts."

"In your case maybe. Mine's more to do with keeping a musket in good order and reading the sign of Cherokee."

"You've had no such trouble where you're settled, I hope."

"Not yet. But I look for it all times. They're still too close for my taste."

The terrible events of the past clouded Jamie's mind—fear-haunted flight, fire and cleavings, merciless engulfment into savagery. ...Must our peace always be got in pitiless ways? Men striking others down for order and peace? And then the blanket of peace never quite smothering old dread.

They talked on awhile about frontier conditions. Finally Allen asked, "You think that Switzer'll come back?"

Jamie was silent. "I don't know," he said at last.

"What did you make of him?"

Again Jamie did not answer at once. "I thought he was a decent man. He meant no harm to your grandmother or Margaret. I think he meant only good."

"Hm. My wife said he was civil-spoken enough when he brought Meg's letter. 'Gentle-spoken,' she phrased it."

"I don't know," Jamie repeated. "I never really talked with him."

"There must be something wanting in him though, to ha' gone off and sent back ne'er a word to her."

"I've thought so," said Jamie. "And yet—what might come over a man's spirit when he's been so misjudged?"

"Well," Allen sighed, "I'm sorry it happened. Understand I cast no blame. All did as they thought best."

"Aye, they did."

Allen sighed again. "If I'd been here I might ha' been one of 'em."

Jamie thought it likely.

Margaret still kept the Sabbath, but if it hadn't been for Jamie, she might not have. If Jamie hadn't come, in spite of a lifelong prohibition against it, she might have kept up the whirr of the spinning wheel or the clack of the loom even on the day her body needed rest. Spinning or weaving, more than any other activity, could best absorb her attention.

A spinster, that's what I am. The word took on new meaning. Hands, arms, feet for motion and rhythm; eyes and fingers to gauge and measure thickness, tautness, length. My being a part of the winding skein, the pattern of dark and light, the old pattern set long ago and a twelvemonth ignored. The weaver a part of her web. My hours and days fixed here. I'm as caught in it as any spinning creature.

This pattern will be finished in autumn. Then to set a new one. Will it be one of my own make? Or one set for me?

As on the weekdays when he came, Jamie did not enter the house but sat out under the oak with a book in his hand. He sat there until the Sabbath sun went down red.

She lay on her bed in the afternoon, willing sleep. Later she sat in the open doorway of the front chamber. Following pattern, she opened the Bible on her lap and looked at the words, but she did not read them. She sat facing two rows of cedars marching up to the house. She imagined a horse and rider suddenly appearing at the end of the avenue, the rider dismounting, moving closer and closer to her. His face was glad, and her feeling tore loose, hurled itself against the sullen earth-dam within her, and she felt the mold of her countenance break up. She stole out the door, slipped away under the apple trees to walk herself weary among the fox and bobcat trails across the ridge.

When Jamie sensed she was gone, he put down his book and sat without looking at it until again he felt her presence in the house.

The next Sunday Margaret set a chair on the porch for him. "There may be more breeze up here," she called.

Thereafter he would sit on the high porch reading, occasionally gazing off as if in some study. Why doesn't he nap? she wondered. Most men nap at least part of a Sunday afternoon. She noticed he brought more than one book. Glancing at the one he held as she went out for water, she saw it was not a Psalmbook or the Bible either; at least, if it was, it wasn't English. Latin, she thought it might be. No, the print looked too strange for Latin.

She allowed the man to move into her thought. Oh Jamie, what do you do here? Go elsewhere. Find some dainty girl who'll adore you. Go to some other country, some place where your gifts and ways will be of more use. To her he was the epitome of male incomprehensibility. When you wanted a man, he wasn't there. Other times you couldn't drive one away. Men consulted only their own wants and feelings, were not to be diverted from them. A man was an entirely separate breed of humankind, she thought, different from anything else in nature.

On a Saturday early in June, Jamie called to her, "Margaret, there'll be Lord's Day service at Wilson's tomorrow if you'll come. A Pennsylvania missioner's passing through the district."

She answered, "Thank you, but I'd not know how to conduct myself among such pious folk."

The next day he would go to all-day meeting, she thought. Yet there he was a little after midday. He'd eaten his dinner at home, she supposed. She never offered him food. When he came to work weekdays, he brought his dinner with him.

It was a hazy-cloudy day with softness in the air, but the clouds were too high for rain. The ground needed rain. That afternoon as she sat in the doorway of the front chamber, the stillness of the Sabbath air like no other, the loneliness of its trees different from any other day, her thought kept turning to the man on the porch.

An hour later to his astonishment she stood in the doorway with a chair for herself. Her hair was smooth and she had donned a dark blue gown with a faint odor of some herb or spice about it.

He got to his feet, placed the chair for her, stood till she was seated.

"Since you seem bound and determined to keep me in half-civilized ways, Jamie, I'll sit and converse with you a spell like a genteel lady."

"I've had little experience of genteel ladies, Margaret," he smiled. "I doubt I'd know how to speak to one."

"Meaning your present company does not fit the category?"

Jamie flushed. "Meaning I'm a clod without wit or manners."

"Now that's genteel speech, to be sure."

She folded her hands in her lap. Jamie's book was still open. At last she observed, "I wonder you have patience to come here day after day. And waste your good talents on such poor substance as you find here."

He met her glance as he laid his book carefully under the chair. "You know I think it not waste."

"What *do* you think, Jamie? Do you think I'll have aught for you anytime soon?"

"Will you?" he asked.

She looked beyond him as if she could see the cedars, the hidden callers, on the other side of the house. "There's too much of hardness in me now," she said low, "to have aught of good for anyone."

He answered, "I know that."

Her glance returned to him. "And if you know it, why do you still come?"

"I told you. Don't you remember?"

She was quiet for awhile. "You didn't care enough to come like this before."

"It's true. But I do now."

She turned in her chair to look at him.

He shook his head. He might have told her that her fire, her utter heedlessness of herself on that awful night had touched something within him like quicksilver—brilliant, perfect—touching and merging into another something in himself to make one shining orb. It had called forth that great loosing he had longed for and it had not destroyed him, though it had brought him pain, yet pain accepted, for he knew now it was the pain that meant life.

"I don't understand you," she said at last.

"No. It's just that I'm not afraid of you now."

She was still. "You're strange to me, Jamie."

"No. I'm like all men. And women. I know now what it is to be—a man in the world. In this world. I mean—" he groped for words, "I can take the hurt of your not caring because I love *you*, Margaret Allen, not just your hand or your cheek—" he paused, "or the shape under your gown. It's you that I care about."

She lifted her eyes to his, their clear gaze no longer a darkness. But had they any softness? "I could wish you had known me sooner."

"You think it too late?"

"Aye."

"Why?"

"Because I have turned down a path away from where you are."

"You think—"

"I'm too far away from where you are! I've had too much of hurt and loss, far more than you have!" She sprang up with the force of a bent sapling released, quivering.

"Oh Margaret," he entreated softly and let a little of his yearning into his voice, "stay a while, do," and at his pleading she turned. "Sit down again, my dear, and rest yourself."

She dropped into her chair, lowering her eyes. Her clenched hands opened.

A flight of crows went cawing overhead. A thrasher scratched at the grassy edge of the yard. Neither spoke for a long time.

He was trying to think of some easy saying when her voice came low. "Jamie, maybe you can tell me a thing. You're a man—" She broke off. Again her knuckles were white, the pure line of her chin lifted taut. But she did not continue.

"Margaret, it may be that Rudi Näffels is too ashamed to come back now."

She looked at him quickly.

"Shame is hard for a man to get over," he said.

"Why?" she demanded. "What has he to be ashamed of? He's no culprit to skulk and run away!"

"No, but to be treated like one, that could go hard with him."

"But what about the loving and caring you talked of, Jamie? If he truly cared— Was I so wrong in my—esteem of him?"

He did not answer for a while. "I cannot tell you that." Then he asked carefully, "Did he tell you aught of his past life?"

"He'd been wed once and his wife left him. She's dead now, he said. Before that—he said little of his life." Her words came slowly. "He has no kin in this country except cousins down below the Congarees. I think he looks up to them. He was not born here, that he told me, but was left orphan very young, just after his family got here. But afterward—and I never understood this part—whoe'er it was raised him must ha' been cruel because he ran off soon as he could."

Jamie listened gravely. "Did he tell you his wife's name?"

"No. But first thing, he told me about her. Though not much. He didn't say much about her. He said she was not true. She's dead now, he said. I believed him."

"Has he ever taken up land?"

"He did. On Camping Creek on Saludy. Granny and I, we were surprised when he told us; at least I was, for I thought all he'd ever done was tramp the woods. But seldom he talked of his past. It was more of now and the things to be done this day that we talked of." Oh, it was the sweetness of our present knowing that filled all our thoughts and the wonder of it! she cried within. "The past did not seem to matter so much to him."

"Maybe it mattered too much. Maybe that's why he seldom spoke of it."

She was silent. "More than I matter?" she whispered at last.

He wanted to say "yes". Easy now to fix it in her mind as fact. But he must speak only truth. He groped for it. "It's not that it matters more than you," he said slowly. "It may be that it's so much part of him, he can't get rid of it. Maybe he wants to get rid of it and can't."

"But to forsake someone dear to you? I'd never do such a thing!" she cried low.

"Margaret, I'll tell you something. It may be there's more of weakness than strength in every man, or more of disease than health, unless—"

She interrupted, "Then I want no such a weak, sick man about me!"

Again he had to say, "But maybe the weakness and sickness came from a thing he could not help. Would you scorn a wounded man?"

Her chin lifted. Her teeth clenched, she turned her face away.

He heard himself say, "Are you so well and strong yourself that you can despise the weak? Besides, what's sick can get well."

"Oh Jamie Fraser!" She turned on him, her eyes flashing with anger, passion, grief—he could not tell. "You're talking like Granny! Who are you to be talking to me like my dear Granny?" Then incredibly she smiled that brilliant smile. The merest ghost of merriment crept around the corner of the house or from out the door or from somewhere.

"Well," he smiled back, "ye need somebody to talk someway to ye now, do ye not?" He spoke in the broadest of Irish accents.

"Oh James Fraser, you're like none I ever knew before! What's to be done about you?"

"You don't have to do anything. Not today. Or tomorrow either."

"And will you come here forever and work for me and wait on me like this?"

"As long as you need me. I told you that."

"It's not right! Don't be such a fool!" she cried, seemed not to notice his flinching, then laughed, "Oh, how can a man like you bear to fill his days with driving cattle and hoeing beans?"

"Well, it's better doing it here than at home. I don't have to step as smart here."

"Pshaw, I've seen you work. You're not lazy."

"Then too, I ha' not to listen to my sisters clacking about who's like to ha' banns read for 'em at every meetinghouse in the country. And they leave me alone about Peg Williams now."

"Jamie, why don't you go down to Charlestown or some place northward, say some great town like Philadelphy, where your learning would be of use to you?"

"It's of use to me here. You think learning's to be valued only for the honor it brings? Or the pounds and shillings?"

"I don't know. I have so little."

"You'll get more," he said slowly. "Though it may be a different kind. Maybe more like your Granny's"

"Granny had not much either."

"You think not?"

"Oh Jamie, Jamie, I cannot tell you how I miss her! No, she did not need letters when she had the heart and the wisdom to make joy beside the grief." Her voice broke.

Jamie breathed deeply, said quietly, "That's what I mean, Margaret. But I think such learning does not come easy."

The shadows grew long as sunlight crept under the white oak's branches. At last she observed, "You're right on one thing. I do need some one to talk some way to me. Even if it's things I cannot fathom or agree with." She rose, her full skirts falling straight, giving finality to her rising. "I thank you for many things. But more than all else—I thank you for hearing—what I could not say."

As he stood looking at her, more comely in the dark blue gown than she had ever seemed to him, he wanted to crush her to himself. But lest she see his want, he groped for the book under his chair, rose again, bowed awkwardly, and said, "I thank you for the pleasure of your company, Margaret," and clattered down the steps.

Oh God, Margaret prayed later, as she took off the blue dress and folded it carefully into her mother's chest, if only— But she did not know what to pray.

Chapter Twelve

Joggi laid down his hoe and wiped his face on his sleeve. He took off his wide-brimmed hat so he could feel the breeze on his forehead. He sank down between the corn hills. There was still some damp in the earth though it hadn't rained in two weeks, and Papa was beginning to get that look on his face.

Joggi stuck out a bare foot—after nine years his mother had finally given in and let him go without shoes—and began to mound the earth around it, packed and smoothed it, then gently withdrew his foot to leave a cave, a neat toady-frog house. He looked about for something to decorate its door with. Nothing but sturdy young field peas which he knew better than to pull up. And grass. At the edge of the field were some orange flowers where large black and orange butterflies clustered. But on the other side of the field, Papa.

Sighing, Joggi stood up and deliberately stepped in the middle of his toady-frog house. It was the kind of thing Heiri or Babeli would make, a girl-thing, a baby-thing. But the cool, packed earth always felt so good on your foot.

The hickory hoe handle was higher than he was but not as big as a man's since it had been made especially for him. It was heavy enough. The corn hills with peas between them were five feet apart, and the corn spears had to be hilled up higher when half-grown. This was late corn, planted where the winter wheat had been. The corn across the creek was already higher than his head. And full of grass.

Joggi sighed again. Hilling up corn was bad enough, but at least you got through with it. Hoeing out grass you never got through with. And it was such unvaried work. Nothing to be seen but the little blue butterflies flitting close to the ground. Sometimes a bobwhite called. The jays in the far woods were making a racket. If it hadn't been for that steadily moving figure across the field, Joggi would have been tempted to go and see why.

Papa was working near the Big Road, mounding up four hills to Joggi's one. "You can be glad it's soft sand and no rocks, young one, and no tough roots either. When I was your age, it was spurge and nettles I had to dig out, such tough roots as you'll never see."

Papa was always telling him how hard he'd worked when he was a boy, how he'd sweated on long summer days. "Longer than these days, and didn't get to take an hour for dinner either."

But when his father spoke sometimes of the sights and ways of the old country—of the high pastures where birds nested in moss and ferns and rock crevices, of the thistle-finch he'd caught and kept awhile in a cage, of a cliff face he'd climbed—Joggi knew his father's boyhood had not been all dreary toil. When his father told of living roofless in the summer pastures except for the few hours of night—Joggi found it hard to envision mountains—"Higher than the river bluff?"—when he spoke of the cold milky brooks, the great rocks, great falls and crashings of snow that could bury you alive, then sometimes his face would get such a look that Joggi knew not to ask more questions. "Why did you leave, Papa?" he asked once but his father's face changed. Not angry exactly but just—hurting?

Mama almost never talked of the old country. Though she sang Swiss songs to them. Once he'd heard his father and mother singing a song for the cows, "Call the brown ones, call the yellow ones," and his mother began to cry. At first he didn't understand why a song about cows would make anybody cry. Then the melody and his father's strange yodeling cry, the way their voices blended made his parents seem suddenly different. His father's voice had almost a wildness, and somehow he *did* understand it was some beautiful lonely thing about mountains, not cows, that made her cry.

Yet although she didn't talk about the old country, she told its stories. About dwarves and giants; about Big Beth and Sturdy Hans, who killed a dragon and married a princess; about the good woman, Verena, who carried a jug and comb with her, for she was always giving children milk and combing their hair. To Joggi a jug seemed an unhandy thing to carry about—why not a pail? As for the comb, well, if he'd seen her coming, he'd have run the other way.

But he did like the story about Tredeschin, who went out to see the world and did missions for the king of France. And though he pretended not to, he, as well as Heiri and his sisters, liked best of all the story of Ida of Toggenburg, whose cruel husband threw her out the window. But she was cared for by God, for she ate apples and berries, and at night she covered herself with a netting of rushes and grass and slept in a cave where foxes and deer and rabbits came to be with her. In Toggenburg. Where his parents came from.

Sometimes he tried to think how it would be if they hadn't come. Who would he be? A herdboy like his father? He sometimes wished he were, rather than to have to hill up corn and hoe grass. He knew he'd like to climb and see where the snow never melted.

Still—not ever to feel this hot sand on his feet and the cool underneath, not ever to play in the creek shallows and the leaf-walled room under the dogwood tree where no one could see you and the rain hardly touched you at all—and not to run home in this scented air, feel the sun-warmed chimney stones at your back as you sat shelling corn. And not to have Bläss—and he wouldn't know Willi and Nissi Rieder either—well, he couldn't imagine it. He wouldn't be Joggi Lienhardt but some other boy.

He was moving his hoe more and more slowly, his eyes on the changeless sand, not seeing it, when the stern voice startled him. "Joggi, what in this wide world have you got your mind on?" His father's form stood real above him.

The boy glanced fleetly upward. The brown face with its deep-drawn lines from nose to mouth looked impassive, but Joggi read well enough its controlled exasperation. He began working. Finally he said, "I get lonesome, Papa."

"You don't get lonesome when you're off in the woods from dinner till dark, do you?"

Joggi did not answer. Who'd ever get lonesome there? he could have said.

"Son, if you're going to live in this world, you've got to learn you can't play all day long! It takes work to live and you've got to learn how to do it!"

Joggi moved away from his father, bent, dragging the earth heavily about the young plants, his shoulderbones showing thin through his shirt, the broad hat hiding his face. His brown feet were shapely in the dust.

Johannes, watching that weary motion, felt a familiar mixture of compunction, amusement and frustration. I would have gotten a good beating for such dawdling. Aye-God, I can't beat him.

"Look, do it this way." He took the boy's hoe. "Pull light. Take five light strokes on each side. Don't chop at the dirt. Scrape along easy. Like this. Here, hold it." Johannes stood behind his son and guided his motion.

"You go six hills ahead of me. See if you can finish two before I catch you. Do it right, now, and you'll finish ahead of me."

Johannes, working behind the boy, saw his shoulders straighten and his movements become brisker. He'll do just what he wants to do, Johannes thought. But, oh, how to make him want to!

"You remember what I told you, don't you? If this field's finished, you can go with me tomorrow."

"Papa, you think Rudi might come?"

Johannes grimaced at the hope in the boy's voice. He answered slowly, "I wouldn't count on it, Son." He was afraid it was the last kind of meeting Rudi would come to. "There'll be so many men there, people from miles around, we'd probably not even see him if he should come."

"But if he didn't see us, he'd look for us. Or he'd come here after it was over, wouldn't he?"

"Yes, he'd do that, I think," Johannes answered gravely. "But I doubt he'll be there, Joggi."

The two worked smoothly together, Johannes four hills, Joggi two, the son's work almost as neat as his father's, even though his strokes were not as broad, for his hoe was smaller.

"If he's too far off, he might not know about it," said Joggi.

"That could be. He goes far back in the country."

Yes, thought Johannes, no telling where the man might be. He hadn't told Madle, certainly not Joggi, but a month ago he'd heard a thing to trouble him. The tale had come second or thirdhand. It was about some hunter up above the Deadfall Line, a Switzer, it was said, whom some Irish had attempted to discipline, only they'd fallen out about it and hadn't finished the work. Johannes probed for details but could learn only that it occurred above Indian Creek. What happened to the man? he asked. Nobody knew. What had the man done? The speaker didn't know, stole something maybe. Then it couldn't have been Rudi.

"Or maybe he just didn't belong up there," said the speaker. "You know how that is."

Yes, Johannes knew. There was a general understanding that German--speaking people between the Broad and the Saluda would keep to the south of what they called the Deadfall Line and the Irish would settle above it, but he'd never heard of any trouble about it before this.

But if the man had been Rudi, what could the trouble have been? Johannes had never known the grown man Rudi to do a morally wrong thing, although there'd been that deed of violence when he was a boy. Poor knocker, brought up no way at all, no teaching, no family, driven to wildness when he'd most needed home and church. It was a wonder he'd become even halfway the essentially decent man Johannes believed him to be. But there was much in Rudi you didn't know. And he had that sensitive, independent streak that made you impatient and sorry for him at the same time.

If only he'd quit his roving ways and settle down! The country was changing. People were getting so they'd no longer tolerate nameless strangers wandering in and out of their settlements. With a wife and children and stock and fields, you had to have more security. You couldn't work in sight of your house all day. People shouldn't have to live in fear. That was why the Regulators had assumed control in the first place. With no relief from Charlestown, they had to do something. And that was what the meeting tomorrow was about.

Johannes had fallen silent. Joggi said, "Papa, tell me about the time it came up a storm and you went in a cave. What was in the cave? If you'd stayed there, would a deer have come?"

Johannes' attention returned to the dusty little figure in front of him. "Once," he said, "I hid in a great old fir tree."

"A fir tree? What kind's a fir tree?"

"Don't slack up now, you're doing a good job. Don't slack up and I'll tell you about it."

The wheat and barley were harvested, the corn was beginning to tassel, and peach limbs were heavy with fruit. It was fine June weather, a good day for the Regulator Congress. Men gathered at the Congarees from all over the backcountry: Welsh Baptists, Irish Presbyterians, German Reformed and Lutherans, English Episcopalians, several prominent Huguenots, even a few Irish Quakers. Friday's Ferry did brisk business. So did the taverns near the old fort and musterground where the meeting was held, yet not so much business as might have been expected, for the great assembly was a serious and sober one.

Johannes was glad he'd left Joggi at the Rieders' to spend the day with Willi. This meeting was no place for a child. Looking about him, he realized he had not been part of such a multitude since he had done service in the Cherokee War. Then, because of language, he had often felt alone even when he was most consciously a part of that disciplined yet heterogeneous mass, the Army. Now, seven years later, he thought he had more in common with those about him, for almost all were backcountry settlers like himself. As he listened, there was little they said that he couldn't agree with.

The men who proposed measures were, for the most part, men in broad-cloth coats from other places, although the Congarees was well represented by William Arthur, Bartholomew Gartman, and John Goodwyn from just across the river. The more prominent leaders were large landowners such as Moses Kirkland of the lower Saluda; James Mayson from Ninety Six; William Wofford of the Tyger-Enoree district; Thomas Woodward, Edward McGraw and Barnaby Pope of the Little River-Cedar Creek area of the Broad; Joshua English and Henry Hunter from Pine Tree Hill, lately renamed Camden; Gideon Gibson and Claudius Pegues from the Pee Dee; and the only prominent lowcountry man among them, Tacitus Gaillard from the Santee, who was also a member of the Assembly. The Deutsch Folk from the triangle between the Broad and the Saluda could look to Robert Buzzard, John and Jacob Fulmore, and Jacob Frei.

Men in homespun and leather like Johannes simply listened.

Speakers urged the importance of voting in the October election for members of the Assembly. "March down in force! They won't dare refuse a thousand of you! March together!"

"We're freeborn British subjects the same as they are! We're taxed the same rate they are! Let those who call themselves 'Sons of Liberty' extend to us the rights they demand of Britain! Let 'taxation without representation' be abolished first in Charlestown if they want it abolished in Britain!"

It was a supreme irony that those gentry who were most exercised over the Stamp Act and other injustices up and down the seaboard had long been guilty of the same injustice to their fellow countrymen beyond the pine barrens.

For years the backcountry had petitioned not only for local courts but also for the organization of new parishes to give them representation in the Assembly. Yet for various reasons—unwillingness of House incumbents to lose power, for the Crown allowed only so many seats in the Assembly—the greed, some said, of Charlestown lawyers who wanted all legal business transacted in that city—their petitions had been ignored. Theoretically the lowcountry parish lines extended into the backcountry, but because voting took place in lowcountry churches a hundred or more miles away, and because parish lines were so vague that most backcountry men did not even know to which parish they belonged, few of them ever voted.

Now the listeners were stirred.

Johannes resolved, I'll do it! I've never done it before, but, yes, I'll cast my vote! I'm a free subject in this Province! I've paid quitrent and land tax for eight years now, I took no bounty from them and they've got my shillings, so why shouldn't I have a voice? I'll go down there in Wine-month and cast my vote as I'm entitled to!

He sensed the excitement in those around him.

But as the afternoon wore on and they came to the main business of the meeting, his feeling of being one with them drained away. Instead of exhilaration he began to feel a stifling, overheated kind of strain as the leaders presented their Plan of Regulation.

Yes, the Provincial Assembly *had* finally passed a Circuit Court Act, and the governor *had* signed it in April, but it was not yet approved in England. And since the country was still without local courts and jails, who knew how long the situation that bred outlawry would continue? There *must* be some control over lawless elements, the leaders emphasized.

According to the Plan of Regulation, men with no visible occupation would be forced to work, given so many acres to tend, or be driven from the Province. Flogging would be the means of coercion. Men of bad morals would be given the same punishment, so many lashes at the whipping post for wrongdoing. Women of like character would be ducked and exposed. Furthermore, to protect their own authority, the Regulators banned the serving of all writs and warrants from the Provost Marshal's office in Charlestown. Except Writs of Debt. The rights of property must always be respected.

Johannes listened with conflicting emotions. He instinctively distrusted Moses Kirkland, a stout, red-faced man; but the commanding presence of Thomas Woodward spoke to him directly.

Johannes tried to detach himself from their authority and influence. He himself was no big landowner with slaves and mills and all kinds of ventures. Nevertheless, he *was* a landowner. In the last three years, partly with the help of a small legacy from Madle's father, but also through his own hard work, he'd managed to add two tracts to his original fifty acres, one up the creek and the other beyond it. That gave him almost two hundred acres.

He worked hard on what he had. It took sweat and daylong toil to clear up newground and make a crop there. He saw his acres of corn bright with last night's rain, his yearlings and heifers shadowed by June leaves, bees working in the orchard, Heiri and Babeli bringing in eggs, Joggi bent over a hoe. His face muscles tightened. Yes. That others could ride in, trample, steal, destroy what they'd struggled for was an outrage. That his family must work so hard for a decent living, while others loafed and preyed on them was intolerable.

So in the end, along with a thousand other men, Johannes subscribed to the Plan of Regulation. What it enjoined was no more than what Virginia, North Carolina, and Georgia already required by law, it was said. South Carolina alone had no vagrancy laws.

Johannes' face was set as he wrote his name. He signed not because he feared the notice of those around him if he didn't. No, it was simply that having become part of this thing, he must follow it through.

For he could have stayed home. Some of his neighbors had.

"I don't know, Johannes. When it comes right down to it, it's going against lawful authority, that's what they're doing now. A man could be liable to judgment for that."

But he'd come here. And he must do what had to be done, like it or not. Yet it seemed to him that more and more nowadays, he found himself in places where doing his duty demanded a hardening within him. His duty to Madle. And to Joggi and Heiri and the little ones.

The thought of those upturned faces was with him as he wrote his name at the bottom of a long column. Still at the back of his mind lurked a question: Is it I, Johannes Lienhardt, doing this?

Ah, the evening air felt good on his face as at last he got free of the home-going crowd. The sounds of the ordinary world could be heard again—the shuffle of horses' feet in the sand, the calling of thrushes in the woods—a quiet refreshment after the day's jangling.

Well, Joggi would have had a high time of it anyhow, far better than if he'd come to the meeting. In spite of the fact that they competed in everything they did, Joggi and Willi Rieder liked nothing better than to spend a day together. The boy would be stuffed full of ginger cakes. Willi's grandmother, Elsbeth, would have seen to that. And maybe switched him and Willi a couple of times too. They'd probably have deserved it.

Now Johannes' problem would be to get away without having to listen to thirty minutes of Elsbeth. Also Hans Jacob would want to know everything said or done all day, and it would be black dark before he got home, and Madle would be anxious. He'd use her anxiety as reason for haste.

Elsbeth had a stone jar of pickled peaches to send home with him, and Hans Jacob a small keg of barley beer, a bribe to get him to stay and talk. Inwardly Johannes sighed.

"Tell Madle she won't find such clingstones anywhere else around here," said Elsbeth, "none to compare with these. Hans Jacob just got me a whole chest up from Charlestown of muscovado sugar and eight boxes of cinnamon and cloves and mace and nutmeg. 'Get a gracious plenty,' I told him, 'I've got twenty-five shelves to fill up. We've got blackberries coming in and apples yet and pear trees loaded, and I want to try haw jelly this autumn. And I'll have six young ones to set picking gooseberries when they come on, then the scuppernongs and bullaces.' Tell Madle she can send the jar back by anybody coming up this way but not to send it by any of that Remster crowd or I'll never see it again."

Hans Jacob wanted to know how many had been at the musterground. "From what we saw pass here it looked like the whole Province."

Hans Jacob was impressed by some of the names. "You don't say!" He sat lounging on the veranda, savoring his evening glass of rum punch. "Jamaica rum, twenty-two shilling, sixpence a gallon," said Elsbeth.

She and her quiet daughter-in-law, Maria, and her oldest granddaughter sat at the other end of the veranda. The children were playing running games at the side of the house. The two men sat facing the darkening east. The shrilling of jarflies filled the air.

As he emptied his glass—Johannes sipped more slowly, seeing Madle's look if he'd had more than one glass—Hans Jacob said, "Some say it won't be long before you'll be hearing from the Provost Marshal. I don't know about you, but I wouldn't care to see Roger Pinkney's deputies ride up to my door." He held out his glass to a black boy waiting behind him. "I've heard a month in that Charlestown jail can kill you." He shifted to look at Johannes. "Of course, big men like Gaillard and Kirkland, they may know how to keep out of it. I know Kirkland does; he's slick enough. I don't know about you."

Johannes laughed. "There'll be many a one of us to go if they try to round us all up. They'll have to build another jail. Maybe it won't be as bad as the old one."

"You say men were there from Pine Tree? How about Joseph Kershaw?"

"If he was, he didn't speak. No, I don't think he's one of them." "Us," he should have said.

"That English parson that wrote up that paper they sent down to Charlestown last year, he's from Pine Tree, and he's on good terms with Kershaw, I hear. You know Kershaw's the one getting ready to open that big establishment here at the Congarees. Funny, he didn't come."

"Well, Hans Jacob, you didn't come either." And Hans Jacob, flattered, laughed. They talked awhile of the new store to be built by the merchants, Kershaw and Chesnut. Johannes was thinking about leaving when Hans Jacob said, "To change the subject, you better let that boy of yours stay up here a few days. Willi thinks the sun rises and sets on him."

"Then he'd be ruined sure enough. I'd never get him back in the field then."

Hans Jacob lowered his voice, "Tell you what, Johannes, I've got a healthy young boy would make you a prime hand in a few years. Smart too. Take his mother and you can have the pair of 'em for two hundred and fifty pounds."

It took Johannes a few seconds to realize what Hans Jacob was talking about. He did not answer.

"Taking him young, you could train him right along with Joggi. They're the same age."

Long ago Johannes had said that he'd never own a slave. Yet now he considered it. Another pair of hands in the field. And more important, a woman to help Madle. "Why do you want to sell them?" he asked.

Hans Jacob shrugged. "I don't necessarily want to. It just occurred to me you could use the help. Your family's not getting any smaller. And your place is bigger. If you add on land, you need more hands. Everybody knows that."

"I'll have three sons to help some day if God spares them. And God willing, maybe others. Though I'm more than satisfied with the ones I've got."

Hans Jacob didn't speak for a while. "How about Madle? She'd be glad of the woman's help, wouldn't she?"

Would she? Busy from dawnlight till after dark. He saw the small figure, just beginning to thicken at the waist with the child she'd have in winter. He saw her bent over cradle, hearth, and garden, coming and going all day long. He saw the worry lines on her forehead, the marks of strain around her mouth. Would having a black woman there add ease to her life? ... He'd have to build a house for them.

"I don't have two hundred and fifty pounds."

"You've got stock, haven't you? Didn't you tell me your herd's up to twenty? I have to admit, last time I got a look at 'em, I don't know how you do it but yours look better than mine. Then that's a mighty pretty little mare Joggi rode up here. He tells me she's foaled. If the filly's as pretty as the dam, I'd allow twenty pounds for her next March. Say ten head of neat cattle, fifty pounds, that's a good price. Thin out your hogs, ten or fifteen pounds more. I wouldn't expect full payment in one year. Say three years."

Two hundred and fifty pounds was reasonable and the terms were easy. "The woman has no more children? How about her husband?"

"Dan!" Hans Jacob raised his voice to the boy behind him. "Go find Simmi. Tell him to come here."

"Call my son too," said Johannes. "We must be leaving."

Very shortly Joggi and Willi appeared, followed by a sturdy, darker boy.

"Come up here, Simmi!" called Hans Jacob.

Even in the twilight Johannes could see that the boy was light-skinned, and that his features and stocky build made the resemblance to his father unmistakable. Johannes felt an overwhelming repugnance. To sell the son of your body! And the woman you'd sinned with.

"Here, boy," said Hans Jacob, "pick up that bench and move it over there. No, don't drag it. Lift it up. Let's see how strong you are."

The boy strained and lifted the oak bench, carried it across the veranda and set it where his master told him to.

Johannes rose. "I must be on my way. Come on, Joggi. Your mother'll be anxious. Frau Elsbeth!" he called down the porch. "Maria! I thank you for letting this rapscallion stay here today."

Maria rose silently. Elsbeth said to Joggi, "Come here, child, let me hug you. Ah, you're getting thin as a rail. You don't remember when I sat up with you all one night when you had the earache, do you, nobody else knew what to do for you, you screamed, you thrashed, you couldn't be still, but I made a strong onion poultice, heated it and held it to that little ear and it did the trick, it did, and then you slept fourteen hours. Johannes, tell Madle she'd better look at that foot where he's jabbed a stick in it."

Johannes forced himself to shake hands with Hans Jacob. The hand felt soft and moist in his hard one. Yet as he turned on the steps he saw the man reach behind him to rub the head of the dark boy.

Willi stood in the shadows trying not to cry because Joggi was leaving. Both boys had begged that Willi be allowed to go home with Joggi.

As he rode home, Johannes thought: It may be the mother as much as the boy he wants to get rid of. He thought of Maria's pale, heart-shaped face, so often vacant of expression. He thought of Hans Jacob's eyes, sometimes friendly and eager, sometimes hard or evasive, the sagging pouches under his eyes. He was a few years younger than Johannes, but there was a paunchiness about him that made him look older. Too much rum punch in the evening. Too many people to do his bidding. Except one, and that one forever dingdonging at him about what his father had done and what Hans Jacob ought to do. Johannes felt heavy.

What a tangle. It's the tangle of sin, he said again as he'd said long ago to Rudi. Aye-God, how could you escape it? Nevertheless, the entanglement of owning slave people was one he never intended to get into.

Joggi, who'd been silent since they'd left, interrupted his thoughts. "Willi finally learned how to skin the cat today. I helped him learn."

"What were you doing cavorting in the barn? I thought I warned you to stay off barn rafters?"

"It wasn't in the barn. It was on a limb."

"Oh? How high?"

"Not too high." Only fifteen feet from the ground, he might have said if he'd known the distance. "Did you have very high trees to climb, Papa, a long time ago?"

Johannes grinned ruefully. The clear voice sounded guileless. "Yes, I did, Squirrel, and it was only by the mercy of the good God I never broke my neck. Once I did fall and had the breath knocked out of me. You'd better watch out or you'll not be so lucky."

"But you had rocks to climb and big mountains."

Johannes did not answer.

"Papa, I wonder if there are rocks and mountains where Rudi goes."

Johannes had hoped his son would not mention Rudi this day.

"Probably are," he said.

"Maybe I'll go with him sometime. And I'll see mountains too."

Chapter Thirteen

Rudi sat beneath the pines trying to make up his mind to go down to the house. It was almost the same spot where he had napped and waited until Johannes called that August afternoon ten years ago. Now it was early July, a sultry day, clouding up. He was angry with himself for his indecision. Stupid to come and not see them. He felt like a spy lurking in the woods, hearing their voices. He could distinguish nothing much, mostly children's prattle, sometimes Madle's ringing voice. No sign of Johannes. Off working somewhere.

Down there everything had a flourishing look. Fruit trees, garden, flowers in the dooryard. Geese and ducks chasing bugs in the grass. Johannes had finally dammed up a duckpond. The new barn was bigger than the old one and farther from the house.

Rudi saw a sturdy child go toward the fowlhouse with a basket. Heiri. He'd be eight sometime this fall. Joggi going on ten. Where was he? ...Just to see them for a few minutes, not to have to say anything, that was all he wanted.

The sky had grown overcast. Thunder rumbled up from the southwest. Wind stirred the pines. Well, if you're going down there, go. No use to stay here and get soaked. He rose stiffly and untethered his horse.

Big drops were spattering the sand when Rudi arrived at the side gate to the dooryard. He had not hallooed to announce his coming, but the geese announced it, and Bläss recognized him and told the world.

Madle appeared at the back door, dusting her floured hands on her apron, and Heiri and a little girl came running from the barn, where they had been shooing a hen and her brood toward shelter. As Rudi dismounted, he saw Johannes and a slender boy hurrying across the field by the creek.

"Rudi?" Madle came down the steps. "Rudi Näffels!"

He put his hand on the gate, withdrew it, waited. Inside, Bläss barked hysterical joy.

Madle and a flying figure reached him at the same time, Joggi glad-eyed and pale under his sunburn.

Madle unlatched the gate. "Dear Rudi!" She put her hands on his shoulders as she always did, kissed him, looked at him. "Dear Rudi, oh, how glad I am to see you!"

Johannes leaned his hoe and Joggi's against the fence and shouted, "Welcome! Welcome in God's name!" They gripped hands. "Man, where have you been so long? We're glad to see you!"

Raindrops were browning the sand. "We'd better hurry in," said Madle. "Come, children, hurry! Johannes, take Rudi in the front way."

Johannes with his hand on Rudi's shoulder steered him through the gate as Madle shepherded all the children but Joggi up the back steps.

"Yes, it's getting ready to pour down," he said. "Joggi, how about Rudi's horse, you want to put him under the shed and see to him? Come on, Rudi, or we'll be soaked. Not that it would hurt us, but I doubt Madle wants us in the house sopping wet."

The two men mounted the front steps and stood on the porch as the rain dropped its white curtain.

"Whew!" exclaimed Johannes.

Thunder crashed and lightning cracked nearby.

"It struck something!" cried Johannes.

"Across the creek," answered Rudi.

The noise of the storm made talk difficult.

"Sit down, Rudi!" Johannes eased himself onto the bench against the wall. "This will cool things off anyhow!"

Both men wiped their faces on their sleeves and sat watching the tossed branches of the trees and the white sheets driven across the field. A torrent splashed into the rain barrel at the end of the porch.

Finally it began to slacken and the noise abated. Madle came out with three of the children, the two little girls' hair freshly braided.

"Cathri, Babeli, you remember Rudi? Greet your cousin now."

The older child was dark-haired like Joggi, the younger one plump and fair. Each held out a hand and said, "*Grüss Gott*, Cousin Rudi," and raised a face to be kissed, but Rudi touched only their hands.

"And here's Hansli can walk now," said Madle. "Hansli, can you say 'Cousin Rudi'?"

"Where are the big boys?" asked Johannes.

"Heiri!" Madle called. "He ran out with Joggi. They're putting on dry clothes."

"I'm sorry they got wet on my account," said Rudi. "I should have come sooner."

"Months sooner," said Madle.

"It *has* been a long time," Johannes said. "How long? Seven, eight months?"

Joggi's rain-plastered hair was black on his forehead, his face rosy-brown. Heiri's shirt was bunched crookedly inside his short trousers.

"Why didn't you come when the other men came to the Congarees?" Joggi asked.

Rudi glanced at Johannes and Madle quickly.

"He's talking about the Regulator Congress a few weeks ago," said Johannes.

"Oh."

"Papa said there'd be so many you might not find us, but I said anyway you'd come here. But then we thought you might be too far off to hear about it."

"Oh, I heard," said Rudi, his lip curling but not in mirth.

"Do you still like *bieberfladen*, Rudi?" asked Madle. "I'd just finished rolling some out when I heard you at the gate. Something must have told me to make a big batch this afternoon."

"Let's cut a watermelon!" exclaimed Johannes. "We've got a couple of good ripe ones already here on the porch. Heiri, roll that one out from under the bench. Madle, bring us a sharp knife. We can eat out here."

Bläss had come up on the porch and lay at the feet of the man who long ago had traded a deerskin for him as a puppy and brought him here to Savanna Hunt. Bläss had a certain attachment for each member of his family from Johannes down to small Hansli, but this man was the first of his family, and though he seldom came to test that bonding, it had not weakened. The dog stayed at Rudi's feet.

The watermelon was good. They cut out crisp red chunks, the men with their knives, the others with spoons. "This is the first I've had all summer," Rudi said. "I always forget how good it is."

"I've got a place down there by the creek that seems to suit water-melons."

"Cathri, are you swallowing seeds? Babeli, make sure she takes the seeds out."

Conversation began to flow. Children's manners and mishaps made a minor diversion. Rudi remembered enough about Johannes' affairs to ask questions. He learned of the new tract acquired last winter.

He mentioned that he'd been in North Carolina at the Moravian settlement of Bethabara. "They're German people. Very religious people. I was there a few days." He told of the town, Salem, that they were laying out. "I even gave a thought to staying there."

Johannes looked surprised. "Oh, you did? Settle up there?"

Rudi did not speak for a moment. "No, I guess I've run loose too long."

"I'd be sorry to see you settle that far from us, Rudi," Johannes said gravely. "Did you ever do anything about your claim on Camping Creek?"

Rudi shook his head. "Last time I was by there, some squatters had put up another cabin."

Johannes was quiet awhile. "Then why don't you come settle here? There's good land back up this creek you can get for fifteen shillings an acre. That's one half what I paid for this and it's every bit as good. Fifty pounds would get you a nice-sized tract. More than I started with anyhow."

Rudi was silent.

"I hear there's some at the head of the creek never even been claimed. You might even get it as bounty. You weren't born in the country. It's all on record, you know. ...Man, we'd be glad to see you settle near us."

"It takes more than land," Rudi said shortly.

"It would be a start. More than I started with," Johannes repeated.

But he remembered that he'd had money for tools—but I worked a year for wages to get some of it—and Madle had brought goods and money for household furnishings. But then Rudi'd had money from the old country too. What's he done with it all? All these years what's he done with everything that's gone through his hands? ...Well, he was robbed of some of it. Still—Rudi was known to be a skillful hunter. And he'd gotten pay for the two or three years he'd ridden with the Rangers. Why should he still be portionless? Mismanagement? More likely heedlessness. But he's had more than one cruel thing happen to him, Johannes reminded himself. He wondered if Rudi *had* been the man he'd heard about up on Indian Creek but did not dare to ask.

"I've got plenty of implements you could use," he urged. "You know, I've always felt I owed you something for all that work you did when I was getting started here. We could never have got in the house that autumn if you hadn't helped us. I've always felt indebted to you."

"You don't owe me anything, Johannes," Rudi answered gruffly.

The storm had moved eastward. The sky lightened and they could see one another more clearly. Rudi's face was thin, his eyes deepset and unsmiling under heavy brows. Johannes thought in dismay, If I'd come up on him somewhere else, I might not have known him. I might even have wondered if it was safe to pass by him. ...But he's Rudi, the man I've worked shoulder to shoulder with!

"I've got a drove of hogs and a couple of cows might be glad to take up with you if you could make up your mind to settle on our creek," he persisted.

"I'm no plow-pusher like you, Johannes. My ways are different from yours. Don't try to make me a dirt-grubber." The harshness in Rudi's voice brought silence to the porch.

Johannes felt himself getting warm. And what are you? Are you so proud of what you are?

Madle cut the silence. "Johannes is more than a plow-pusher, Rudi. He's a good husband and father and provides for these children. He does more than feed us too. He gives us protection and he works for *us*, not just himself. He gives us all he has." She stood up. "Joggi, get a basket. Children, collect these rinds. Babeli, get a broom and sweep these seeds off the porch." She picked up Hansli and went inside.

The men did not speak. Johannes was deeply moved, yet distressed. Rudi was a turmoil of emotions. The children eddied about in obedience to their mother. When Babeli came out with the broom, Bläss went stiffly down the steps and under the house.

"Looks like it's passed over," Johannes said to break the silence. Random drops hit the puddles. He would have gotten up to be about his work but he could hardly leave one so newly come. Though it was too wet to continue hoeing, there was plenty else to do. "More rain, more grass. How about it, Joggi? Think we'll ever get the cornfield clean?"

Joggi groaned and slid down the bench closer to Rudi, looked up at him. "Rudi, are there caves where you go? Did you ever go in a cave to get out of a storm?"

"Oh yes. More than once. And sometimes I came out quick too."

"Why? What was in it?"

"A nest of rattlers one time. Another time I backed up into a bear's den. Bobcats, wolves, bears—they like caves too."

Heiri said, "God took care of Ida of Toggenburg in her cave. The animals liked her. But," he added, "I think I might be scared to go in one."

"I don't know that caves are much worse than other places, Heiri. You take chances wherever you go." The edge to his words sounded inappropriate spoken to a child.

"How about the Moravian settlement?" asked Johannes. "You said you went up there. What crops do they raise? What else do they do besides farm."

"They do some of everything. Sell goods. Tinker. Make pots. All kinds of metalwork. They've got good grainfields. Raise just about everything you do. Except they raise sheep."

"Strange you thought of staying there."

Rudi did not answer immediately. They speak my tongue, he might have said, same as you do; there my tongue doesn't set me apart. I would have been one of the single brothers if they'd accepted me. But the main thing, the strangest, was their music. I never heard such music, and their service, their worship, though I took no part in it, it gave me such a quieted feeling. Like when Granny washed me. "Yes, it was strange," he agreed. ...But to live cooped up with that many people, to have to do everything their way, no. In the end he could not submit to it.

The rain ceased. Watery sunshine made the puddled sand and the wet fenceposts glisten. In the field to the east, young peavines lifted their drowned shoulders. Johannes hoped the high part of the newground he'd been terracing with brush wasn't washed too badly.

"Like to walk out with me?" he asked. "I'll show you what I've been doing across the creek. You've seen more ways of farming than I have. You might know a different way I can handle the washes over there."

Rudi was tired, for he'd been traveling since daybreak, and the hour up in the woods had not rested him. Yet to refuse the invitation would put more distance between them.

He rose, and as the two men went down the steps, Johannes turned and called into the house, "We're going across the creek, Madle. Be back in an hour or so."

"Can I go too?" asked Joggi.

"Me too, Papa?" begged Heiri.

Johannes looked down. "No, you two stay here and help your Mama. Stay close in case she needs you for something. No more hoeing out grass today, Squirrel. But don't run off anywhere." He put sternness in his voice.

"You mind me!"

We shouldn't have asked, thought Joggi. We should just have followed without asking.

At their drooping faces, Johannes said, "You'll have plenty more time with Rudi! He'll be here yet awhile, I hope."

Johannes did not suggest riding, for he still had the old-country habit of walking wherever possible. You could look at things better on foot.

Where formerly there'd been only a trail, now a wagon road and a plank bridge led across the creek. Rudi observed that the canebrake across the creek was greatly diminished, but the corn that had taken its place was magnificent.

"I want you to see my cotton. Second year I've tried it. Once you get the seed out, it's less work than flax. Even the little ones can help with it. Though Madle still likes linen best."

In contrast to the corn, the young cotton plants were neat and low to the ground.

"I had to card cotton and spin both when I was a boy. It was work to do inside when you couldn't get out. But now swingling flax, that's got to be an outside job. ...I think back sometimes about all the different things we had to do there just to live. We went to school but there was no after-school play for us, I tell Joggi."

"Does Joggi like to card cotton and spin?"

Johannes laughed. "I have enough trouble keeping him at work outdoors. No use asking for more."

They stood a moment observing the grassless, orderly field, each plant like the others.

"I want my sons to know how to work, but I don't want to make slaves of 'em. Not like some men I know. Though Joggi will make you wonder sometimes if you're not treating him like one."

"He's smart," said Rudi. "He remembers everything you tell him." How an eagle will take a fishhawk's prey. Gray foxes live in hollow trees.

"Pastor Theus tells me he's his best scholar," Johannes said simply. "He gets that from his mother." Johannes turned. "I want to show you the place that's gulleying in my newground. Tell me what you'd do about it."

They strode through a tract of fine hardwood. "See that big poplar? I've got my eye on it for some troughs."

Rudi said, "Johannes, I'm sorry for the way I spoke to you back there at the house. Tell Madle I'm sorry for the way I offended. You meant well. I know that." He wanted to say more but did not know how. He wanted to say, What's wrong with me that there's no place on this earth I can live at peace with others just the way I am?

Johannes was silent, for he too had something difficult to say. That was why he'd not let the boys come along. He'd hoped there might be an opening. "Rudi, I don't know how to say this. I hope you won't take me wrong. I'm worried. Concerned, I should say."

"What about?"

"About you."

Rudi stopped still, looked at Johannes. His face darkened. "You're worried about *me*?"

Johannes heard with dismay the hard note in Rudi's voice. "You know this country's changing, Rudi. You know the way we lived ten years ago when I first came here, unsettled as things were then, Indians in and out our doors whenever we turned around, we were closer together then. We worked together and we trusted one another more. It's not like that now."

"What's that got to do with me?"

"Rudi, it's just that every man now, almost every man that's not—" Johannes searched for the right word, "attached to some place, with neighbors that know what he's about, that understand his comings and goings, he's looked at with suspicion nowadays."

"You think I don't know that?"

"In fact," Johannes continued, "he's liable to find himself treated—in ways I wouldn't like to see anybody I cared about treated."

Rudi's short laugh held no mirth.

"You heard about that meeting here three weeks ago," said Johannes doggedly.

"Oh yes. I know all about it."

"I was there."

"I knew you were. Joggi said as much. I wasn't going to say anything more, but since you bring it up, I'll ask you. Did you sign it? That paper they drew up?"

"Yes," Johannes answered heavily, "I did."

"That paper that said men that don't live according to your style will be tied up and lashed?"

Johannes said, "That's not the way I understand it. It's against vagabonds and idlers that prey on others."

"And what am I but a vagabond? Is that why you're worried about me? Let me tell you something, Johannes Lienhardt!" Rudi's voice rose. "I know a thing or two about slavery. You know about work. But I know about slavery! I know about being driven and worked to the point you don't care if you live or die, yes, and being tied up and lashed too! I broke free of it, and how I live now is my business to decide! And nobody's going to force or cajole me into anything different, you hear me?" He shouted, "You understand?"

"Rudi, I—it's not intended to—"

"Oh, it's not? Make a man tend so many acres, lash him if he won't! What's that but slavery? No, I don't have cornfields and cottonfields and a house and barn and stock, not that I've got anything against them that want it, I'm glad you're accumulating, you need to, but I supply goods to merchants same as you do, maybe more, and I never heard of a merchant scorning good quality buckskin! I pay for everything I use except for what's free in the woods! And I've never done harm to any man that wasn't out to harm me first, not even a red one! So how in the name of God can you subscribe to some stinking paper that would treat me like a damned runaway slave?"

"Man, it's got nothing to do with you personally!" Johannes' voice rose too. "You know that! It's just that— You know what happened here last fall! You were here when it happened!"

"Was I one of 'em out there burning down your barn? Tell me that! Was I one of 'em?"

"No, but—"

"Listen here! They tell me I had two brothers named same as your sons. I've tried to think sometimes what it would be like to have a brother. You and Madle, I thought you were as near a brother and sister as I could know—but, Johannes—I can't—" His voice broke; he moved away. "I can't see a brother turning against—"

"Rudi, listen to me!" Johannes shouted. "Nobody's turned against you! Why do you think I spoke in the first place? Are you satisfied with the way you live? A man—how old are you now? Twenty-seven, twenty-eight, no home, no family! Are you satisfied to spend all your days roving the woods and nobody but the buzzards to know if one day you don't get up?"

Rudi whipped around, bearded lips drawn back from his teeth, eyes black as the bottom of a well. "Shut up! No more! You've got so much, all you rich, satisfied boars and stallions, who are you to gloat over the rest of us God-forsaken beggars? Leave me alone! Go look at your fine crops by yourself! You've seen the last of me!"

"Now wait, Rudi! You've gone crazy! Madle and the children—"

"They don't need an ignorant woods-rat like me around! Your young ones might pick up my ways!"

"Man, you talk like a fool!" Johannes strode forward, intending to put his hand on Rudi's arm.

"If you touch me, you might be sorry." The younger man stood at bay.

They eyed one another. Speechless, Johannes turned back.

Rudi walked fast across the plank bridge, past the watermelon patch, and between the corn rows, where raindrops still clung to the blades.

Joggi saw him saddling his horse under the shed, but before he could reach him, Rudi had trotted his horse out of the lot and gone, not by the road but over the ridge through the pine woods as he had come.

Chapter Fourteen

Jamie was no woodsman. He could plow a straight furrow, and he could wield an axe with strength and accuracy and even a blow of his fist when he was roused. He could thread his way with precision through a Virgilian line, and with his unerring feel for the shapes of words he was slowly working his way through the Greek New Testament Mr. Richardson had left with him. But he had trouble finding his way through unfamiliar woods.

He missed his way three times on the way to Ninety Six. All creeks and hills looked alike to him. Paths had a way of disappearing into thickets which no human had ever penetrated. Landmarks he was told to look for were not there.

The second day his horse went lame, and he knew it was his own fault for forcing the beast down a pathless hillside. Yet somehow by the grace of God, he thought, and the people he strayed onto or met up with, he stumbled into Ninety Six just after dark on the third day of his journey.

There, after two days of inquiry, he was rewarded if somewhat daunted by reliable information. The man he sought was camped some six miles below the Indian town of Seneca, well within the bounds of the Cherokee Nation.

"Go straight up the Road," the trader told him. "Cross Twenty Six Mile Creek, come to Twenty Three Mile, but don't cross it. Turn downstream, it's a fair trail, cross two, three little branches maybe, and you'll find the place. It's a meadowlike place, some old town site, I reckon. It lies in the forks of them two creeks about five hundred yards up from the stream."

"You're sure he's still there?"

"If he aims to go out with Running Elk this fall, he is. That's where he's known to lie out at."

"He hunts with Indians?"

"With one he does. Ye don't hardly hunt in them parts without friends."

Seneca, where the trader lived, was a sizable Cherokee town sixteen miles below Keowee, built after the destruction of the Lower Towns in the late war.

"I would have thought it dangerous for a white hunter there."

152

"I'm not saying it would be a good idea for some, but he's got to be on right good terms with one of their headmen."

"And you're sure it's the man?"

"Oh yes. I been knowing him from way back."

But the trader could not guide Jamie to the place, for he was bound for Charlestown, and Jamie could not wait till his return.

He knew it would be foolhardy to venture out alone—perhaps foolhardy in any case, he thought ruefully. There was not now as much danger from Indians and renegade whites as there'd once been; still it was better to travel with company, even when the way was well-known.

Again he was fortunate. That same afternoon a small party going up the country stopped at Goudey's, among whom was young Thomas Rohan, the halfbreed son of another trader. He was on his way to old Fort Prince George, now more of a trading post than a garrison. Rohan said he knew the site Jamie described, and though it was off his path, he would take him there. So next morning Jamie set out with a party of nine—his guide, two traders, and six packhorsemen.

It was no pleasant trip. It was the third week of August, and the air was thick with heat, mosquitoes, black gnats, and horseflies. Great drops of blood rolled down the horses' flanks. Jamie suffered almost as much as the horses. Even in the cool of night he had no peace because his whole body was infested with the almost invisible red mites they called seedticks. Day and night they tormented him under his clothes, inside his shoes, between his toes, in tender parts where he couldn't scratch. Also he'd gotten stung on his cheek, neck and hands by yellowjackets, and neither mudpacks nor tobacco wads seemed to alleviate the bone-deep pain, itch, and swelling.

No one else was as afflicted as he was.

"What do you do to keep 'em off?" he asked.

"Ye get tough and lean for one thing. They don't much bother old leather. They'd rather bait on fresh meat. Wouldn't you?"

"That's your trouble," laughed another. "You're fresh to the woods and they like you."

"Grease yourself up with some bear grease and salt," advised a packhorseman.

He tried the remedy and exchanged the torment of itching for burning and stinging that made him want to dance. When that torment subsided, he felt more loathsomely hot, greasy, and miserable than before.

Also he began to be bruised and saddle-galled. He had left his own horse at Ninety Six and against his better judgment had hired a rangy, ill-broken brute that was always balking and shying. Jamie was not a bad horseman, but more than once he was nearly thrown. Moreover, the horse had an aversion to crossing streams—until a packhorseman seized its head and bit its nose. After a couple of these treatments, the horse's aversion left him. Fortunately the creeks were low because of dry weather. Even so, the footing was often slippery and the air was dank under the heavy-leafed oaks, hickories, and poplars.

The ancient trading path that led all the way up from Charlestown to the Cherokee Lower Towns was now a well-marked road, so that Jamie would have had little trouble finding his way alone even beyond DeWitt's Corner, which was near the border of the Cherokee lands. However, south of Twenty Six Mile Creek his guide said it was time to leave the main path and the rest of the party.

Jamie questioned him. "I thought we had to cross this creek and cut off south of the Twenty Three Mile."

"This way is nearer," said Rohan. "This way you get there tonight."

Jamie could only follow. The path was difficult and barely marked, the country much broken with streams and hills. They were continually scrambling up and down banks, and they led their horses more often than they rode.

It seemed to Jamie that his guide was forcing their pace. A time or two he was out of sight for twenty minutes or more. Finally Jamie hallooed. The thought crossed his mind, Would he try to lose me? I have not yet paid him. But he could lose me, sneak back and do me mischief and rob me. Jamie carried a pistol and a musket which he had not used since setting out. If he tries a trick like that, he'll be the one to pay, Jamie decided grimly.

But there around the bend stood Rohan impassively waiting, and Jamie felt ashamed. "You'll have to remember I'm not so fleet of foot as you are," he said.

"I thought you'd want to get there before night."

Jamie forbore to say, Don't you see I'm half lame? However, after that, Rohan slowed his pace and they toiled on without speaking.

Jamie did not mind the silence, for with his guide in sight he could give his mind completely to what he was going to say and how he would say it when he got there.

Find the man.

When the thought first struck him, he had asked, How could I possibly find him in all this backcountry? Hundreds of miles perhaps, to the north or south or west, I don't even know the direction. He could be in Florida or Pennsylvania for all I know.

Well, try! came the command. At least you can try!

Late in the afternoon they crossed rushing, rock-broken Twenty Six Mile Creek, and after they clambered up its hollowed-out bank and around a great fallen treetrunk, then, as they climbed a path between rising ranks of trees, they saw a clear space between the trunks ahead. And just where the trader had said it would be, lay a small meadow of long grasses and wild peavines with a horse grazing peacefully. On the far side stood an opensided lean-to, roofed with poles and branches.

Both men stopped. "He's not here," said Rohan. "He'll come back soon."

Jamie moved forward to look around him, then glanced at his guide, who seemed already to be fading into the forest behind him. "You're not ready to leave, I hope," he called. "What if he doesn't return for some time?"

Rohan motioned toward the grazing horse.

"Well, how do I know whose horse it is?" Then he thought, Of course, I know him. How could I fail to recognize that short-legged mongrelly brute?

He went to give the young man the money they'd agreed on, the price of a gallon of rum. Jamie was still reluctant to see him leave, but Rohan gestured, "Sun's low," and disappeared into the woods.

Slowly, thoughtfully Jamie unsaddled his own horse, and just as he finished hobbling him to graze, a man appeared from behind the lean-to with a string of fish in his hand. Dark-faced and thinner than when he'd last seen him. Jamie recognized the Switzer.

Rudi was slower to recognize his visitor. He saw a tall, limping, white man in what had once been good settlement clothes. His skin was blotched with insect bites, what part wasn't streaked with grease and dirt. One eye was swollen half-shut, and his forearm had a bloodcaked gash on it. As the man came toward him, Rudi recognized him with shock.

"Fraser? James Fraser?"

Jamie managed a deprecating smile. "I think by this time you might rightly name me 'Fool Fraser.' I'll be bound that's how you see me."

As Rudi stared, almost open-mouthed, Jamie said, "I can tell you're astonished. Well, you're no more astonished to see me than I am to be here."

"How did you come here?"

"Right now I can hardly tell you. I don't know how many days or nights I've been coming—it's all one to me—for it's been nothing but scratch and gouge all over my poor carcass night and day, and tug and yank and be jerked about with that misbegotten nag yonder what time I wasn't half down on the ground—and me trying to get him somewhere instead of him working for me. And for no other purpose than to find myself in country where all that's wanted of me may be my scalp—but, Näffels, I tell you now—" he broke off and paused for breath, "I know you're fair amazed to see me and maybe one of the last persons you'd ever want to see either, but if you've got a grain of pity in you, you'll not run me off." He raised his voice, "And you'll do something to help me get ease of these damned bug bites and I don't know what else I've got!"

It was not at all what he had composed to say. Yet Jamie could not have opened with a better speech.

Rudi was utterly unable to repress the gleam of mirth that shot up through his wonder. He gazed a moment at his visitor. "Best thing would be tobacco. You got tobacco?"

"No, I don't use it. Besides I tried it and it did little good."

"Then try something Indians use. Cut up some witch hazel and boil the juice out. Try witch hazel." Rudi couldn't help enjoying himself.

"Witch hazel? Does it grow hereabouts?"

"I think I noticed some in the woods up that way." Rudi waved his hand vaguely to the right.

Jamie looked helplessly that way, then back at Rudi.

Rudi found the grain of pity. "First thing I'd advise," he said, "is go wash yourself in cold creek water. A kind of fern grows down there, whether it's the kind I've heard folk call 'poor man's soap,' or not I don't know, but you break it up and scrub with it. It helps clean dirt off. And that cold water'll numb up the feeling."

"Which way?" asked Jamie. "The way I came?" He dreaded to toil down that tree-hung depth again.

He looked so pitiable standing there in his grease, sweat, dirt, and the blood-caked snags in his clothes that Rudi, still mystified, was moved, had to be moved to downright compassion. He couldn't help remembering the last time he'd been in Jamie's presence; yet this ludicrous reversal of circumstances for the moment smothered its darkness with laughter. Not that the man's misery was funny, but it was simply the incongruous situation and the way he expressed himself that appealed to Rudi's never quite obliterated sense of humor. He decided to take charge.

"You go this way. I'll show you, it's not far. It's easy all the way. The creekbed's shallow and clear down there. But cold," he warned. "I'll make fire and boil up a mess of witch hazel. You got rum? Put it in rum to make it feel good on you."

Jamie had whiskey.

"That's good. You soak yourself all over with that mixture and you'll feel better. Looks like maybe you got a little poison ivy too."

"That's a thing I usually know to stay out of, but it's possible. I could have landed in it once when I fell up a hill."

The path Rudi showed him was on the other side of the meadow. It was broad and open between shrubs and low trees smothered with grapevines. In a very short time Jamie heard rushing water, then saw it glinting between the trees, Twenty Three Mile Creek. Though it was swift where the trail came out, its water was no more than waist deep. He stripped and plunged in.

Once half-submerged in its biting cold, after he had caught his breath a time or two, he willed himself to a pleasurable numbness. He lay back, submerged in the hard rippling flow. After a while he looked up and saw it—the evening sky through overarching beeches, cucumber magnolias, and maples along the banks. Sunlight yellowed the highest leaves. Some bird flew across the blue space in curving flight.

Then as he lay in the creek, a strange kind of peace came upon him such as he had never known. It was peace in the midst of wildness, of loneliness. Utterly exposed as he knew himself to be among men of other tongues and nations, yet he felt himself at the center of a vast wheeling concourse of forces beyond his understanding. Naked and exposed as a baby. Yet somehow he knew a strange sense of cherishing—or of being cherished? He could not tell which. Who? Himself? Or another?

The roughness of broken fern rubbed some feeling back into his skin, yet for the time being, not the itch. He wished he'd thought to bring clean drawers and a shirt from his saddlebag. The air felt so good he hated to put on anything. The sun had long gone down when he climbed to the clearing.

Woodsmoke scented the dusk. Rudi sat before the fire.

"I'm using your kettle," he called. "I need mine for the hominy."

Fish was cooking over the coals.

The smoke smell was sweet in the chilling air. The fire warmth was good.

"Sit down," said Rudi. "We'll eat soon."

Jamie sat down. "Aye, I do feel better," he sighed.

Rudi's brown face had a hawk look in the firelight but not predatory. It was simply alert. Some old god of wood and stream might have looked like him, thought Jamie. Rudi tended the fire, handled the cooking, rose a time or two to get something from the lean-to.

Jamie made an easy decision. Say nothing tonight. Unless he brings it up. Let this peace endure.

They ate fish and hominy. The trout was exquisitely tender-fleshed and done to a turn. Jamie could have eaten twice as much. "I'm sorry to have eat up so much of your supper."

"I could have caught more if I'd known."

Jamie thought of the bread in his saddlebag. He rose painfully to get the rest of his loaf. He broke it and offered half to Rudi, not knowing that Rudi had not tasted such bread in six months.

Rudi passed a small Indian basket to him. "Have some grapes." They had a dark winy taste, as good as any he had ever tasted.

Jamie sighed again. "This is the most enduring ease I've had in a week."

Rudi too felt the peace. He had braced himself for words, but in some subtle way the man made him know that none were to come tonight. The silences between them were long and companionable.

I've broken his bread, Rudi thought. He's eaten my food. That's as it should be. Brothers. The word "brother" was not at all strange.

"I think your mixture has boiled down now," Rudi said, "if you got something to pour it off in. Pour in about a cup of your whiskey, and it'll be good skin medicine. I don't say it'll cure but it'll help."

It helped enough so that for the first night in almost a week, Jamie slept soundly. He slept outside the lean-to, out from under the trees, and gazed for only a minute at the patterned sky. He drowsed to sleep to the distant crunching of grass in his horse's teeth and the calling of night birds. He did not hear the far cries of predators.

Rudi lay awake a long time, still bemused. There was no use trying to guess why the man had come. It was outside his own experience.

On waking next morning, he wondered for an instant if he'd gotten hold of some kind of potent brew from Running Elk and drunk himself into hallucinations. But his head felt perfectly clear, and there in the early mist lay that long, inert figure rolled up in its blanket.

Jamie brought out his dried beef and coffee to go with the corncakes Rudi was baking. He observed baskets of dried beans and corn suspended from the poles inside the lean-to. His host said he often got such garden truck from the Indians.

After breakfast Jamie took his horse to the creek for watering and offered to bring back a pot of water if it was needed. Rudi had already taken Stony into the woods lest he overgraze. "He'd founder in this peavine if I'd let him."

When Jamie came back from the creek, he didn't see the other man anywhere and he had a moment of apprehension. Then he heard him call, "I'm over here."

Rudi sat in the shade at the edge of the clearing, his back against a granite boulder, his knees drawn up and his elbows resting on them.

Jamie walked slowly over and sat beside him. He drew up his knees in the same way.

They looked out across the open space. The sun had burned off the mist. Butterflies worked back and forth across the meadow.

"I left home eight days ago," said Jamie, "and went to Ninety Six. I kept asking till I learned your whereabouts. A man named Ephraim McGill told me. You know him?"

"I know him."

"I left there the next day with a party coming up to Fort Prince George. Thomas Rohan, son of some trader. You know him too?"

"I know of him."

"He brought me here."

"Which way did you come?"

"Not the way McGill directed. We left the road some distance south of that creek down there."

"That was a rough way," said Rudi.

"He said it was a nearer way and I judged I had no choice but to follow him."

Both men sat awhile in silence. Rudi had taken out his knife and was making some kind of snare from a length of vine.

Jamie said, "Come back to Indian Creek."

He saw the man's body stiffen.

"You've treated her badly. Margaret."

Still Rudi did not speak. Then he drew a long shuddering breath. "Yes, I did. How else could I treat her?"

There were other things Jamie had intended to say. It wasn't her fault. You owe her something, don't you? Instead he said, "If she never sees you again, she'll not die. She may even more or less forget you." And I may get her for myself. He sighed lightly to cover his feeling. "Still—there was a thing begun there that's not been worked out. It must be worked out. Or at least given a chance to."

"Oh, I thought it was. Worked out and finished by your brother and the others in your settlement."

"And who are we to decide the course of another man's life?" Jamie asked fiercely. "Not to mention a woman's. Don't leave that burden on us! We are just—they are just—no more than bystanders—pests, you might even call 'em. Think of 'em that way anyhow."

"Is that what you are? A bystander?"

"I'm one that's perhaps thought a bit more deeply than some have. I seem to have more opportunity than some men." He tried to speak in measured tones.

"You're a thinker, so you leave your ways and country for eight days for what's not your country or your ways, and you come here where men of your kind come only in packs of thirty or fifty with guns and legal papers. I don't understand you."

"I love Margaret Allen with my whole life," Jamie said softly.

"Did she send you?" Rudi asked swiftly.

"No! And I've been racking my brain to hit on some way to keep the deed from her!"

"You said she'll forget me. Then why you want me to go back? Can't you get her for yourself?"

Jamie gazed across the sunlit meadow into the forest as if there were a thing there he might discern. "I cannot put it into clear words. Also I find it difficult to say to another person." He shut his eyes and was silent so long that Rudi thought he was not going to speak again and moved restlessly. Then the man's words came as if he were learning their truth only as he spoke them. "You see—if love is given to you—for so long I did not have it, what seems to come so easy to others—you must honor it. I know I am given a rare thing. So I cannot dishonor it by having her now—when I know it would come from the evil that was done to you."

And there it moved before them, between them, the darkness of that night.

Jamie's words came in a rush. "There is so much of evil gets in our lives, Rudi. But something else must overcome it. Light, if you will. That's gospel."

Butterfly wings moved lazily in the sunshine. Rudi's hands drooped and were still.

The light on the box by the window. Sunlight on willow boughs when he'd first talked with Johannes. Gold poplar leaves in the path of his bright bay horse as he trotted up to the Congarees, his legacy from those in the old country who still remembered and loved him. The light not visible in Granny's touch and voice.

"It's little I've known of evil or misfortune compared with you." said Jamie. "I do not know why men's lots differ so. Save for when I was wrenched from my books and study in Virginia. ...Oh, there was fear of death there, but it did not touch me personally. I know I have been little touched by other men's troubles. But I also know that for me to profit from the wrong done you—and yet," he interrupted himself, "they were not bent on evil as such! They were ignorant, unknowing! They let their minds get twisted to a thing not intended. It's happening all over this Province! You know it! You were one of its victims."

"And I'll not be a victim!"

"You cannot say that! You were, and you could not help it! A man like you could not help it! And know this, Rudi Näffels—and this is what I came to say—it's the victim makes the best giver. Not everyone can have that privilege."

Rudi's tone was dull. "Privilege. Makes no sense to me."

"No. ...To most men it would not. But yet—let me tell you how it's come to me. See, I do not know all that's happened in your life. I sense it to have been more than common misfortune. But it can give you a power if you can ever get over it! And maybe you already have that power somewhat." Jamie spoke slowly but urgently. "I have meditated much on you, man. You have got to get over being afraid! Listen now, hear me out!" His voice rose. "You have much to give. I say it again. You have much to give! You must already have given it to Margaret and her grandmother or they would not have loved you so!"

The dark-browed man subsided. Nothing moved but the great monarch butterflies feeding on the orange bloom at the edge of the meadow.

When he finally spoke, Rudi's voice sounded muffled, almost sullen. "Leave me alone awhile. Let me think about what you said." He did not look up but was again working the vine loop in his hand, tightening it, loosening it.

Jamie got up stiffly. He was still sore all over. "All right, think. Be sure you think. Don't feel, just think. And remember."

Jamie left the shade, crossed the clearing and descended the path to the creek. He wanted to get rid of the intensity that energized him, get rid of the sound of his own voice. He wanted to know again the peace of yesterday evening. But it did not come.

The place was still beautiful. Sunlight dappled the water, glinted on rocks. A trout's shadow moved on the gravel, light illuminating its iridescence. Great dragonflies darted over a mass of red-jeweled touch-me-nots. Across the stream a small gray-blue bird flitted above dark banks of rhododendron. High in the trees a phoebe bird called.

What if he will not go? What then?

He'll have to go. Jamie felt the unaccustomed compelling force within him again. He must go.

He did not hear the footsteps till they were almost on him.

"I'll go back with you. But I must ride first to Seneca."

The journey down the country was physically easier for Jamie than the journey up, but he did not ride with elation. As they neared the end, he was oppressed more and more with weariness, dejection, even self-pity, and disgust with himself because he recognized his self-pity.

He had not accompanied Rudi to the Indian town. Interesting as the visit might have been, he simply did not feel up to it. He wanted only to rest

at the campsite as long as he could. Rudi by himself would have left for
Indian Creek that afternoon, but it was the next morning before they burned
the signs of habitation in the little clearing, Rudi having packed his goods
the night before.

The first day of their journey they were still the good companions of
that strangely intimate friendship they'd begun at the meadow. Both spoke
of their early life. Jamie asked Rudi very few questions, but he learned more
about Rudi than Johannes, Madle, Eva, or even Margaret had ever learned.
Language was no barrier, for each probed cleanly, economically till he
understood the other. Jamie felt more and more a swelling compassion that
was new to him.

Rudi in turn acquired from the younger man's sparse comments a
conception of a different kind of dead-ended frustration. He gained an
enlarged perception that made his own problems seem less darkly central
in the universe.

For every advantage there's a cost, he thought. He's tied up in loops
and knots I've never been tied in. The things I've most envied him, his
chances and his schooling, these can complicate a man's life too.

The next day their silences were longer, and by the time they reached
Ninety Six all Jamie wanted was to get home. He was glad to have his own
reliable horse under him again and was even more eager than Rudi to leave
Ninety Six. The last day they rode in silence.

What will it be like not to see her every day? What will my life be now
with her cut out of it? I'll have to go elsewhere, just as she told me. I must
leave this country. Then the demonic thought kept sidling in, Perhaps she'll
reject him! ...Oh God, that I could be as I once was, not caring! That great
peace he had felt five days ago was almost gone from his remembrance.
Even his satisfaction with the success of his mission was gone.

Rudi's thoughts were confused by guilt and longing, mixed with
apprehension. How must she feel? What can I say to her? No excuse for me,
none at all! How can I ever make it up to her if she'll even let me? His
dammed-up feelings flooded him. He swam in adoration of her dearness and
beauty. Hurry! he kept saying. How will I dare to look in her face?

In all their conversation they had spoken little of Margaret, but on the
day they neared Indian Creek she was at the center of each man's thought
and feeling.

Chapter Fifteen

The flax fiber had all been spun into thread, the lot that had been broken and scutched last fall and combed in winter, long fibers drawn again and again through hackles, the tow combed out of the line for the spinning of fine thread. The skeins were put away in the chest, for she could no longer bear to weave in the dark heat of the house. They were put away too because of words that clung to them. "This will make fine linen. I'll sew you a shirt one day. Would you wear a white shirt I made you?"

She did not remember his answer, but she remembered the pleasure that suffused his face.

"What can't you do?" he asked. "You can do most things I can and fifty I can't."

"Let's see. What fifty? Thread a needle's one. Make soap. Have you no art to make soap? Or rob bees? Have you never robbed bees? Churn butter, that makes four."

"You can read and write."

"Oh Rudi, I had my mother spared to me. It was not your fault yours was not." My dear, I'll teach you one day to read when I've learned from you. The room had become large in the shadowy firelight and larger still the rooms beyond, larger and larger rooms she had not dreamed of, yet prepared for her all along.

Now these cluttered rooms stifled her.

"This old loom, David'll not want to take it. No way to take it, I suppose, even if he did. Leave it here to rot. Nancy'll have her own."

As she came and went outdoors, she held imaginary conversations with someone, Jamie perhaps. "Build up and leave. Clear, plow, and then let grow over, move somewhere else. Let all go wild again. That's the way of it here. Build, tear down, build a bigger one somewhere else."

She was dismayed to discover how much she missed Jamie. Where had he gone? What was he doing?

"It's necessary I be gone a week or two, Margaret," he had said one afternoon. "I hope you'll not have need of anything while I'm gone." He gestured toward the fields and outbuildings. "I think all's in good order."

And with that he was off.

As if he feared I'd pry in his business! I hope I've more conduct that to pry into a man's business! At least Granny taught me that.

But what could it be? Something about land or property? Could he be taking up land? It was a good week's trip or more to Charlestown and back. Some errand for his father, no doubt. Family business. Yet she found it difficult to think of Jamie with family obligations. He seemed such a lone kind of person, not related even to his own kin.

Maybe something about the meetinghouse. He'd told her they were going to build one this fall. A trip to presbytery to request a minister again? But that would take more than a week if he went to Virginia. Or was there a presbytery now in North Carolina? ...Maybe he'd gone to the Waxhaws to see Mr. Richardson. She knew he continued to read and study in the books the minister had left. Did he hope to be licensed himself someday? Jamie a minister. He did not talk to her directly about religion, and yet in some ways the idea of Jamie as a minister seemed right. But in others, no. ...He'd need more schooling, she thought. He'd need to go somewhere else and bend his mind only on that. As I once urged him to.

She was disquieted by the idea. She realized now that she'd begun to think of Jamie only in terms of service to her. But I didn't ask him to come here! I didn't ask him to make it so I'd get to depend on him!

It's been over a week. It's been almost two weeks. She grew anxious. What if something's happened to him? If I knew where he'd gone, I'd know more how to judge.

"As selfish and inconsiderate as anyone!" she exclaimed aloud in a flare of anger. "To go off with no more words than that! Come and declare faithfulness, come faithfully for three months, then up and leave one day with no more words than that! Just up and leave!"

And then without warning the memory of that other leaving devoured all thought of Jamie, uncovered the deep well of crying that still woke her in the night.

Oh God, dead somewhere and me not knowing it! Some bullet or knife wound and no one this time to get him up off the ground and hold him! Sick of some fever, sick of smallpox. Dead in a grave for aught I know. Or dead and not buried—light gone—carrion in leaves and grass.

She wrenched her waking mind from such pictures.

Yet nothing could stop the cry out of sleep—oh God, where? Why?

What could it be but that he's not *able* to come back?

She awoke like this one night and, unable to sleep again, she went heavy-headed into the morning. Only care of the creatures shaped her hours—the two horses, the cows, the fowls that had not been caught by hawks or foxes. Their calm dependency, their mild-eyed trust governed her daylight hours. She talked aloud to them.

The air was sullen and leaves hung still in the August glare. She heard squawking at the sandy run below the spring and got there in time to see a snake slither into the bushes.

"Why will you bring your biddies into such a place, you old fool?" she cried at the hen. "No wonder you've got but the five left!" She stood a moment, hands on hips. "Wild is overtaking this whole place."

She brought a hoe and an axe and attacked the bushes, weeds, and briars that had grown up around the spring. The air was so humid that soon she was drenched with sweat, and her ragged-tailed skirts stuck to her legs. She let her drab-colored shift hang loose, but she skinned her hair back tightly, knotted and tied it with a thong to keep it out of her face. Thinking she ought to wear shoes for this job, she had put on an old broken pair that had been her father's.

What does it matter? Who's to see or care what I look like? The cows don't. I doubt Molly and Dan do.

She flailed at bushes, tore out roots, hacked off young saplings, chopped and crushed the tough and the tender together. At length she sank back to rest on a half-buried rock above the spring.

How can I keep on fighting it alone? Why did I not go with David? Afraid of loneliness there, afraid of intrusion. My hope here. What hope? To struggle on here with no hope.

She looked about her at the waste of wilting vegetation she had made, leaves turned whitely to the sun, a few yet crisp, not knowing they were on the way to death.

She got to her feet, dull-eyed, her strength sapped by sleeplessness and exertion in the heat. What she'd cut down was too green to burn, but soon as it dried out, she'd set it afire. She must go for a rake to get it into piles.

Coming out of the barn with her rake, she stopped still. No creature had given her warning. There was only the slight jingle and creak as he dismounted, for he was ever a one to move quietly.

A man of inconsequential stature he seemed to her now, used as she had gotten to the size of Jamie.

He met her look straight and said her name.

She turned sideways, stepping down from the barn floor, then paused where he had stood that night to face his attackers. She looked at her rake, felt locked in dumbness, was conscious of her sweat and dirt.

"Margaret?" He took a step toward her. "Have you no word for me?"

She observed that though his face was leaner than she remembered, he looked brown and healthy.

"I could ask where you've been." Her voice sounded dried out as if from disuse.

He said slowly, "Yes. I'll tell you that." He paused. "But it's not to tell you all that that I've come."

"Why have you come?"

He had dared to hope there might be some gladness in her eyes, that she might seed a gladness in him to swallow up his guilt.

"I've come to ask forgiveness. I was wrong to leave as I did."

She turned away from him, stretched to put her rake back inside the barn door. She felt her torn skirts drag against her legs, sweat trickle behind her knees, down her ankles into the ugly worn-out shoes that had trampled the weeds.

She said, "Let's move out of the sun. It's too hot to stand here clacking."

He followed after her till she stopped under the great tree where she had last seen him in the glare of torchlight. When she turned again toward him, her face with her hair strained back showed no softness.

"You say it was wrong of you to leave as you did. When did you first reach that conclusion?"

"Margaret, I always knew it was wrong." He spoke in a low, halting voice. "I lacked courage—to face it—and to face you."

"And I'd thought you a man of courage." Her words seemed to come of themselves.

"And too," he said heavily, "I thought—what did I have for you? A man shamed—and hated by your people—little as I had to give you, better, I thought, to leave you alone, since I had nothing for you."

Her brain, tongue, and feeling fused. "No, you had nothing. True. You had not the common decency to tell me so to my face." The thrill of her anger cleared her mind. "Not even the common consideration to let me know you'd go and not be back. Just up and leave without e'er a word!"

"Margaret, I cannot tell you, I have not the words for my feelings then, all that I felt—only I thought—I hoped you might understand."

"Understand? Understand what? That I meant no more to you than some squaw woman maybe you'd take up with and leave for a sixmonth and then straggle back to when the notion struck you? You think I'd have no feelings? Let me tell you something, Rudi, I'd never ha' treated you that way!" Words she had cried a thousand times. "Never, never," she cried, "would I ha' treated a one I cared about in that way, no matter what might ha' happened!"

"Oh Margaret—"

"Don't come near me! Left to all manner of grief and distress, not knowing but that you might lie dead in some savage place and me never to hear a word of it! Then you come calmly, stroll back one morning, say, 'I've decided I was wrong. I decided I'd come back to you!'"

"I didn't say, I didn't mean it like that! You know I didn't!"

"I don't know what you *do* mean! You say, 'understand.' What am I to understand? That you ha' not the spirit to face down your enemies? Did you think I was on their side? You speak of *your* feelings! What of the shame to me? Stand up for you as I did afore all of 'em, and then you leave me to be the laughingstock of the country! 'More fear of *them* he had, than love of Margaret Allen, to be sure!' Oh yes, that's what they'd say! You think I'd have no feelings of pride or shame either?"

His face was gray. "Oh, it was wrong." he said weakly. "It was the coward in me. I can only say—" He turned to look toward the house, toward the garden as if there might be someone there to hear him. "It's not easy to face truth. I come now to try to face it. I ask you again—help me!"

The word "help." It made its appeal, stronger than anything he had yet said. She saw him again riven, the great gaping wound only half healed over. But the charge of anger still controlled her. Its currents had raced through her too long, too deep. The questions had tormented her too long.

"Help? And how can *I* help *you?* You're the man, aren't you? Do you mean," she looked about her, "do you want a horse? Maybe another one to help you on your way? I ha' not too many goods left here."

He was still. She heard her own words in the air—the caw of a crow, the screech of a jay.

She saw whiteness at his mouth. Then she saw a crumpling in his face, a misting of his eyes that incredibly reminded her of Granny, a crumpling and softening, a relaxation about the mouth. Still he did not speak.

"And you think all you've got to do is come back here and look pitiful," she said, crying, "and work your tricks again?"

Light moved into his eyes. Though he stood motionless, in his spirit he gathered her up, cradling and stroking, gentling. Oh Meggie, Meggie, no one to love you when you had most need! In his spirit he reached under the rough mass of her hair to touch the nape of her neck. She was only twenty years old. All she's endured here alone, too young to have endured it alone.

"Margaret, Margaret," he said at last. Then, "Meggie, dear Meggie." Such depth and richness she had never heard in any voice. Startled, she felt and saw herself not a squawk-voiced crow but a loved child.

She whirled once toward the house, then away, and began running down the field toward the woods above the creek.

He followed her with his eyes. Maybe after a while she'll let me come to her, he thought.

He went to tend Stony left standing in the barnlot. "Not yet, old fellow. Not quite yet." He stood a long while with his hand caught in his horse's mane.

He was overcome by knowledge. She doesn't have to understand me. What matters is that I understand her. That's where the light is. That's what he was talking about. A power. Given.

Nothing to do with status or man's pride but a power enlightening the eyes, giving wisdom to the mind. A little like Granny's? he wondered. Do I have any of that light?

He found her sitting at the foot of the chestnut oak that was covered with wild grapevine, sitting there with her head on her knees drawn up under her torn skirts. Though most of the muscadines had been eaten by animals and birds, a few dark berries still hung on the vines, a few still lay sunken and drying on the ground.

She did not look at him but turned her swollen face away as he eased down beside her.

"I won't trouble you long," he began. "I have little more to say, Margaret." He looked earnestly at her averted cheek. "It's true. You didn't lose much when I left you. I wasn't much to lose. You said right. I was only—maybe—the promise of a man."

He saw a long angry scratch on her shoulder where her dress was torn. It would have come from some rough place she'd been or some rough work she'd been doing.

He continued haltingly, "I don't know—if you can find in your heart—any feeling of what you once had for me. More than anything I want—the chance to be with you again. ...But I know—to come here as sudden as this...." He let the words die away. "I see clear what I did. I did you worse harm maybe than they did me. But I didn't see then as I see now."

The stillness was broken only by the rattle of a woodpecker, the thump of a nut falling in the grass.

"Always my problem is lack of means, lack of a place to give you. But I see now I must have a place for myself before I have one for you. You may not want me or what I have. Still I must find my place here. I can't rove always among Indians and outcast men."

She drew a long shuddering sigh and turned her head to look in front of her. He wanted to untie the gray thong that pulled her hair back so tightly.

Her voice was hoarse from crying. "I hope you find it. Your place."

His voice gained confidence. "You spoke of standing up to enemies. There's a man I go to speak with, a man who's against these wrongs they do to people here like me. I think I may offer service to this man."

"Who is he?"

"Edward Musgrove, a man of authority. And no one can say he's not a man of good name."

"I know naught of such matters."

"Can I come back?"

"I thought you said you wanted your own place."

He winced, said gently, "I mean, to see—if you have other words for me. That's all I mean."

"I may not be here. I promised my brother I'd go to him in the fall."

He was glad but dared not say so.

"I'll find you," he said strongly after a while. "I know where your brother lives."

They sat quietly. She plucked trash from her skirt.

"One thing more. I must tell you this. I owe much to James Fraser."

"What? James Fraser?" She turned to look at him.

"He's the one came and talked sense to me."

"Jamie went and talked to you? He's the one talked you into coming back here?"

"Yes, but—"

She rose in one lithe movement. "Jamie dared go and meddle—"

"Margaret!" He too rose swiftly and put his hands lightly on her arms. "The man loves you! He's a good man. If you could have seen him, what he went through to find me and get to me, you'd thank him—"

"I'll thank him to keep out of my concerns! And so he talked you into coming back here!"

"No!" he cried. "I came because I've been wanting to day and night since I left, but I had not the sense to see what a fool I was—"

"So you both decided it was you instead of him was to have me!"

Her wrath was contagious. His humility and repentance were suddenly swept away. "Woman!" he shouted. "How'll any man ever be able to get along with you? What's to be done with you?"

"Nothing by you!" she cried. "You can rest assured of that."

"Oh yes, it is!" Swiftly he seized and kissed her a long kiss.

When he let her go, they were both trembling. Then she wove her fingers behind his head again, feeling the spring of his hair like young vine tendrils. But softer now, she thought, finer than anything of wild.

At last he said, "It may be some time before you see me again. When all's settled, I'll come back, either here or to your brother's. Be angry when you will, but you wait for me, hear me, Margaret?" They drew apart to look each other in the face. Light and dark flashed between them. "Hear what I say?"

"I hear you, Rudi Näffels. Next summer maybe I can look for you. Or two, three years after that. But if you don't come in five, I'll maybe send Jamie after you." Her smile struck him down anew.

When he was gone, she leaned against the oak that itself leaned against the hillside covered over with sweet-fruited vines. A breeze moved through the sun-laden air and she felt its coolness on her neck. Absent-mindedly she reached up to untie her hair. She had already kicked off the old shoes.

"I'll wash in the creek this evening, wash my hair too, wash all over. I'll burn this old shift and petticoat. That's all they're good for." She looked distastefully at her father's shoes. "But I'd better not throw these away. You never know when such might be needed." She lifted her hair, felt it swing free.

"If it cools off a little, I might try to weave some this afternoon."

Chapter Sixteen

In the fall of the leaf, as they said in this country, Johannes rode with several hundred men from the Congarees and above it, rode a hundred miles to the elegant little church of Saint James Goose Creek in the very heart of the lowcountry, there to cast his ballot in the parish of Saint James. The Province was electing a new Assembly.

Hundreds of other backcountry men also voted in the nearer parishes—Saint David's, Saint Mark's, and Saint Matthew's—and they elected their candidates: Claudius Pegues and Benjamin Ferrar, who were Regulators, and William Thomson, who sympathized with them. In only one parish, Saint Bartholomew's, were the Regulators turned away.

Riding into that still, flat country with its moss-hung oaks and cypresses, Johannes had much to reflect on. He remembered his first journey through it. Now after twelve years, his sense of its power and mystery was as strong as ever.

He remembered the man with whom he'd first viewed it, Matthys Tschudi, his friend and rival. They'd come all the way from the Upper Toggenburg to their Congaree landing. For it was the herdboy Matthys who had first dreamed of Carolina, or West India as they called it then, a place of wonder, a new Eden. But Matthys had died within a year of his arrival, overcome by the freedom and wildness of it all and by malaria fever.

And Johannes remembered the slow journey up this road a year and a half later with his still-faced bride. She had married him only because she did not know what else to do with Matthys dead—the lover she had traveled so far to find. Madle, where are you? he had cried in his heart many a time that bittersweet spring as they progressed up the road from Charlestown in their borrowed wagon. Now he might have asked her again, Are you still there, the girl I tried to comfort in Jeremiah Theus' parlor that chill day? Occasionally he still caught a glimpse of the eager-faced child who had run up the Toggenburg meadows after him and Matthys, but never since Joggi's birth had he seen a hint of the merchant's daughter, the fairytale princess who had lost Matthys. Had she died with him? Or was she only hidden away like the Chinese plates in her chest?

172

Such thoughts rarely troubled him nowadays. Yet perhaps he had sensed that revisiting this lowcountry would rouse them, for he had not returned since their marriage.

He seldom thought of Matthys the man, though often of Matthys the boy when he told his children of his own boyhood. Yet a time or two he'd found himself thinking, Is it possible for one man's spirit to influence another's son through the mother? Johannes asked now, What would they have thought of each other, he and my son? Would the child too have been drawn to Matthys? Johannes did not like those questions. He's my own child in every way, nothing of Matthys in him. Yet he remembered the idling herdboy's "I'll go there. I'll see those places one day. ... When I get there I want it still wild, not cut back for fields and villages."

As Johannes rode, he saw the country again as if through his lost friend's eyes, as if that first trip were only yesterday. Then he tried to see it through his son's. What would the boy think of these black waterways, the great lazy-winged herons, the brilliant little parrot-birds—and of Charlestown?

Oh, I must bring him this way soon. Poor little fellow, I want for him more than ignorance and common drudgery. How his eyes will widen at streets and buildings. And the sea.

But as they neared the coast, thoughts of old world cities possessed him as if he were reversing that first journey—Amsterdam, Basel, Zurich—and that strange yearning vision he had known twice before rose in him again. It was less clear than formerly, yet still connected with passage. It assumed the shape of a spire like that of the great cathedral at Strasbourg, floating baseless beyond some river. He closed his eyes to try to assimilate its stonewrought soaring but almost immediately he saw only reaches of water and shadowy banks. What beyond? For whom?

On their left, the Santee was a river of cypress swamp, alligators, and snake-necked anhingas. So many kinds of beasts and beings, so many ways of striving, how to understand it all? Ah God, I thank You for my fields and woods on Savanna Hunt. I'd not exchange them for all the goods of Zurich or one of these mansion houses either.

They caught few glimpses of the great planters' homes, for most of them were set far back from the road, nearer their river ricelands.

Goose Creek Church was as lovely a building as he'd ever seen. Johannes' craftsman's eye delighted in its workmanship, its symmetry, its elegant simplicity. Though it had no steeple—what use for a steeple and bells to call worshippers when the nearest might live five miles away?—yet its arched windows and its classical pediment and pilasters were beautifully set in red-stuccoed brick walls, white-quoined at the corners. It had been built fifty years ago by Englishmen from Barbados.

He thought of the rough-boarded meetinghouse below Tom's Creek. Well, the Father can hear people in Saint John's as surely as Saint James', he thought. I'm glad He knows German as well as English. Nevertheless Johannes sighed lightly. Not for us these high-panelled pews and polished walnut. But I can admire the joining of them, can't I?

The parish officials received the newcomers with consternation. This their polling place? Were they not mistaken? did they not belong to Saint Matthew's?

The leaders of the cavalcade explained that they had met to determine parish boundaries, and they were definitely excluded from Saint Matthew's. Saint James' *was* their parish. They were all qualified freeholders, and they respectfully requested they be allowed to exercise their right to vote.

The churchwardens consulted. The visitors were surprisingly well-mannered. Still it was difficult to conclude that men from so far away were entitled to vote *here*. But there were quite a number of them and they really were somewhat insistent.

"If we err, let it be on the side of liberality," one urged. "Let them vote and let the Commons judge the validity of the election."

They could hardly have decided otherwise, these gentry who had recently protested so much in the matter of Liberty and the Rights of Free Men.

The backcountry cast their ballots, and their number assured that their choices would predominate: Tacitus Gaillard, Moses Kirkland, and Aaron Loocock, who was a Charlestown merchant connected with the Kershaw-Chesnut enterprise in Pine Tree.

They were jubilant as they rode away. "See how they stepped back? As polite as to a lord. It was well worth it we came."

"Now they know we're not lawless scum. We have gentlemen among us too."

"We want only our lawful rights! We're as peace-loving as anybody!"

Well worth the time and cost, Johannes said to himself. How glad I am I came! Observing the lion and unicorn above the chancel, he'd thought, My king too; and for the first time he had some sense of being one with all these men, lowcountry and upcountry alike. All freeborn subjects of the same king, he mused. Me freeborn in mountains five thousand miles from here, and now subject to an English king, though I'm not an Englishman either.

...Who was Johannes Lienhardt? American? Carolinian? He worked the soil of this land. His children had never breathed any other air. He'd traveled this province from the sea to the mountains. And here his body would go to earth. Again he felt the strong, sappy pull of new roots.

At Moncks Corner Johannes bought a parcel of Irish linen for Madle, five pounds of raisins, some spices, and a nutmeg grater. He bought worsted stockings for the children, and with some hesitation small penknives for Joggi and Heiri, then handkerchiefs for the girls, and a bit of white and brown candy for Hansli.

The former proprietor of the store, now dead, had been Simon Theus, a brother of Christian Theus and of Jeremiah Theus of Charlestown. The Theuses on his mind, Johannes thought that he'd like to see again that hospitable, goodnatured Charlestown portrait painter. He shows what a man can be and do if he's upright and honorable. Came not over fifty miles from where I did, no more English than I am, yet as respected and well-established as any man in Charlestown, though maybe not as rich.

Johannes wished now he'd ridden on to the city, near as it was. He would like to have bought Madle something silken and blue, blue as her eyes when she'd run in alpine meadows.

I'll go down there again, he said. After the child's born, soon as it's weaned, God willing, I'll go down there and take her with me. We'll go in our own wagon this time and bring back a well-joined bed or table. Maybe bring back glass for the window panes I promised her one day. If God wills and He prospers me.

Four days later he knew profound contentment in the midst of his family in the cool October dusk. Small and common as his house might be, it was his own mansion, his home entirely.

"Ah Madle," he said low, brokenly, "there's no way I can tell you— how glad I am for you and our children."

In late November, however, Johannes' satisfaction was marred, as was that of most Carolinians. Governor Montagu dissolved the newly elected House of Commons because it had endorsed a circular letter from Massachusetts urging opposition to the obnoxious Townshend Acts. Furthermore, soon afterward came news that the King's Privy Council had rejected the Circuit Court Act sent so hopefully across the sea in April. Once again the people of the backcountry felt disenfranchised, cheated by a swirl of events far away.

"Try again," some urged. "We can go again in March. We can't afford to give up now."

Their sixth child was a girl. "Verena" said Madle; "Verena for my dear Aunt."

After the Peace of Paris in 1763, letters from Wildhaus had found them every few years. The last one brought news of the death of Verena Bittlinger, Madle's great-aunt and Rudi's grandmother, who had said she would pray for them every day she lived. Johannes was sorry they'd not remembered or had time to tell Rudi she was dead. Well, he'd hardly given them time, had he? Would they ever see him again? Johannes didn't like to think about Rudi these days.

He himself became more and more disquieted by what some Regulator bands were doing. "Too harsh, too extreme!" he protested when he heard how they'd whipped a man for an hour because he was only suspected of being a horse thief.

"And played the fiddle and beat a drum all the time they were lashing him," came the report.

"I'll never be party to such as that!" he muttered to himself.

He wondered if some men were using the Regulation to satisfy private grudges. How else explain attacks on such men as John Furnes on Bush River, a man said to be of good repute among his neighbors? Of course, Joseph Curry, whom the Regulators opposed, was known to be as crooked as anybody, but then what about his Regulator opponent, Moses Kirkland? How Kirkland had ever got claim to the old Saxe Gotha Township common lands was a mystery to everyone. Heinrich Gallman, now six months deceased, who'd lived in the area longer than almost anyone, had shaken his head. Johannes didn't like to think that Kirkland was a prime leader of the Regulators.

And what about John Musgrove on Saluda, twice flogged by Regulators and lately forced to leave home? Johannes knew little of John except that he was a large landowner and had been a militia major in the Cherokee War, but everyone knew that his brother Edward, also accused by Kirkland of being "a conniver of thieves and robbers," was a man who had served the backcountry well. The Musgroves thieves? Or upholders of them? It seemed unlikely.

"I'll take no more part in it!" he told Madle one day.

But events that winter forced him to change his mind. Indeed, the Regulation had gone too far, decent men everywhere admitted and began to draw back. The attack on Musgrove, along with more brutal attacks on lesser men, brought sharp reaction.

It brought the sharpest reaction of all in Charlestown when Jonathan Gilbert, a justice of the peace from Beaverdam Creek on Saluda, took affidavits to Governor Montagu and his Council in February. They related details of Regulator activities and asked for relief from their menaces, from men who'd controlled the backcountry for over a year now. As a result, the Governor and Council stripped the Regulators Gaillard, Mayson, Cunningham, Buzzard, Frei, Teiger, the Fulmores, and Wofford of their commissions as militia officers or justices of the peace; in the case of Gaillard and Mayson of both commissions.

Men like Johannes would have accepted this turn of events without violent agitation, but what none of them could accept was the commissioning of a certain Joseph Coffell.

Coffell was well-known for a rogue and ruffian, no better than a thief himself, and this same Joseph Coffell was commissioned to arrest thirty-five Regulators. Furthermore, Coffell, who called himself "Colonel," along with John Musgrove as major, began enlisting troops to suppress the Regulator movement, promising them twenty pounds a month pay. It was too good a chance for those who'd been hounded by Regulators to miss. Within a short time Coffell had a following of over a hundred men, some of whom were said to be former members of the gangs.

Meanwhile, John Musgrove, Gilbert, and others more reputable than Coffell were organizing the counter-movement of so-called Moderators, and Governor Montagu was talking about sending British troops into the backcountry.

After some skirmishing, Coffell and the Moderators arrested six

Regulators, mostly Germans, and sent them to Charlestown. This action was inflammatory enough, but most infuriating of all was the news that Coffell's men were plundering and raiding farms under the guise of impressing provisions, that they were terrorizing men, women, and children just as the thieves had done. Again the backcountry was in turmoil.

On a March evening in 1769, Johannes took down his musket and cleaned it, and the next morning he rode away. He did not look back toward the house. Madle did not come out to see him off. She had not remonstrated with him for going. She seemed not to care one way or the other. They had buried their infant daughter five days ago, little Verena, the first of their children to be put into the sand.

Madle seemed beyond his comfort, frozen-faced as he remembered her from long ago. Strong as was their bonding, there was ever a place he could not enter. As there was something of himself he could never express to her. Each knew and accepted it in the other. Still it was hard not to be able to comfort her, hard to have to hold his own grief inside.

Rains had been heavy. The river was flooding and sloughs were full of water. Low-lying fields were drowned, and water covered the bridge of Congaree Creek. Black willow branches trailed green in the creek water; the bases of swamp gum trunks were submerged.

Johannes' face was lightless, for he had no pleasure in this going. He doubted that many from the Congarees would be at the meeting place. He himself was coming late, for most of the Regulators had begun to assemble several days ago. No, he did not want to go. It was simply that having made up his mind to a stand, he must hold to it. Now as at other times it was not a matter of doing what he wanted to but of doing what he had to. As when he shot a fox. And sometimes a hawk.

There had to be a showdown. Men like him had to take sides. If they didn't show strength now, the country would again be overrun. For fifteen months his family had known relative security, mainly because people had joined together for what on the whole was a good cause. Yes, it did get out of hand, he admitted, but why send criminals to prey on us? Now people were being robbed and plundered all up and down the Saluda River, some left to starvation, almost as bad as before! Surely the authorities in Charlestown didn't know what they'd done! But to shrink back submissively and pretend you were sorry you'd ever opposed such outrages was unthinkable. Arrest me if you will, said Johannes. I'll not turn my back or hide at home! It's my country too. All I love's been entrusted to it.

He joined several men near the old Congaree fort. At Friday's Ferry a few more latecomers rode up from east of the Congaree, and after they crossed the Saluda at Kirkland's Ferry, they came up with the main body of men.

They all moved up the north bank of the river, and by nightfall over six hundred were camped near Bear Creek. They were mostly from creek valleys along the Wateree, the Broad, and the Saluda. They had begun gathering the week before.

Word came that Moderators too were assembling up the Saluda at John Musgrove's, hundreds of them.

"Good! We'll have it out with 'em once and for all. If we can't stand down a bunch of thieves and ragtag such as follow Coffell, we deserve to be plundered."

"We'll see how they like stopping our lead."

At dawn the men continued up the north bank. Johannes had not been this road before. He was struck anew by the richness and variety of the country. The soil of these bottomlands was deep red clay, heavier than what he was used to. These great tulip poplars always meant rich land. They crossed Camping Creek.

Where had Rudi's tract lain? Anger and grief tore through him. Such good land as this, I'd swap a hundred acres of mine for fifty of these! Why wouldn't he try to hold on to it and make something of it? As good farmland as any you'd find anywhere in Carolina!

The fierce face confronted him again. "You've seen the last of me!"

But Johannes saw it now at the other end of a gun barrel.

This was a possibility he'd been trying not to think about ever since he'd left home. He did not know it for fact, but he had a strong feeling that Rudi Näffels was in some way allied with the other side.

But surely Rudi wouldn't serve under a villain like Coffell! No, but were they all villains on the other side?

Again Johannes felt himself sinking into the quandary that had tormented him during and after the Cherokee War. He'd asked himself a hundred times afterward, If I had it to do again, would I go? He did not know. And what would he do tomorrow if he saw Rudi looking at him on the other side?

...No, Rudi was miles away. Surely he wouldn't involve himself in these brangles. He was too detached a man to come so close to other people. He was so chained up in his own feelings he couldn't even tell a child goodbye. It would be a long time before Joggi and Heiri would forget the hurt of that leaving.

...The faces of his children. The mystery of their persons. My son is not me. He's not his mother. No, Johannes told himself, but the heart of being a father is responsibility. Though our images in some way may be imprinted on them, we had nothing to do with that part of it. But we had everything to do with the fact that they're here. We *are* responsible.

...Oh God, what else could we have done when that little body struggled so? We tried everything we knew! Oh God, if I'd kept the house warmer, if I'd held her longer while Madle was busy that morning when she was first stopped up with cold! That sheepskin we could have put in her cradle, I didn't even think of it then! If I'd prayed more! Took too much for granted. Five in good health, always blessed with recovery. Madle, oh Madle, it was *not* your fault! Oh my Madle, you did all you knew to do! So many of them now, you can't be six pairs of hands at one time!

...Those wide blue eyes had followed them all over the room. The tiny hand that had fastened so strongly around his forefinger—how could I let it go?

But under his wash of grief came another voice: You had no will in it. She was given only for a little while. Rain torrents washing the cedar shingles. Christian Theus' voice: "'The Lord giveth and the Lord taketh away.' Six given and five entrusted to you still, Johannes. Grieve for the one taken, but give thanks for those that remain."

How to serve them. To protect them, provide for them, teach them. What I do now is for them, he told himself.

But some wouldn't see it that way. You could be putting your family in peril, they'd say, and you risk death for yourself. But I take risk every time I step out of the house, he answered. When I kill a rattler, there's risk. Everytime I go in a canebrake, every time I fell a tree. All I can do is take care. As I will tomorrow. I'll not make myself an easy target for anyone's bullet.

At four o'clock that afternoon they reached the south bank of Bush River just below where it entered the Saluda. Across Bush River in the forks of the two streams was John Musgrove's land where the enemy was said to be waiting. They decided not to cross now, for dusk would come early and they were tired.

The woods were alight with their campfires. Some men sat up all night because of the cold. The hard ground and the cold may have roused Johannes long before daylight, but it was neither that kept him awake.

He cried out, Rudi! Are you over there, man? Again and again he rehearsed the reasons Rudi might or might not be across the river. But no matter how many negative reasons he thought of, the conviction remained: He's there.

How can I go over? he cried in the black of night. That man stood by me in my own house with enemies outside. He risked his life to get in and stand by me. It's a lie! he cried to Rudi's accusers. He was never an associate of thieves!

...He helped build my house. He helped me raise the timbers that shelter us every night of our lives. His hands helped me hew those roof beams; his shoulders helped put them in place. Johannes saw the young man's face, the boy's face, so eager and hopeful when he'd first known it.

Johannes sat up, saw the shapes of other men, restless around the fires—tall, red-haired, swarthy, freckle-faced, long-headed, gaunt, wiry, stocky like Rudi and himself.

...Young as he was, even then he had the look of his grandfather in his shoulders first time I saw him. Old Melchior. He's a Toggenburger like me. He was born under Säntis same as I was, even if he can't remember it. Our grandfathers were friends. Old Melchior and Johannes, they were boys together, I've heard old Granddad say so.

...I killed that Indian. Sure as I sit here, my bullet tore a hole in his chest. And it tore something loose in me too. If I fire a bullet to kill *him*, kill Rudi—can I look my sons in the face? Can I look at myself?

Johannes got up, stamped his feet, and walked away from the campfires. He walked till he came to the clearing they had skirted yesterday. It was already plowed for spring planting. Today was the twenty-fifth day of March.

He looked at the sky and saw it was clouding up again. Though there was frost out from under the trees, he felt a softening in the air. In the distance he heard a cock crow, then another and another. The sleeping farmstead was not far away.

The men across the river there, they had guns too, horses, determined faces. Would men like Coffell hesitate to ride down on that farmer if it suited them, hold his girl-children hostage? Or shoot a boy that dared oppose them? He remembered his wife's white face that October night. He thought of his brave son slipping through the darkening woods.

And remembered the bullet holes that would be in the front of his house-wall as long as it stood. Felt again the menace of riders who came out of the dark with lightwood torches, with no respect for God's law or man's law either. For whom a man's land and home meant no more than an anthill to be kicked over and stamped on, a squirrel nest to be shot out of a tree, the little ones no more than blind vermin to be knocked out of a nest or to be fired out of some burrow.

Johannes stood a long time looking back down the way he had come yesterday. He saw far down the river to where it entered another one. He stood until at last he saw the sky lighten, the farm buildings take shape, the clods in the field. His mind cleared.

No matter who those men were that waited over there, they had raised their hands against what had been entrusted to him or to men like him. Their faces became one, a darkness, and Rudi's was no longer among them. Everything settled and came clear. They had one nameless face. Those who joined such men did so at their own risk. No matter who they were.

He turned back to his own camp.

Chapter Seventeen

On the other side of Bush River men were cooking breakfast. The smell of frying pork and sizzling cornmeal permeated the spring-washed air. Rudi, waking, had almost forgotten where he was. He'd slept hard, for he'd ridden hard the day before. He'd come down from Squire Edward Musgrove's on the Enoree with a letter for the Squire's brother. He'd known ahead of time the business at hand and needed no urging to remain. A month ago he'd seen the festering back of another poor soul whom the mob had beaten, who'd lain in a fever for days afterward. He knew well that desperation in the face of John Musgrove, who had twice endured similar humiliation.

"Accuse you of villainy!" Musgrove's voice last night rang out. "They're the most lawless villains ever walked this earth!"

Eyes narrowed examining the bore of a rifle or musket. Barrels were cleaned, grease boxes filled, more patches cut, more powder and bullets shared out to those who had not enough.

Now in the dawnlight Rudi felt his rifle beside him, ready for the day's use. It had been some time since he'd handled it against men. He'd done so in the days of the Indian War and a few times afterwards when threatened. Other times he would have if he could have gotten to his gun or could have come up with his enemy. He'd never had scruples against giving back what a man was trying to give him.

Rudi would not take service with Coffell, but he was glad to serve the man who'd befriended him. Squire Edward Musgrove was a gentleman. He didn't make you feel like a dumbhead because you weren't English or Irish. He valued a man for what he was, not the origin of his name.

Squire Musgrove had remembered Rudi from his service with the Rangers. He heartened him with his words. "You're too fine a young man to let suspicion and a little rough treatment get the better of you. You know what that mob say about me? And no doubt would do to me too if they dared!"

He encouraged Rudi to remain in the upcountry. "You'll find it different in a year or two. I have great hope of changes here. But they must come legally. That's why I opposed the Regulation from the beginning. I knew what it would come to. And," he added dryly, "I knew a few in it."

He offered Rudi wages to work at his gristmill during the fall and winter. Though a slaveholder, he was a just and compassionate man, Rudi thought, with an air of authority that somehow gave you confidence in yourself.

Rudi knew he might have made more money from pelts, but then that money had a way of getting away from him. Earning his shillings at Musgrove's gave him a sense of earning more than his wages: the respect, the good will and friendship that came with them, he thought. And he was earning it for Margaret.

He'd sent her a letter in October, written for him by Musgrove himself. He'd hesitated a long time before asking the older man to write for him, but later he was glad he had, for he'd enjoyed Musgrove's surprised approval. It was a plain, rather formal letter, wishing her good health, telling her where he was and what he was doing, assuring her of his continued regard. The letter was entrusted to an itinerant minister who planned to visit the Long Canes area, near which Margaret's brother lived. I'll go to her in March, Rudi promised himself. I'll have something solid behind me then. We'll decide then where to take up land and how to begin.

He remembered that Johannes had worked for wages when he first came into the country. "To learn more," he'd told Rudi, "to establish myself better, to have a chance to look about me and be sure of the right step."

Cautious Johannes. Careful, steadfast, not to be moved once he'd made up his mind to a thing. And yet as good a man as ever breathed. How'll I ever make my peace with him? Rudi asked. Go back to Savana Hunt? Not yet. Not for a while yet.

But recent events had blotted out all Rudi's personal concerns.

This morning, March 15, like yesterday and the day before, was given only to the needs of the moment. Today his mind was fixed wholly on his present allegiance, which sprang from indignation, old conviction, and new gratitude. He knew who some of the men at these campfires were—some of them perhaps barnburners, yes pilferers, a few of whom he wouldn't have wanted to turn his back to alone on the trail. But many weren't that kind, and even those who were might not have been if they'd been given a little more of—what? The lifting up he himself had known a few times. It was wrong as sin to trample a man in the dirt because of what he didn't have, that he couldn't help not having. He knew, he knew.

How had he learned it? Not just because of the bad that had happened to him, he thought, but from the good too. From Granny maybe. No, before that. From Johannes and Madle when he'd lived at the Congarees. Or maybe somehow even before that. That memory, the light.... He'd also learned it from Jamie.

Jamie came strongly into Rudi's mind as he dipped his rations from the pot. Jamie here or over there? Neither place, he felt sure. He wondered about Aleck Fraser and found himself hoping Jamie's brother wouldn't be there either. Strange he felt that way. He remembered Granny saying, "The Frasers were always known as good neighbors." Aleck had helped to bear her coffin. He was Jamie's brother.

Who were they over there? Mostly from that hotbed east of the Broad and beyond the Wateree, he'd heard, though plenty from hereabouts and around Ninety Six too.

"We heard 'em a couple of times last night. You might hear 'em now if everything was still."

"Wouldn't doubt if we don't see some heads poking up through them bushes soon."

"Oh no, they're not big enough fools for that. They'll go further upstream to cross, come down that way. Another hour and a half maybe and we'll see something."

"Why don't we move up too?"

"Somebody'll tell us to, soon."

But instead of moving up Bush River, they were ordered to draw back a quarter of a mile up the Saluda, where there was more of a slope to the ground and they could take positions on the hillside.

"They'll find us, never you fear, but we'll wait on our own ground."

New grass was heavy with river damp. The red clay was slick. As men scattered up the slope, Rudi remained in the van near the river, using the multiple trunks of a large old river birch for cover, its branches peeling their red-brown flakes in front of him.

Waiting like this was second nature to him. His body was an alert stillness, mind focused to simple watching, no movement of twig or bird or waterdrop unnoticed. Since branches were still small-leaved, his view was fairly unobstructed. Keen-eyed, far-sighted, he observed swallows beginning their spring excavations in the bank downstream.

The sky was overcast, but the air was clear. Across the river beyond the line of trees lay an open field. Once Rudi heard talking across the river. Then he caught another sound, the sound of horses down the valley.

"There they are, just like we said!"

Lounging men stood up. Rudi swung himself into the crotch of two birch branches for a better look. He saw horseflesh, a shoulder, some heads, all as solid as—no, more solid than the scaling trunk under his hand. The rich gleam of leather, the stock of a gun, strength of thigh and forearm, and the power of a strong-jawed face. Appeared, then disappeared. They too were deploying carefully.

Yells broke out along the hillside.

"Come on, ye yellow-bellied bastards! Show us what ye can do in daylight!"

"We're ready for ye this time! Let's hear your fiddles and your drums now!"

There were no answering cries, but the still air brought sounds of distant commands. The enemy were dismounting.

Rudi watched the appearing and disappearing shapes come closer. Soon they'd be in range. Then he swung down, reached for his powder horn, for because of the morning damp he had not yet loaded his rifle. As he poured out a measure of powder, his hand began to tremble in delayed reaction. His entire body was afire and ice-cold at the same time. He continued to load swiftly, automatically, wrapping the bullet in its greased patch, ramming it down the muzzle.

It could not have been Johannes. Just a glimpse. A stern-set face with no light of kindness on it. Not Johannes from down the Congaree. Rudi held the rifle in firing position, his eyes straining for a sight of that face.

But why not? He'd put his name to their paper. He'd owned it to Rudi's face, never hesitated to style himself a Regulator.

Rudi's hand hovered at the cock of his rifle. His eyes were misted. Why didn't it enter my mind he'd be here?

Would it have made a difference?

It sure as hell makes a difference! he exploded. Man, what in God's name are you doing here?

Rage and frustration churned inside him. He stood oblivious to sounds and movements. Just like him! I should have known! Why, who'd have thought he'd join up that time in sixty-one? Never forget him come hunting through sixteen hundred men in Grant's camp till he found me! Once he's made up his mind to some damned thing— But how can he do this, how can he be so damned wrong-headed?

"Rudi, do you know that men of our race make some of the best soldiers in Europe?"

Memories of Johannes that night in his darkened house when another mob raged around it in torchlight. Children and their mother huddled upstairs.

An earlier memory: a child on his father's shoulder in the March dusk at Gallman's Fort, a little face alight with glee.

Rudi turned slightly and stepped back. He looked about him at his waiting dark-faced companions. He glanced toward John Musgrove fifty yards away. He saw the burly figure of Coffell as the two consulted.

Rudi drew a long ragged breath. He stood up straight, glanced down at his rifle and lowered its muzzle groundward. He did not look at anyone again but turned and began to walk up the slope.

For a minute no one seemed to realize what he was doing. Then someone called, "Where you going?"

He did not answer.

The jeers began. "Look at him! Scared in broad daylight!"

"I heared how they catched him once! Must ha' give it to him right hot to ha' scared him this much!"

"Hey, you white-livered Dutchman! We won't let 'em get you this time!"

Neither glancing at them nor speaking, not hurrying but not hesitating, he made his way through the six or seven hundred men, many of whom were acquaintances, several of whom he called friends. Among their leaders were some of the most influential men in the backcountry. Almost all of them saw him leave. Only a few recognized that there was nothing of fear in his going and observed him with wonder. But most glared at him with anger and contempt, though no one tried to stop him, for they must pay attention to what was in front of them.

As his distance from them lengthened, Rudi's pace quickened. Just to get to his horse now, that was all he had to do.

Since there was nothing furtive in his manner, the black men watching the horses did not question him. As he rode off, he heard gunfire behind him.

He rode a mile up the Saluda past the shoals. Though the river was high, he was able to ford there, and twenty minutes later he came out on the Cherokee Road.

He stopped, looked up and down the road. West past Ninety Six toward the Long Canes settlements and Savannah's Little River? Or east toward the Congaree? He had come away under compulsion. He let compulsion rule him now and turned east along the old road he'd traveled a hundred times before.

I'll be there when he gets back. I hope to God he gets back. God!—it was a prayer—make him get back! Rudi was not sure why he himself wanted to be there. The same reason he had to ride away maybe.

He could not frame the reason or reasons clearly. Something to do with who or what he was. I am myself. I myself. Not in me to do such a thing. I will not shoot down a brother. No matter what he might do. His responsibility, not mine.

Not to win all the favor and goods in this country, he kept telling himself. Go my way lone till I die, I'll not do it.

The taunts and accusations faded. He felt a freshening in the air. He crossed Little Saluda, then Rocky Creek in the middle of the afternoon, Hollow Creek an hour later. He did not push his horse, for yesterday had been hard on the beast. Late in the afternoon it drizzled rain. An hour before dark, Rudi found high ground off the road and matted himself a shelter of pine branches after he found young cane for Stony near a small branch.

He chewed a strip of jerked beef and ate a handful of wet meal but he did not make fire.

He lay sensing rather than hearing the softness of rain sinking into the sand. It slid down pine needles, formed droplets on twigs, caught at the ends of tiny new leaves. Occasionally he felt a drop on his face or hand and shifted a little.

What John Musgrove or Edward Musgrove or Johannes think of me is not my lookout. Let them judge me how they will. I will not set myself up to kill a brother.

Squire, you may have that duty. Thank God, I have not.

As he lay on the earth, sheltered a little from rain, sounds of the spring night shrilled and receded around him, and contentment came over him. Home, he thought. This is my home place. Not just this place on the ground, but the place in me now where I'm free of all judgment and blame.

Chapter Eighteen

In the drizzling dusk Rudi came to Savana Hunt. He hallooed as he emerged from the woods fronting the house, the square-logged little house looming high in the gray evening. But no dog barked, no child came running, and no door opened to show light. They must not have heard me, he thought, and hallooed again.

Still there was no response. Then it came to him: fearing for their safety, Johannes had taken his family elsewhere. They weren't at home.

Rudi looked about him at the dark green wheatfield, the newly plowed ground down by the creek, then toward the empty barnlot. All sheltered creatures must already be bedded down.

He was deeply disappointed. So he might as well not have come. Ten years earlier he would have found a way into the house and made himself at home. Now he couldn't think of it.

Even so, he decided to ride in and look about.

He paused at the side gate. The new barn was certainly bigger than the old one. But was it as big-timbered? He rode nearer to peer through the gloom. No. It was well-built, but the logs were not of the size that he and Johannes had hefted. As he turned away, he noticed the back door of the house ajar. They must not have shut it securely. Or had someone entered in their absence? Or *were* they home?

He dismounted, though as he looped the reins around a post, he thought, If there's been plundering, you shouldn't be here. Still he opened the gate, and as he did so, the back door opened.

Relief surged through him. "Heiri!" he called. "It's me, Heiri! It's Rudi!"

The little figure stood still.

"Where is everybody? Where's your mother?"

"Papa's gone." The boy's stillness seemed unlike him.

"How about Joggi? Is he here?"

As Rudi came up the steps and looked into the darkened room, Heiri stood back. "Where's your Mama, Heiri?" Coals glowed dimly on the hearth, but the room felt cold.

"Mama's lying down. Joggi hasn't come home yet."

"How about the little ones? It was so quiet I thought nobody was here."

"They're asleep. I was too, but then I woke up. I heard something and came down 'cause I thought it might be Papa."

Rudi stood perplexed. "Bläss? Where's Bläss?"

Heiri did not answer at once. Then he said low, "Bläss died."

"Ohh." Rudi sank onto a bench. He wanted to pull the little boy to him. He reached out and touched his arm. "He was older than you, wasn't he?"

"He was older than Joggi. ...Our little sister died too."

"What?" Rudi asked sharply. "Who, Heiri? Babeli? Cathri?"

"Our new little sister. She died."

Rudi rose. "Your Mama, Heiri, she's not sick, is she?"

"Mama felt so bad we all lay down. After the man came and fed up, Mama said for us to go to bed too."

Now he saw an indistinct form in the doorway of the inner room. "Rudi?"

He moved swiftly to her. "Madle?"

"I thought I heard calling, but I couldn't wake up." Her voice sounded heavy.

"My dear Madle!" All he had ever felt but had never spoken was in his voice. As he put his hands on her shoulders as she always put her hands on his, he kissed her gently.

She was still a moment, then unbelievably put her head against his shoulder and began to cry in small broken whimpers, and Heiri too began to cry. Rudi felt the child pressed against his leg and reached to caress his head. He held them both; all he could do was hold them.

She said, crying, "I'm so glad you came! Johannes—he's not here. I'm so glad you came!"

"I'm sorry," he said, "the way I left last time. I had to come back."

"Yes. Well." She drew a shuddering breath, as if striving for control.

"Heiri told you our sorrow." Her voice crumpled again. "I'm sorry I'm so—"

"Yes, Madle, it's all right, it's all right," he kept whispering. His tenderness came to him as easily as if the two were his own, overwhelming him, for he had never soothed a woman or child this way.

When at last she drew away with a convulsive sob, Rudi picked up Heiri and sat on the bench, then set the little boy beside him and covered a small hand with his own. Still he could find no words.

"Light—" Madle said brokenly, "we must have light and fire."

He rose quickly. "I'll make up the fire."

"There's dry wood under the shed."

Outside, he couldn't think which way the shed was till Heiri's shadow called, "It's over here, Rudi."

The child by his side, he brought in great armfuls of oakwood and hickory. Though Madle had left the room, he built up the fire, and as the flames licked the wood, he saw Heiri more clearly, barefooted in only his shirt. The child was pale with stains under his eyes. What's happened to this family? Rudi asked in panic.

He looked about him in the growing light. The room was orderly though crowded. Yet it seemed empty, far more empty than that day long ago when he'd slept here with only Madle and her baby in the house, the day he'd ridden in to tell them of Indian attacks.

She came in again, went to the cupboard, stood there picking up and putting down plates and bowls.

Rudi said, "Joggi—where's Joggi, Madle?"

She did not answer at once. "I must trust God to bring him home safe."

"Where is he?"

"I don't know."

Rudi was silent. "When did he leave?"

"This afternoon," she sighed. "I don't know. He does this." She came to the table with a cup and bowl. "He goes and comes home at dark. I used to whip him, but it does little good. Each day I pray God to bring him home safe. That's all I can do." She turned toward the hearth and passed her hand across her forehead.

He did not know what to say. Oh, how I wish— What? That Johannes and Joggi were here, that all of you were here as you were that day in August when we sat together after the rain. That I could have that time over again.

The firelight was harsh on her tired face. "Not much left," she said as she lifted the lid from the great kettle. "We left some for Joggi. And I thought Johannes might come."

"Madle, try not to worry about Johannes."

The lid clanged. "You know where he is?"

"I was there," he said swiftly. "But I rode away before anything happened." The words came of themselves, for he had not intended to tell her this.

"You were with him?"

"I was on the other side. I could not—after I saw him, I could take no part in it."

"Ohh!" Her cry was long and deep. She groped for the table and drew a deep breath, buried her head in her arms and began to sob great exhausting sobs as if all that was in her were being wrenched out by the roots.

Rudi sat down beside her with Heiri on his other side, Rudi's arm loosely about the little boy. Never in his life had he heard such weeping. He ached at the child's hearing it, for he felt the small body tremble. The firelight grew brighter and the room warm. Still she wept, great laboring sobs, but he said no word. Finally he was aware that their anguish was diminishing. Then her shoulders were still.

Burning sap sang in the chimney. They sat in stillness, the woman with her head on the table, the man and child beside her.

She sat up and blotted her eyes with her apron, wiped her face. "Forgive me," she whispered. She sat a moment with her apron over her face. "It broke loose," she whispered. She reached across Rudi for Heiri and said the little boy's name.

Rudi passed Heiri in front of him for Madle to enfold. "Mama's better," she whispered. "Don't worry anymore, Heiri." She spoke louder. "Mama's better now. You mustn't cry anymore either."

The three of them sat still for a while, Heiri sniffing and Madle whispering, "It's all right now, I'm all right now," wiping his eyes and dabbing at her own with her apron. Rudi was still shaken. Though he had known them in trouble before, never had he associated anything with this family but well-being.

"I'm sorry we give you such greeting," said Madle at last. "You must not have known what to think of us."

"I thought you weren't here. I almost left. Then I saw the door wasn't shut." After a while he observed, "The little girls must be sound asleep."

"Yes, and Hansli too." She got up, stood a moment as if to make sure of her balance. "But I must go and see."

As she went out, Heiri tiptoed close behind her. It was a few minutes before they returned, but when she spoke, her voice sounded almost normal. "They're sleeping peacefully, thank God, all three. It's the rain, I think, puts them to sleep."

Rudi rose. "I'll go see to my horse now."

"I'll have supper set out when you come back."

He noted that her movements were more purposeful. He hesitated. "Madle, if I called Joggi, you think he might come?"

"You can try. I'll tell you though—" She paused. "Joggi loves you, Rudi. It was hard for him—when you left."

He had no answer but stood irresolutely at the door, then turned with a heavy tread and went out.

The light was almost gone when he called, "Joggi!" He walked beyond the barn and called again and again, "Joggi! It's Rudi!"

"He goes that way."

Rudi glanced behind him at the dim little shape.

"Over the ridge there is where he goes now."

Rudi walked on and called again. Worry quickened his voice.

"Sometimes he'll hear and not come," said Heiri.

Rudi put as much power as he could into his call. "Joggi! Come home! It's late!"

They were out of sight of the house. The rain had stopped and darkness was complete. Anger began to mingle with Rudi's anxiety. That boy ought not be allowed to stay off like this!

"Does he do this often?"

"Not when Papa's here. He knows what Papa'd do to him."

Rudi's mouth tightened. And what I've a good notion to do if I can get hold of him—or would if he was mine.

"Joggi," shouted Heiri, "if you don't come home, Rudi might leave and you won't get to see him!"

"I don't care if he does!" came an answering yell.

Rudi's distress roared into anger. "You young whelp, you, if you don't get yourself back down to that house, you're going to wish I *had* left!"

There was silence.

"Your mother, all she's had to grieve her and your Papa gone, I'd have thought you'd be man enough to stay there with her," Rudi shouted, "instead of going off like that to yourself!"

His words reverberated in the cool dark. When their irony struck him, it was his first taste of what it felt like to be middle-aged.

A shape loomed near them. "I'm coming," Joggi said sullenly. Rudi turned away and strode toward the house. Heiri ran at his elbow; presumably Joggi followed.

At the gate, however, Rudi waited. But as the older boy came up, Rudi did not say the words he wanted to say: I'm sorry the way I left last time.

The old relationship could not be restored, he knew to his sorrow, perhaps should not be. It's the cost of my fear and anger. It's what it cost him then. And it costs me now. My cost greater than his because it was my fault and I can't undo it.

When the three came into the fire-bright room, Madle took one quick step toward them. Joggi went to her. "Mama, I won't do it again," he whimpered. "Please, Mama, I won't do it again!" His head burrowed into her apron.

And somehow with that one exchange, Rudi thought, their world turned right again.

Madle tipped her son's face up to look at him but did not answer. They both knew what she was thinking. You will. You may not mean to now, but you will. "Well," she said, "sit down and eat with Rudi. Though I think you'll have to make out with bread and hominy. Rudi'll have the stew."

Rudi did not protest, but when they were seated, as soon as Madle turned away, he spooned some stew into Joggi's bowl. Out of the corner of his eye he saw Joggi hesitate, then keep on eating. He was as bedraggled a little woods rat as Rudi had ever seen.

His mother said, "Don't dawdle now, so you can get those wet clothes off and go to bed. I've put clean shirts there by the fire for you and Heiri both. I want you to rub yourselves dry, and upstairs then to bed. Not another word from either of you."

"Can Rudi sleep upstairs with us?" asked Heiri.

"Yes, his bed's made up." Her brisk voice had only a trace of hoarseness. Their mother was herself again. As the boys got ready for bed, a scuffling between them and a giggle from Heiri told their relief.

Rudi and Madle sat before the crumbling fire.

"I cannot wholly understand why Johannes does things sometimes," she said. Their low exchanges were separated by silences. "But I must believe it's part of his care for us. I know a man's way is different from a woman's."

Rudi looked somberly into the darkness above the coals. Finally he said, "No, we may not understand the other person—but we care about them."

"Yes. ...That's how the pain comes."

"I've learned that."

"It goes on and on. That's the part that's so hard."

"But it may bring—" he turned to Madle, "a thing that's as restful and good as—clear water."

"Yes, that's true," she answered eagerly. "I've known that. Out of it, grows something later like spring. I knew it the second spring I was here. Out of all my sorrow there came that second spring with Johannes. And I know now, even with my little girl gone ..." Her voice died, came again swiftly, "Oh Rudi, the sand was full of water, her grave kept filling up with water, and they said they'd have to wait till the rain stopped. But Johannes found another place to dig—" She closed her eyes awhile, tears welling under her eyelids, grief moving over her face again, but easier now it seemed, like wind across a field. "She looked so much like Joggi. She'd have been most like him of all my children, I know. ...Rudi, we can't stop hurt and caring."

"No."

"We shouldn't try to, should we?"

Thick walls shut out the noises of the spring night, yet not for Rudi the noises of another March and April twelvemonth gone.

"You cared and so you came back," Madle said. He heard a fluid quietness in her voice again, not the rigidity of ice-jammed emotion, but the quiet of its melting.

"I had to. The way I left last time, I had to come and tell you how sorry I was."

"I know you were. Many a time I'm sorry for things I say. Sometimes I hurt Johannes, and then I'm bitterly sorry."

They fell silent, thinking of where Johannes might be this wet March night. Yet something seemed to turn their thought, even to negate their anxiety.

"So strange, Rudi, that I tell you these things. ...It may be we can't ever give all our thought to those we love most."

He wondered if it was true. He wondered if he could ever give his inmost thoughts to Margaret. "It may be," he answered finally. "But we give them ourselves. And they may not need our thoughts."

"Yet how it rests one to speak of them sometimes. You cannot know how it rests me. ...Our grandparents were brother and sister. It may be because their blood is in us that we speak to one another. Do you think so?"

Rudi turned toward her with quick joy, washing away years of loneliness. He said, "It's the same light. My earliest memory is of light."

"Why I loved Wildhaus," she said, "and hated the dark of Zurich."

Afterwards he lay under the roof that he too had helped build. He heard the even breathing of the little boys. Yet he lay in a wholly different room now, one he had never entered before.

He thought, What if I had not come?

Johannes returned next day. His face whitened when he saw Rudi, then flushed with some other emotion Rudi didn't recognize.

"When did you come?" Johannes asked wearily.

"Yesterday, just before dark."

"Did you come down Saluda?"

"Yes, and I want to hear what happened. I hope you'll tell me about it later."

Joggi and Heiri were at school, but the little girls and Hansli had run to clamp themselves about their father's legs. Then Madle came out and Rudi walked away for a while.

Johannes shut his eyes in thanksgiving as he held his wife. He sensed her thanksgiving too, and he saw a different look in her eyes from the one she'd had when he left. He thought, It's passed. Thank God it's passed. Another part of his mind calculated: I wasted no time getting here. If Rudi got here yesterday, he couldn't have been there. Thank God!

After a midday meal of sauerkraut, sausage, and thick-crusted bread, the two men went outside. They sat on a bench against the south wall of the barn, Johannes content to be idle for once. Though the sun was shining, the wind was blowing up cold from the southwest.

"It feels like frost tonight," ventured Rudi.

"Yes," Johannes sighed. "I'm afraid it'll nip the peaches."

"Maybe this will be the last one."

"Sunday's Easter. It should be."

They were silent awhile. Rudi had decided, Let Madle use her own judgment about telling him what I did Saturday morning. I'll say nothing unless he asks me.

"Johannes, I know what was planned up near Bush River," he said in a low voice. "How did it go? What happened?"

"Nothing happened."

"What?"

"There was no battle. Both sides disbanded."

Rudi absorbed the statement. "You mean there was no fighting? Nobody killed?"

Johannes shook his head slowly.

Rudi thought, But I heard gunfire!

Before he could speak, Johannes said, "Oh, it started, all right. It was starting up, but just as the shooting began, well, you wouldn't believe what happened. Three men rode up. Colonel Richardson—Richard Richardson from over on Wateree—and Colonel William Thompson, you know him—and Colonel Daniel McGirt, a man I don't know but everybody seems to respect. Well, these three men rode right up between the two sides and stopped it. As brave as anything I ever saw."

"Is that the truth!"

"Yes, they'd come up from Charlestown riding as fast as they could. It seems they took it on themselves to go down there and let everybody know, the Governor and everybody, what was going on up here. And the upshot was they brought orders for Coffell and his gang to break up. Seems Coffell didn't have the authority he claimed to have. Or at least, if he did, they took it back from him."

Rudi digested it all. "And everybody just went home?"

"Oh no, not at once. You can imagine, with everybody's feelings being what they were, it wasn't as easy as that. No, we all stood there half the day, and they parleyed back and forth between the two sides."

If the backcountry had had an order of nobility, Richard Richardson would have been a duke and William Thompson of Amelia Township an earl. Because none of the three conciliators had been partisans in the recent turmoil and because they had given long and honorable service to the region, especially during the Cherokee War, they probably had more influence than anyone else in the backcountry.

Johannes said the three men literally talked both sides into laying down their arms. The orders from Charlestown were not quite sufficient.

"When their side finally consented to break up, that whole crowd of 'em," he said, "since Coffell's commission, or whatever it was, was taken back, we did too. Seems the authorities never intended them to do the things they did. I knew that all along. Still we couldn't sit back and let it go on happening."

And what about your side? Rudi wondered but did not ask.

"Our side," Johannes said, "what we finally agreed to was, there's to be no more Regulation. No more use of the word even, no more Regulators." After a moment he added, "I can't say I'm sorry."

Again Rudi did not comment. Finally he said, "I'm glad there was no bloodshed."

"Oh, I can't tell you how glad I am!" It was the mercy of God, he would say to Madle later. It was a downright miracle!

He looks so much older, Rudi thought. Maybe it's because he's tired. Yet for all his tiredness there was a look about him of—well, a little like Squire Musgrove's, Rudi thought. He's a man who knows himself. ...And so am I. So am I.

They sat feeling the sun and the brisk air flowing on their faces. Above the deep green of the wheat fields rose gray clouds of leafing trees against a bright blue sky.

"Rudi, I hope I've done with such going out," Johannes said heavily at last. "It was no easy choice, I can tell you." He hesitated, continued, "I know you disapprove of things that were done—that I put my name to. I did too—of some of the things. I want you to know that."

"I don't disapprove of a man defending his own, Johannes."

"But where to draw the line—between doing that—and going against some other man's right, that's the hard part."

Both men spoke slowly.

"It's the many against the one I disliked," said Rudi.

"Yes." After a while Johannes said, "But in a court of law that's how it's got to be finally. Many against one."

"But was it a court of law?"

Johannes did not answer.

I've gone too far, Rudi thought. He said, "Maybe it boils down to this, Johannes. What is a court of law? Who makes the law?"

"I know the answer to that one. Law belongs to God Almighty. He entrusts it to men. But as you say, which men?"

"The best men," said Rudi. "The ones that don't judge a man by what he is but by what he does."

"I agree with you."

Again they fell silent. Rudi was thinking, There's more each of us could say, but do we need to? It's true, you don't have to tell your whole mind to a person to come close to him.

Johannes thought, Thank God, he's not like he was last time. What's happened to him? Was it just time? I wonder. Well, I thank God he's himself again.

He remarked, "They say we're bound to get our courts soon. They say this new Assembly's drawing up another bill to send to England, and this one's bound to go through. They say it's unlikely they'll turn such a bill down a second time if it's written the way it should be."

"You think there'll be a court here?"

"In Ninety Six probably. And one in Orangeburg and another one in Pine Tree, or Camden, as they call it now."

Edward Musgrove was right, thought Rudi. The country will change. I admit it may be for the better. "Well, there are some that may have to clear out from these parts," he said.

"But not you," said Johannes.

"Oh no, not me."

Chapter Nineteen

Rudi remained another day with the Lienhardts. The next morning he boldly undertook to deal with a very personal problem. Somehow he did not want to ask Johannes directly, so he approached Madle when she was alone in the house.

"Madle, do you think Johannes would lend me his razor? I've decided to get rid of this brush."

She was silent a moment, trying to hide her surprise and pleasure. At one time Rudi had gone clean-shaven for six months, and she always remembered what a good-looking young man he had been. "Of course, he will, Rudi. You can use my scissors too if you need them."

"I don't know what happened to the gear I had. I must have left it somewhere. Or lost it in the woods. I'll get a new outfit tomorrow when I pass through Congarees."

Alone, Madle and Johannes smiled at each other. "Who do you think it is?" he asked. "That Irish girl?"

"What Irish girl?" she demanded.

"The girl and her grandmother that took care of him summer before last. When he was hurt. I told you about it. Why don't you try to find out?"

"Oh no. He'll tell us if he wants to."

Rudi did not tell them. He was not absolutely sure he'd have anything to tell. So they could only hope and speculate.

"I'll be back," he said next morning as he prepared to leave. "Johannes, I may talk to you sometime about that land up the creek. I don't know yet. I have much to decide."

Johannes' face spread in a smile, but he said only, "I'd be more than glad."

They gripped hands. Rudi embraced Madle and squatted to tell the three small children good-bye. Heiri and Joggi would accompany him as far as Pastor Theus' on their way to school. The rest of the family waved him out of sight till the woods hid them. Rudi's last look showed him Johannes with Hansli on his shoulder.

Heiri rode behind Rudi on Stony, and Joggi rode the chestnut mare. The older boy kept stealing glances at Rudi. He looked so different with his beard gone, thought Joggi, He was no longer a man of far and wondrous places but more like his own father. Or some other man of the Congarees. Part of Joggi hurt all over again by a feeling of loss, but the hardened part said, I don't care anyhow.

A rabbit flashed across the road.

"Is your Papa going to get another dog?" Rudi asked Joggi.

"Maybe," he answered. "I don't know."

"Mama said we'll never get another one as good as Bläss," Heiri said.

"He was a good dog," Rudi agreed. "He served you long and well."

"Willi Rieder's dog might have puppies," Joggi contributed finally. "We might get one of them."

They rode most of the way without talking. The sun was just rising and Heiri was still drowsy. Joggi was saying to himself the Latin paradigms he had for today. Also he was deciding that he'd go ahead and turn loose outside the little broken-tailed lizard in his lunch basket that he'd found in the sun yesterday.

"I'll ride in with you for a few minutes and speak to Pastor Theus," Rudi said as the low tree-smothered house appeared.

When they turned off the road, Joggi rode the mare to a small pasture. Rudi dismounted and stood uncertainly near the dooryard while Heiri ran inside to tell the Pastor who was there.

Theus came out. "Why, Rudi Näffels!" His round, gray-stubbled face was alight with pleasure. "*Grüss Gott*, my friend! I'm very glad to see you! What's brought you to the Congarees?"

A little stouter, Rudi saw, as plain as ever, but still cheerful and easy.

"You're keeping these Lienhardt boys in good order, I see," Rudi said.

"Oh yes. At least one of them. And I haven't given up on the other."

"I hope you don't, sir," smiled Rudi.

Joggi had come up with another boy who had just arrived. Rudi looked at Joggi. Never in his life had he wished more for the gift of eloquence and wisdom. However, all he could do was to tousle the boy's head roughly and say, "Watch out where you go now. Be careful and watch the path."

Joggi glanced up swiftly, for a moment the old glad light in his eyes. He said, "If we get the puppy, I'll call him 'Felsi.'"

"What?"

"You know. A *Fels* is a rock. Like 'Stony.'"

Before Rudi could answer, Joggi dashed off calling, "Come on, Willi!"

Rudi bade Theus good-bye, then bent and embraced Heiri quickly. As he rode away, a smile stayed in his eyes a long time.

At the Congaree store, along with his shaving gear, Rudi bought a bleached holland shirt, a pair of shoes with steel buckles, and a good beaver hat. He deliberated for quite a while over a light-colored pair of cloth breeches and a brown holland coat, but decided that his present refurbishment would be enough. Anything else in addition to his shorn state might be too much of a shock to those who had known him formerly. After much deliberation he bought a small pair of scissors with chased handles and a silver chain and hook on them, as pretty as the pair he'd seen Madle wear at her waist. All of the purchases except for his hat he packed in his saddlebags.

His treasury was not too greatly depleted, for he had not had occasion to spend money lately. He hoped there'd be no difficulty about the wages due him. If there should be—he shrugged—he'd not contest it. He'd go by Squire Musgrove's mill on the Enoree later. Today he was headed toward the creek valleys of the Savannah.

The weather clouded up again with one day of fine mist, and it continued chill through most of the week. But Friday dawned fair and warm, and Saturday, the first day of April, brought gladness to everything that crept, swarmed, or flew. Vixens led their open-eyed young out into the sunshine. Wild throats pulsed in cascades and creeks of sound. Nests were lined with fine new grasses. Mothering hovered and brooded. The chrysalis was broken. Wings hardened, shimmered, lifted in warm bright air.

The valley of Savannah's Little River was afloat with tier above tier of white dogwood, its air fragrant with opening sweet-shrub. Violets, wake robins, pale anemones, the small pink spring beauty, and wild ginger hid or starred the ground. Wing, water, leaf, and sunshine, petal and perfume brought all that the Carolina woods could hold of Eden.

Yet Rudi rode in increasing disquiet. Why did I wait so long? he asked. Seven long months!

He encountered more and more signs of new settlement: smell of smoke, sounds of axes, raw-stumped clearings. Once he stopped to hail a man and talk. These newcomers were mostly Scots-Irish, he learned, like those they were joining—Calhouns, Norrises, Pattons, and Alexanders. A woman to stay single so long among so many of her kind? How could he have expected her to wait? And who was he for a woman to wait for anyhow?

But I sent her a letter. But then how do I know she got it? He thought of a dozen mischances for his letter: the carrier's pack washed down some creek, pack stolen and letter thrown away; carrier sick or hurt or dead; carrier lost in the woods and not even going so far, forgetting the letter, leaving it with some careless illiterate who'd forget the direction.

Will she even be there? At least, he knew she'd left Indian Creek, for he'd gone by the place once to view its loneliness. Now other possibilities rampaged through his mind: accident, sickness, fever, smallpox, an isolated Indian attack bringing death or captivity. Or had she simply turned from him? Family influence, ardent courtship, anger at his long absence—what might these have accomplished?

That morning he had again painstakingly shaved his naked face, combed and tied his hair back as neatly as he could with a new black ribbon, and put on his new shirt and his good shoes. The day before, he had cleaned Stony's gear, and early this morning he had brushed his coat till it shone. But what a fool he'd feel if she shouldn't be there. Or if she was, what did Margaret Allen care about a man's shoes or the shine of his horse?

He worried, laughed at and cursed himself by turns.

The planting of the garden, begun on Good Friday, was almost done. "I'll finish, Nancy. It's only the beans to drop soon as I finish digging the hills."

They were clearing up after dinner. "I could use the time for ironing," said Nancy. "If you'll do that, I'll flute up your cap for you. I ha' mine and Issy's yet to do." She added anxiously, "You *will* go to meeting with us tomorrow, I hope?"

"You wouldn't want me to stay here and keep the young ones?"

"By no means! Easter Sunday? I'd not have you to stay here on any account. There'll be others there to help mind young ones. Or if need be, I'll stay out."

Well, let Nancy work with hot irons in the house if that was what she wanted. Given a choice how could anybody stay indoors today?

The soil was crumbly damp, a deep red clay under the rich mold. Already David had won his reward from this ground and talked of adding to his tract and getting people to help him work it.

Margaret dropped seed and stooped to cover each hill, firming it with her hands. She looked about at the neat new fields, so different from the old ragged ones she'd left. But for all its joy, this scented air was tinctured with pain. It brought too much of memory—of a hillside where the earth had been dug into deeper than this.

She remembered this time last year when the struggle was ending, flesh grayed and stilled. ... And the unsleeping cruelty of moonlight, night after night. Moonlight was just as white on Allen's Creek as anywhere else.

Issy came out, breaking her thought. "Mammy said I could help you, Aunt Meggie."

"Well. You want to drop the beans? See, drop three to a hill."

Margaret was glad of the child's coming.

"Let's sing, Aunt Meggie!" Issy called back, as she moved ahead with her bag of seed.

"What would you like to sing?"

"Sing 'Bessy Bell and Mary Gray.'"

Because of the children's demands, Margaret had recovered dozens of riddles, songs, and stories from memory, bringing back old scenes and voices.

> "'Oh, Bessy Bell and Mary Gray,
> They were two bonnie lasses.
> They biggit a bower on yon burn brae
> And theekit it o'er wi' rashes.'"

There were no mountains here as there had been in Ulster and in the Shenandoah to name in memory of those sad girls of Perth who had died of plague away from their kin, but among the beanhills of the South Carolina Piedmont the small sweet soprano and the strong contralto still sang of Bessy and Mary's plight.

"Let's sing another one, Aunt Meggie. Sing 'Bonnie Barbary Allen.'"

Bean planting slowed as they sang the many mournful verses about the unkind Allen girl and Jamie Grove.

"But why did he die?" asked Issy.

"Because she would not have him."

"But why wouldn't she have him?"

"Because he slighted her."

"But why did he slight her? If he loved her."

"I don't know," said Margaret. "It doesn't tell that."

And why are all song ballads about either cruel lovers or lovers who never return? Must love be always grief and pain?

"Let's sing 'My Love Will Come A-walking Yet,'" said Issy.

Margaret felt a surge of pleasure, for this was a song she had made up herself though the children didn't realize it. She had put it to a tune that could be either rollicking or sad. She sang it mostly to herself and Issy, and there was something about the way Margaret sang it, the interchange of quick and slow, that made Issy like it. Margaret began softly,

> "Ohhh, my love will come a-walking yet,
> A-walking in the night.
> His horse is lame, his feet are bare,
> But, oh, his eye is bright!"

The child's voice joined hers to sing the refrain quickly,

> "Oh, come, my love, and come right soon
> If that ye'll find me here.
> But if ye wait until the frost—
> Ye must find some other dear!"

Issy kept her eyes on Margaret's face as they sang the last verse slowly,

> "My love will come a-walking yet,
> A-walking in the gloom.
> Though his clothes be torn, his pack be gone—
> I pray he may come soon."

"Oh, Aunt Meggie, let's sing it again!" Issy breathed.

"No, that's enough. We'll sing it another time."

"Aunt Meggie, will you go to meeting tomorrow and wear your pretty cap?"

"Who'll mind Billy and Hugh?"

"I don't know. Will you go?"

"We'll see."

"Oh, I'll run tell Mammy!"

Margaret had forgotten that to a child "We'll see" meant "yes."

Well, why not go? She was not a heathen, was she? God shouldn't be blamed for her trouble and grief. It was people, proud narrow-minded people. ...If only she could feel herself more in charity with her fellow worshippers! ...But tomorrow was Easter Sunday. And it was God, not men, you went to worship, Granny always said. Would *she* have approved of her staying home? Margaret knew the answer to that. ...And no, you didn't have to pay attention to calf eyes, clumsy jokes, and double-edged questions and comments at noon dinner and after meeting.

When the last hill was covered, Margaret straightened and looked across the wide garden. Would she be here to eat its yield? Most likely, she thought in near despair.

How she longed to be back on Indian Creek. She knew now she had not valued Jamie's shield nearly enough. In one important way it had been much stronger than her brother's.

Hardly a day passed that she did not feel assailed by relentless questions. Where are you going? What are you going to do? Make up your mind.

Not that anyone ever said a word to her directly. The pressure she felt was what was not said or in such phrases as Nancy's "some day" or "when you have your own."

And the visitors. Margaret was not vain, but she couldn't help knowing that she had the looks, age, and family to suit quite a number of the dozen or so single men in the Long Canes-Little River area. They made sure she knew it. One man had even come down from Rocky River to see David. And it was always worse when she went into company. The region was becoming more populous. They had their own minister and meetinghouse now, and the growing population meant not only more weddings and funerals, but other social events. It was hard to be a recluse in such a community, not without embarrassing David and Nancy.

Margaret sighed. No use to be angry with anyone, not even herself. And she remembered Granny's saying one time, "Meggie, when you do not know what to do, do not do anything, and let the good Lord Himself show you the way. Or sometimes He'll bring a thing to pass in His own way, though it may not be yours." But another time Granny had said, "To let go and to let some one else do for you, that's the hardest lesson you'll ever have to learn, child. You're a born doer, not one to sit and wait with your hands in your lap."

Nancy was so neat and careful of her appearance that Margaret was forced to think more of her own. Nowadays she seldom went about without a cap or bonnet, never barefoot or even without stockings. Nevertheless, as she shut the garden gate behind her, she took off her bonnet to let the breeze fan her temples, and she had a sudden impulse to take off her shoes and stockings, to run across the plowed field and find a low-limbed oak or hickory and pull herself up into it.

As she gazed toward the woods beyond the fields, a horseman emerged. Somebody coming. Young by the looks of him. She sighed. And David working across the hill. Well, maybe he'd have seen him. If not, let Nancy take care of him. Besides, how come you to think it's for you? Oh, you're getting a great conceit of yourself!

She was about to turn toward the house when she noticed something familiar about the horse. Short-legged. The blaze on his forehead. The workmanlike, tolerant look of him. But his brown coat was too shiny. The rider had his hat on. She caught her breath sharply. It could not be! She'd never seen that smooth face before. Smooth-shaven. He swept his hat off, called, spurred his horse.

Wide-eyed, open-mouthed, she gazed a moment longer, then began to run across the plowed ground, careless of corn spears, her shoes and stockings, everything.

"Oh Rudi, Rudi!" she cried over and over, weeping, laughing, her hands on his face, pulling his head back to look at him. "How could you do this to me? Look at you now! Come up fine as a lord and if it hadn't been for Stony—oh Rudi, Rudi!" She could not get enough of saying the name she'd barely spoken for seven months.

Nor could he look enough. Young and sure as when he'd first seen her in his haze of delirium on the forest floor. Warm and beautiful in the white sleet, strong as that log she'd been trying to tumble about. "Oh Margaret," he kept saying, "did you get my letter? You knew I'd come, didn't you? You knew I'd come!"

She could only hold him, draw back to look at him, laugh and hold him again. Rudi felt light-headed, wondered if he would faint or float. They grew aware of observers: a man, a woman, a baby, and three children.

"Daddy, it's the man that gave me the play-pretty!" Issy sang out.

As they turned and drew apart, Rudi missed the man's momentary hesitation, saw only David Allen coming toward him with an outstretched hand.

There was nowhere to sit in the evening but in the one common room. David said, "I aim to build on next fall. Another room the size of this one with a big loftroom. It's getting too little here, even for my crowd."

Rudi would not let them shift and make room for him in the house that night. He'd be comfortable enough in the barn, he said. Or in the woods for that matter, he thought, but did not say so.

"You'll go to meeting with us tomorrow?" asked Nancy.

"Aye," said Margaret, "go with us."

"I'm—I'm not a—Presbyterian." He hoped he said the word right.

"No reason you can't go to meeting with one, is there?" Margaret asked.

Later she walked outside with him. "We can sit here a little while on the steps," she said.

"You're not cold?"

"Not now. Let's sit out from under the shadow. Sit out where I can see you."

Moonlight flooded the valley, whitened the fields, whitened their hands, darkened their eyes.

"But why did you play me such a trick as to shave off your beard?" she asked after a while.

"You don't like it?"

"Well, yes—only—you're so handsome now—why, you're even better looking than Jamie, and folks will think I'm wanting you for your looks. And I'd not have anyone thinking I'm that light-minded."

"And why is it then," he asked laughing, "that you're wanting me?"

"I think it's because Granny liked you."

"What! Your Granny liked many people!"

"Aye, but if she hadn't taken you in hand, what would you ha' come to? And with her gone, who else is to see to you?"

She was teasing, of course, but he answered slowly, "I think when she took me in hand, she took me to—a place of goodness. It's where I hope we'll live, you and me."

Well, they would begin on Indian Creek. For in the end Rudi had no more to offer than himself, but for Margaret it was enough, and her brother consented.

"I said the place would be hers when she married. I'll see it's deeded to you when you've wed. It's a rundown place, I'm sure you've noted. You'll have your work cut out for you, to get it in shape again." Cut out for you in more ways that one, David thought wryly.

But Rudi was ready to work. For her, he'd be a plow-pusher or anything else, he vowed. Though as to the where, he wasn't sure of his feelings. Whether he could ever feel at home in that neighborhood he'd have to find out. But the least I can do is try, he thought. There has to be bigness in taking as well as in giving. He would leave for Indian Creek on Monday to begin spring planting, for it was not yet too late to put a crop in the ground. David said he should take Dan. Stony too would have to learn to plow.

Often had David and Nancy talked of these possibilities in the months past, and although every conversation had ended with David's "Wait and see," yet their talk had prepared him for the seeing. Different the man was, but not disagreeably so. And when was an Allen ever to be thwarted in the want for something different? David asked himself.

They had not yet discussed the date of Rudi's return to Allen's Creek, but in her mind Margaret fixed a period of four weeks. This time, she would tell him, if he was not back at the set time, she would come and get him. She meant it, and she would let him know she meant it too.

"Would you like for David to speak to the parson tomorrow about publishing our banns?" she asked softly.

"Aye," he answered. "As well make an Irish Presbyterian of me now as later."

After all, it was what Granny had been.

Epilogue

On Easter Sunday in the new log meetinghouse on Indian Creek, the elders asked Jamie to read the New Testament Scripture. They had yet no minister and scant hope of getting one. He read from the Gospel of Luke about Christ's appearance on the road to Emmaus.

As he read about Jesus' meeting with the men who did not recognize him, of his expounding to them the Scriptures, and the burning of their hearts and the opening of their eyes, the heart of James Fraser too began to burn. The words assumed radiance, power. They became for him the Word.

Next day, as he'd long planned, Jamie told his family goodbye for the beginning of his journey northward. The hollow place in his chest he would take with him, he knew. Yet he thought it might diminish, perhaps matter less as new compulsions filled his heart and his mind.

Aleck went with him across Duncan's Creek to the ford on the Enoree. Beyond it lay the path that would eventually take him northeast to the Waxhaws, where he'd spend a few days with Mr. Richardson if he was home.

"Jamie, you can't miss it. Just follow this path about four miles and it'll take you straight across Tyger. And when you cross Tyger, it's a plain, well-marked road you can take straight to Fishdam Shoals on the Broad. It's a good shallow fording place. And from there on it's another well-marked road to Land's Ford on Catawba. Which is what you're heading for, though I understand Parson Richardson lives back a way this side Catawba."

"How well-marked?" asked Jamie. "Are you sure it's well-marked?"

"It's a traveled road—or path anyhow. Surely you can tell a traveled path when you see one? Now it's thick-settled where you're going," Aleck instructed Jamie severely, "so if you miss the way, just hire somebody to guide you."

Aleck watched his brother out of sight. Sunlight glinted on the fair head. Will he get where he's going? He will. Though no telling how.

Jamie did not miss the way that morning. He found Tyger and crossed it. After that, he decided to quit worrying about trails and landmarks and to think instead of his general direction. He'd pay more attention to the lay of shadows morning and afternoon, and he'd not stir for an hour at midday, nor would he continue for more than a quarter of an hour after sundown, no matter where he had to lie out. After all, he'd gotten to Ninety Six, hadn't he, and that other place which now seemed almost mythical. He knew the Broad and the Catawba Rivers were there and when he got to them, he'd beat up and down the bank till he found a fording place. And who knew what persons he might meet up with on the way?

He thought of brown-clothed woodsmen, the one he'd followed up the country from Ninety Six and the one he'd come back with. How did you get to be so sure of yourself in the woods? You looked about you for one thing. You kept your mind not only on where you were going but on where you were. He thought of William Richardson, whose comings and goings were almost as frequent as a hunter's. Had Richardson ever been lost?

A strange thought struck Jamie. Lost not in the woods maybe but somewhere else. There was deep trouble there. Maybe had been for a long time. In the man or in his situation.

Jamie rode gravely as he thought of lonely paths, gloomy paths, no longer noticing the way the shadows leaned. How do you keep from getting lost? How do you find your way through this labyrinthine rich green world?

Still the trail remained plain for Jamie that April afternoon. His horse was a careful stepper and Jamie let him amble at his own pace. The weather was pleasant. So far he had not been bitten or stung by anything.

He kept thinking: The road you went or where you were going, which mattered more? Both mattered. You had to know your destination, but you had to know the road too.

The men who went to Emmaus, which mattered more to them?
Neither mattered.

It wasn't their road or their destination either; it was the one they met on the road, the one who met them. Because didn't they turn around and come straight back to where they'd started from, Jerusalem?

The same destination? No, all was changed. It wasn't the trail or the ford or the city either that made the difference. It was the person on the way. The persons.

Late that afternoon about sundown, Jamie came down to the Broad

River and was relieved to see the zigzag chain of rocks the Indians had built there, the rocks that meant Fishdam Ford. He was even more relieved to see low buildings and horses on the other side.

Afterword

A well-documented study of the Regulator movement in South Carolina is contained in Richard Maxwell Brown's *The South Carolina Regulators* (Harvard, 1963). I have followed Brown's account rather than those of older historians, which differ in some particulars as well as in the spellings of names. The events in Chapters Five and Ten are fictitious but are typical of the time and place. The aborted battle between the Regulators and Moderators is historical, also the Regulator Congress at the Congarees, the descent of the backcountry men into the lowcountry to vote, and other developments referred to.

Many real persons are mentioned or described in the narrative, a few with invented speeches ascribed to them, but of those who play any extended role in the story only the ministers, Christian Theus and William Richardson, are historical. William Richardson's life ended tragically and strangely in 1771. He was found dead on his knees in his study with a rope around his neck suspended from the ceiling. Christian Theus lived to be an old man. He and his sons were Patriots during the Revolution. He died some time in the 1790s.

A colorful although biased account of this period is found in the writings of Charles Woodmason, an itinerant Anglican minister. These have been edited by Richard J. Hooker in *The Carolina Backcountry on the Eve of the Revolution* (Chapel Hill, 1953).

All place names in the story are real except "Allen's Creek". However, given the number of creeks in South Carolina, there may well have been one so named.